The Matchmaker is both charming and beautiful. Sarah Price writes with an authenticity that pulls at the heartstrings and triumphs over self in a way that gives you renewed faith in love and friendship, showing us all the hand God has in our lives.

—SUE LAITINEN
DESTINATION AMISH

In her own distinctive voice Sarah Price has created a wealth of memorable, delightful characters in *The Matchmaker*! Readers will love this unique blend of the Amish and Jane Austen's classic tale *Emma*—the story of a meddling, opinionated young lady who must learn the hard way that best-laid plans may sometimes go awry! With unpredictable twists and turns that Sarah Price is so well known for and a charming main character that is not your typical Amish heroine, this harmonious mix is truly a "match made" in heaven!

—DIANA FLOWER
SENIOR REVIEWER AT OWG BLOG

Once again Sarah Price has woven a tapestry of beautiful imagery, timeless wisdom, and sigh-worthy romance into her most recent work, *The Matchmaker*. Endearingly sweet and positively delightful!

—NICOLE DEESE
AUTHOR OF THE LETTING GO SERIES
AND *A CLICHÉ CHRISTMAS*

Sarah Price's retells *Emma* in her delightful novel, *The Matchmaker*. This sweet rendition is both authentically Amish and true to Jane Austen's story, while full of whimsy, romance, and heartfelt redemption. Thank you, Sarah, for a truly enjoyable read!

—LESLIE GOULD
CHRISTY AWARD–WINNING
AND BEST-SELLING AUTHOR

Just like *First Impressions*, *The Matchmaker* combines two of my favorite things: a Jane Austen's book with Sarah Price's unique and engaging storytelling. Sarah Price does a brilliant job of intertwining Amish life into a much-loved classic while staying true to the themes in Jane Austen's *Emma*. Her characters are three dimensional, relatable and, more importantly, entertaining. Sarah's Emma is just as lovable and full of error as Jane Austen's heroine, while Gideon is as dashing and honorable as the incomparable Mr. Knightley. The story is so captivating that it pulls you in and leaves you wanting more from this very talented author. If you love Jane Austen as much as I do and are looking for a book that brings a fresh perspective to a retelling of a universal story, you do not want to miss reading *The Matchmaker*. I, for one, am looking forward to reading more from Sarah Price.

—ERIN BRADY
AUTHOR OF *THE SHOPPING SWAP*
AND *THE HOLIDAY GIG*

Highly recommended to anyone who reads Amish romance!

—BETH SHRIVER
AUTHOR OF THE TOUCH OF GRACE SERIES
AND *LOVE'S ABUNDANT HARVEST*

The MATCHMAKER

AN AMISH RETELLING OF JANE AUSTEN'S *EMMA*

THE
AMISH CLASSICS
BOOK TWO

SARAH PRICE

REALMS

Most CHARISMA HOUSE BOOK GROUP products are available at special quantity discounts for bulk purchase for sales promotions, premiums, fund-raising, and educational needs. For details, write Charisma House Book Group, 600 Rinehart Road, Lake Mary, Florida 32746, or telephone (407) 333-0600.

THE MATCHMAKER by Sarah Price
Published by Realms
Charisma Media/Charisma House Book Group
600 Rinehart Road
Lake Mary, Florida 32746
www.charismahouse.com

All Scripture quotations are from the Holy Bible, New International Version. Copyright © 1973, 1978, 1984, International Bible Society. Used by permission.

Cover design by Bill Johnson
Design Director: Justin Evans

Visit the author's website at sarahpriceauthor.com.

Library of Congress Cataloging-in-Publication Data:
An application to register this book for cataloging has been submitted to the Library of Congress.
International Standard Book Number: 978-1-62998-004-1
E-book ISBN: 978-1-62998-005-8

First edition

15 16 17 18 19 — 9 8 7 6 5 4 3 2 1
Printed in the United States of America

To my dear friend Erin Brady,
for encouraging me to take my writing
to a new and very exciting level
of literary exploration.

❧ A Note About Vocabulary ❧

THE AMISH SPEAK Pennsylvania Dutch (also called Amish German or Amish Dutch). This is a verbal language with variations in spelling among the many different Amish and Mennonite communities throughout the United States.

In some regions a "grandfather" is *grossdaadi*, while in other regions he is known as *grossdawdi*. The word for mother is *maam* in some communities, *mammi* in another, and still *maem* in yet one more variation.

In addition there are words such as "mayhaps" or "reckon," the use of the word "then" and "now" at the end of sentences, and, my favorite, "for sure and certain," which are not necessarily from the Pennsylvania Dutch language/dialect but are unique to the Amish and used frequently. Other phrases such as "oh help," "fiddle faddle," and "oh bother!" are ones that I have heard repeatedly throughout the years.

The use of these words and phrases comes from my personal experience living among the Amish in Lancaster County, Pennsylvania. For readers who are not familiar with such terms, I have italicized the words and included a glossary at the end of the novel.

❧ *Preface* ❧

THE IDEA FOR this book was a long time in coming. I started to read quite early in life, and my taste for books transcended the typical chunky books that preschoolers are made to read. I confess that my first love was Laura Ingalls Wilder's books, which I devoured practically on a daily basis. To say I was a bookworm would be putting it mildly. Children would take bets whether or not I could finish a book a day—a challenge I won easily on most days.

So my transition to classic literature came at an early age, with my favorites being Jane Austen, Charlotte Brontë, Emily Brontë, Charles Dickens, Thomas Hardy, and (a personal favorite) Victor Hugo. Christmas was fairly predictable in my house. Just one leather-bound book always made it the "bestest Christmas ever."

In writing Amish Christian romances, something I have been doing for twenty-five years, I have always tried to explore new angles to the stories. I base most of my stories on my own experiences, having lived on Amish farms and in Amish homes over the years. I have come to know these amazingly strong and devout people in a way that I am constantly pinching myself as to why I have been able to do so. I must confess that on more than one occasion I have heard the same from them: "We aren't quite sure what it is, Sarah, but...there's something deeply special about you."

Besides adoring my Amish friends and "family," I also adore my readers. Many of you know that I spend countless hours using social media to individually connect with as many readers as I can. I found some of my "bestest friends" online, and despite living in Virginia or Hawaii or Nebraska or Australia, they are as dear to me as the ones who live two miles down the road.

Well, something clicked when I combined my love of literature with my adoration of my readers and respect of the Amish. It is my hope that by creating this literary triad, my readers will experience the Amish in a new way. They will experience authentic Amish culture and religion based on my experiences of having lived among them and my exposure to the masterpieces of literary greats from years past.

I thank the good people at Charisma Media for sharing in my enthusiasm, especially Adrienne, who reached out to me and listened with an open mind.

It's amazing to think that a love of God and passion for reading can be combined in such a manner as to touch so many people. I hope that you too are touched, and I truly welcome your e-mails, letters, and postings.

Blessings,
Sarah Price
Sarahprice.author@gmail.com
http://www.facebook.com/fansofsarahprice
Twitter: @SarahPriceAuthr

❧ *Chapter One* ❧

LEANING OVER THE back of the kitchen chair, a very busy Emma Weaver struck an unknowingly pretty picture as she bent forward to rearrange the yellow and purple flowers in the glass jar. The late summer blooms had been plucked from her flower garden only an hour before, and their sweet scent wafted through the room as she moved them around for the third or fourth time in less than ten minutes. Satisfied at last, she stood upright, nodded her self-approval toward the bouquet, then quickly assessed the rest of the room with her cornflower-blue eyes.

The table was set with plain white linen and her *maem*'s best china, a gift from her *daed* when they had just been married. It was something that Emma loved to use when guests came for supper, especially on Sunday evenings. The sitting area was freshly cleaned just the day prior, for it was forbidden to clean on Sunday, regardless of whether or not it was a church Sunday or a visiting Sunday. The blue sofa and two rocking chairs with blue and white quilted cushions looked welcoming for their soon-to-arrive guests.

"Ah, Emma!" a deep voice called out from the staircase.

She looked up in time to see her *daed* shuffling down the stairs, taking each step one at a time as his weathered hand held the railing. With his long, white beard and thinning hair, he looked older than his sixty-five years, a fact that worried Emma on a regular basis. "I thought you were resting, *Daed*," she said as she hurried to meet him at the bottom of the stairs. Taking his arm, she led him to his favorite chair: a blue recliner that was covered with a pretty crocheted blanket she had made for him last winter.

"Such a quiet house nowadays," he mumbled as he sat down and raised the foot of the chair so that he could rest his legs. "How sad for you that Anna went off to get married!" He clucked his tongue a few times and shut his eyes as he rested his head on the back of the chair. "Poor Anna, indeed! Why ever would she want to do such a thing anyway?"

Emma laughed, the sound light and airy. "*Nee, Daed*," she quickly retorted. "We must be happy for Anna! Old Widower Wagler seemed right pleased last Tuesday, and I dare say that Anna was radiant in her blue wedding dress!"

"Radiant indeed!" her *daed* scoffed. "Left us alone is what she did. Who shall entertain you now, my dear Emma?"

"Now, *Daed*!" she reprimanded him gently. "I don't need anyone to entertain me and you know that. We have quite enough to keep us busy, and I'm happy for cousin Anna to finally have a home of her own."

Without giving him a chance to retort, Emma turned and hurried back into the main part of the kitchen. Everything was set up for their soon-to-be arriving guests. The bread she had baked just the day before was sliced and on a plate, covered with plastic wrap so the flies wouldn't land upon it. The bowls of chow-chow, beets, and pickled cabbage were likewise covered and set upon the counter. Only the cold cuts and fruit spreads remained in the refrigerator.

For a few long, drawn-out moments Emma fussed at the

table, wanting everything to be absolutely perfect for their dear soon-to-arrive guests.

"Careful there, Emma," her *daed* said, lifting his hand to point in her direction. "That's a sharp knife there on the edge of the table!"

Laughing, Emma put her hands on her hips and frowned at him, a playful twinkle in her eyes. "*Ach, Daed*! I'm not a child anymore! I *see* the knife!" As if to make a point, she picked it up and wiggled it in the air. "No danger here."

"Emma Weaver!" a disapproving voice came out from behind her.

Startled, she dropped the knife and jumped backward as it clanked on the linoleum floor. "Gideon King! You scared me!" she cried at the sight of the man standing in the doorframe. Annoyed, she quickly bent down to pick up the knife. Wiping it on her apron, she set it back on the table before hurrying over to greet their first guest.

"And *you* were teasing your *daed*!" he said, a stern look upon his face. "Good thing I walked in when I did! You could have cut yourself!"

"I almost did cut myself!" she retorted, making a playful face at him. "No thanks to you for scaring me so!" Despite her words it was clear that the presence of the newcomer pleased her. She reached up her hand to make certain that her chestnut brown hair was properly pinned back and hidden beneath her freshly starched prayer *kapp*, the ribbons tied neatly as they hung from the sides. Even if it was only Gideon, she wanted to make certain she looked proper and plain, like a good Amish woman.

"That's no way to greet our guest, Emma," her *daed* chided. "Come, Gideon! Greet this old man!"

The tall Amish man with thick, black hair and broad

shoulders crossed the room in three easy strides. He shook the older man's outstretched hand. Emma watched with a smile on her lips, knowing that it had been a long week for her *daed* without Gideon stopping in to visit him. With no sons of his own, her *daed* had come to look upon Gideon as a son of sorts. Since Gideon's younger *bruder* had married Irene, her older and only sister, Gideon was as good as family. And by the way he constantly reprimanded Emma, his voice more oft full of criticism than pleasure, she often felt as if she had, indeed, acquired an older *bruder*.

"It's *gut* to see you, Henry," Gideon said. "Looking well, as always."

Henry gestured toward the sofa, indicating that Gideon should sit down. "Have you just returned, then?" He didn't wait for the man to answer before he continued. "Tell us about your trip."

Without waiting for an invitation, Emma joined the two men, plopping herself on the sofa next to the new visitor. "*Ja,* Gideon. Do tell us about Ohio. We missed you at Anna's wedding last week!"

Stretching out his legs, Gideon smiled at the young woman next to him. "I wouldn't have missed it if I hadn't needed to attend to some business in the Dutch Valley," he said. "I rode out with a couple who were going to visit their *dochder* who recently married a widowed bishop out there. They were traveling with a young woman from around here."

"From around here?" Emma's mouth fell open. "Do I know her, then?"

"Lizzie Blank," was the simple response.

"Why! I wonder that she must be related to Widow Blank and Hetty!" She looked from Gideon to her *daed*. "Have we met this woman, *Daed*?"

Henry seemed to ponder the name for a moment, his brows knitted together and his eyes squinting as he did so. "I'm not so sure of our being acquainted with a Lizzie Blank," came the answer.

Emma, observing Gideon brushing some dirt from his pants, smiled to herself at how fastidious he always was about his appearance, especially on Sundays. He glanced up at her, catching her watching him, and sighed, the hint of a smile on his face. "You can't know everyone, Emma. I know how hard you try, but it would be quite impossible, it seems."

"Gideon! You tease me so!"

He laughed. "I am all but a *bruder* to you, Emma. Isn't that what *bruders* are supposed to do?" He changed the subject back to his trip. "It was a pleasant journey and she is a lovely young woman. A shame you *didn't* know her, Emma. Her wit would have amused you immensely!" With a pause he turned his gaze to her *daed*. "Ohio was sure nice, especially at this time of the year. The rolling hills and winding roads make for a lovely backdrop for the long drive there."

"Such a romantic!" Emma teased, which prompted Gideon to frown at her. Still, the fierce look on his face could not hide his pleasure at being reunited with his good friends after being away for so long.

"Speaking of romantics," he replied, a mischievous gleam in his dark brown eyes, "who shed the most tears at Anna's wedding, I wonder?"

Henry laughed and pointed at Emma. "You know her so well, Gideon. Surely you are aware that Emma wept through the entire service and the singing afterward."

"Oh, *Daed*!"

But it was true, indeed. She *had* wept, mostly out of elation for dear sweet Anna, who, after so many years living with them, had finally found happiness and married good ole Widower Wagler.

Only two months prior Emma knew very little about Samuel Wagler except that he had recently moved into a ranch house within their *g'may*. Prior to that he had lived with his older *bruder* and family in a neighboring church district, residing in the *grossdaadihaus* until it was needed by his *bruder* for his oldest son, now married and with an infant on the way. That was when Samuel had moved into their *g'may*.

Emma had noticed the way his dark eyes seemed drawn to Anna during his first church service in his new district. It had taken Emma only a few minutes to formulate a plan and invite Samuel to share supper with them. And from that moment on she had been delighted to watch the commencement of Samuel's courtship of Anna. Delighted, that is, until she realized that by marrying Samuel, Anna would be moving away to live in that ranch house with her new husband.

That realization had saddened Emma and had been the other cause for tears during the wedding.

After all, Anna had been like a mother to Emma and Irene. After their *maem* passed away, when Emma was not even in school yet, their *daed* vowed to raise his two *dochders* on his own. He had married later in life and his *fraa*, while younger than he, had great difficulty in carrying her pregnancies to full term, making the two children who did survive all the more precious. Henry doted on his two *dochders*, a fact that contributed to his decision to remain single. So, while other widowers tended to marry within a year or two, Henry Weaver refused to consider that option. Instead, he readily agreed when his older *bruder* volunteered Anna, his eldest and still unmarried *dochder*, to move to the Weaver residence and care for the children. What had been offered as a temporary solution soon became permanent for Anna. She enjoyed tending to the needs of her two young cousins, and with the full appreciation and support of her *onkel* Henry Weaver, she found that she had no reason to leave.

That was until, fifteen years later, Emma introduced the now forty-five-year-old Anna to Old Widower Wagler.

"*Ja vell*," she said dismissively, trying to downplay the memory of her emotions at the wedding service. "Anna sure did look right *gut* standing next to Samuel, and any emotion I felt was from sheer joy at her marriage! A strong marriage is a *wunderbaar gut* thing, ain't so?"

Both men cleared their throats and shifted in their seats in response to her statement. After all, with neither being married, how did she expect them to respond?

She looked pleased with their silence.

"And you may have forgotten that it was I who helped arrange the match between the two," she added, her pride of having a hand in the match more than apparent. "And this, after so many had speculated that Old Widower Wagler would never marry again."

The two men looked at each other, a brief glance that said more than words could communicate. While Gideon merely shook his head, it was her *daed* who commented. "Emma, it's not for you to play matchmaker. Promise me you will do no such thing."

"*Nee*, *Daed*," she retorted. "Not for myself, of course. But it gives me such joy to see others happy! Just think...after so many years Samuel has a new wife and, as such, a new life! Perhaps now his son Francis shall return and live with him once again. Why! We haven't seen Francis since his *maem* passed away. When was that, *Daed*? About sixteen years ago?"

"Just before your own *maem* passed, I believe," Henry added, a solemn look upon his face.

"Think of how happy that would make Samuel!" She practically hugged herself in delight, the thought of Samuel being reunited with his son bringing her a great deal of joy. "I must acknowledge my success in having made such a match for both Samuel and Anna. And with that in mind how could I possibly not strive to do the same for others?"

At her words, Gideon leaned forward and stared at her. "Success? If you noticed the interest that Samuel had in Anna, you merely accommodated it with an invitation to supper. Nothing more, Emma. I wouldn't call that a 'success' as if you had a hand in making a 'match.' It was bound to happen with or without your interference. And should you persist in trying to arrange such matches, you are more likely to do harm to yourself than good."

Clearly his words did not suit Emma and she scowled. Still, despite Gideon's reprimand, she refused to let her mood be altered. "I have one more match to make," she announced. "Why, our very own bishop's son, Paul Esh, seemed to hang on every word of their wedding service. I'm certain he is longing to settle down himself." She looked at her *daed*. "And rightfully so! He's almost an old bachelor like someone else we know so dearly!"

"Emma!" Henry coughed at her statement and glanced apologetically at Gideon. Being sixteen years Emma's senior, Gideon more closely shared Henry's concerns and mind-set than Emma's. "Marriage is not for everyone."

The members in the *g'may* had stopped speculating long ago about when Gideon King, a well-established and prosperous Amish businessman in his own right, would settle down and start his own family. He seemed more than happy to relish in simple things such as weekly visits with friends. Still, Emma's statement had caused a degree of discomfort in the room, at least for Henry.

"I so agree!" Clapping her hands together, she quickly changed the direction of the conversation. "I understand that Gladys is bringing a young woman with her today to visit and share the supper meal."

Last Sunday after worship service Emma had invited *Maedel* Blank and her *maem* as well as Gladys Getz to join them for supper the following week. While the Blanks were regular guests at the Weavers' Sunday gatherings, this was only the second time that Emma had extended the invitation to Gladys, who had never married but had taught school for years.

When Anna had lived with the Weavers, both she and Emma had always enjoyed inviting people to their home for Sunday meals, selecting those who might not have other family in the area with which to share fellowship. Henry certainly never seemed to mind, enjoying the time spent with new and interesting people. Emma's eclectic mixture of guests always seemed to bring a lively energy to the *haus*.

Today, however, promised to be especially entertaining, for Gladys had mentioned that she would be bringing a guest with her, a young woman, who had recently moved in with her. She had referred to the woman, Hannah Souder, as her niece, but last Thursday during her weekly visit to the Blanks, Emma had learned from Hetty that the only relation between the two was of the heart, not the physical body.

Now Emma turned her head to look at Gideon. "Have you met her yet, then?"

Gideon shook his head, his dark curls falling over his forehead. *"Nee,"* he responded. "I have not." Leaning forward, he stared directly at Emma. "She arrived at Gladys's just the other day, I heard. Apparently she was staying with another family south of Strasburg beforehand, but I do believe that she is originally from a community in Ohio. Outside of Berlin, I think. She lived with Gladys's *schwester*, if I recall properly."

"Ohio?" Emma said, lifting her eyebrows. She had forgotten that Gladys had family in Ohio. "Whatever is she doing here, then?"

"Visiting." The answer was direct and simple as if it explained everything. But it was clear that Emma's curiosity was piqued. "Knowing Gladys, this Hannah Souder is a lovely, God-fearing woman, even if so little is known of her family."

It was the sorrowful way that he said those words that caused Emma to gasp. "Gideon! Pray tell!"

He took a deep breath and sighed as he sat back in his seat. "I should have said nothing. I'd prefer not to spread idle gossip, Emma. It's not fair to say." He hesitated, leveling his eyes at Emma. "Or to judge. After all, the Bible tells us 'to aspire to live quietly, and to mind your own affairs, and to work with your hands.' Mayhaps you might want to reflect on that. Gossip is surely the work of evil."

She looked visibly put out and made a face at him. "I should say so," she responded, although her expression hinted at some disappointment that Gideon was not going to explain his comment about this Hannah Souder's background. There was no time to further the discussion as they were interrupted by the sound of a buggy pulling into the driveway. Glancing over her shoulder, she sought the view out the window. "It appears our guests have arrived!"

Her *daed* quickly put the recliner into an upright position and looked around the room. "I hope it's not too warm in here for them." A look of worry crossed his face. He looked first at Emma and then at Gideon. "*Mayhaps* we should visit outside in the breezeway. You know that when the air is so still that it's not good for the lungs."

Emma shook her head as if dismissing his concern, even though she hurried over to a closed window and lifted its lower pane. A gentle breeze blew through the opening as Emma turned back toward her *daed*. "Is that better, then?" She didn't wait for an answer as she hurried to the door to greet the Widow Blank and her *dochder*, Hetty.

"Our dear Emma," Hetty gushed as she led her aging mother by the hand through the door. Both women were rather petite, although the elder Blank walked with great difficulty, hunched over and shuffling her feet. Hetty, however, was bright and alert, with round glasses that often slipped down to the edge of her nose. "How right *gut* of you to invite us to supper! I was just talking to my *maem* about how kind and thoughtful you are!" She turned and peered at her mother. "Didn't I say that, *Maem*? About Emma being so kind and thoughtful?" She didn't wait for an answer as she turned back to Emma. "And such a lovely home it is! I don't think we've ever been here when it hasn't always looked just perfectly maintained!" She enunciated the last three words as if making a point.

Emma smiled but did not respond.

Hetty hurried by Emma and greeted the two men who were in the sitting room. "Henry! Gideon! So nice to spend some time with you both!" She smiled as she looked from the one to the other. Her glasses tipped down on her nose, and with a shaking hand, presumably from excitement and not nerves, she pushed them back so that she could see properly. "You have a most thoughtful and kind *dochder*, Henry. Reminds me so much of my dear niece, Jane!" With a delighted laugh, she glanced over her shoulder at Emma. "Did I tell you that I received a letter from her a few days ago? Shall I read it? She always has such *wunderbaar gut* stories!" She started to reach into the simple black cloth bag that hung from her wrist.

"Nee, Hetty," Emma was a little too quick to reply, but kept a pleasant smile on her face. The last thing Emma wanted was to encourage the dreaded reading of Jane's weekly letters to her *aendi* and *grossmammi*, especially with other company on the way. While the reading was inevitable, trying to limit it to a single iteration was most likely the best that Emma could hope for. Besides, she didn't want to remind Hetty that she had already been subjected to the reading of Jane's letter just three days ago. "I hear another buggy pulling into the driveway, and it would be most disagreeable to have to stop in the midst of the letter when they walk inside. You'd only have to start all over again, and I would think that would be rather tiring on such a warm day, *ja*?" Emma didn't wait for her guest to answer but politely excused herself as she started back to the door, more to escape the constant chatter of Hetty Blank than out of curiosity as to who had just arrived.

Pushing open the door, Emma was pleased to notice that it didn't squeak as it normally did. Her *daed* must have fixed it during the latter part of the week, she thought. Such a *gut* man, she pondered, then turned, just briefly, to gaze at him. He was hovering near Hetty and her *maem*, wringing his hands as he inquired whether the two women thought it was too warm inside for visiting or if they were comfortable enough. Shaking her head to herself, Emma stepped outside and waited to greet the newly arrived visitors.

Gladys exited the buggy first, her prayer *kapp* slightly askew on her graying head, and waved at Emma before she slipped the halter over the horse's head. She moved the reins safely back and constrained them so that they would not slip over the horse's croup and spook it while it was hitched to the side of the barn. Emma waited patiently for Gladys's guest to emerge, and when she did, Emma was immediately intrigued.

Hannah Souder was not exactly a pretty young woman, but the wisps of ginger hair that stuck out from beneath her prayer *kapp* and her bright, big eyes immediately spoke of an eagerness to please and learn. Her beauty seemed to radiate from the inside. Her steps conveyed the impression that she was bouncing behind Gladys with such eagerness that Emma found herself smiling, already liking this new addition to their Sunday supper gathering, even if her prayer *kapp* was not heart-shaped like the Lancaster Amish. Instead, it hugged the back of Hannah's head, more rounded and stiffer like the rest of the Amish women wore in her Ohio settlement. Even her dress, a pale pink in color, which Emma thought did not particularly flatter her coloring, was slightly different in design.

"*Wilkum!*" Emma greeted Gladys with a warm handshake before turning to Hannah. "And you must be Hannah Souder! I have heard much about you and have been looking forward to meeting you!"

"*Danke.*" The response was simple and soft. She was shy. That was apparent from the way she couldn't quite meet

Emma's eyes. As she made her way into the house, Emma observed her with curiosity. She noticed right away that Hannah barely exhibited any form of social grace as she was introduced to the Blanks, Henry, and Gideon. Despite the smile on her face, she stared at the floor shyly and made certain to stand behind Gladys, rather than next to her. She even hesitated to shake hands with Emma's *daed*. Still, there was a kindness about the young woman's face that made her immediately appealing to Emma.

"I have the Scrabble game set in the sunroom," Emma announced.

Hetty clapped her hands and glanced around the room. "Oh, how I love Scrabble! Such a fine way to spend time together. I'd love to play, wouldn't you, *Maem*?"

When her mother squinted and frowned, clearly not hearing what her *dochder* had said, Hetty repeated her question louder. "Scrabble, she said. Scrabble!"

Emma smiled as the two women hurried into the sunroom, joined by Gladys and Hannah, to play the game while she finished preparing the supper meal. She worked in the kitchen, preparing the platters of food while listening to the laughter and arguing in the other room over their selection of words. Her *daed* and Gideon sat on the sofa, talking about local news and occasionally interrupting to share their opinion about the validity of a word used in the board game. For Emma it was the perfect Sunday afternoon, and her insides felt warm with the love that was permeating her home.

It was close to four o'clock when the gathering moved to the table for the light supper. With everything properly prepared earlier, Emma had little to do but set the platters and bowls in the center of the table before calling the guests to come for fellowship. *Daed* took his place at the head of the table and Emma was quick to sit beside him.

"There's an extra place setting," Gideon pointed out as he sat at the other end of the table. "Are you expecting another?"

There was no need to answer as the door opened and a young man walked through. "My deepest apologies, Emma," he said as he removed his hat and greeted the gathering. "My *daed* asked me to visit with the neighbors, and the time got away from me!" He smiled at the others who were already seated around the table, his eyes falling upon Hannah. "Why, I do believe that I know everyone here except for one! Do introduce me, Emma!"

With his freshly shaved face and bright blue eyes, Paul Esh brought a crisp liveliness to the gathering, and Emma was quick to introduce him to Hannah. When she lowered her eyes and blushed at his attention, a thought struck Emma in regard to the young woman's social inadequacies and apparent shyness.

I can help her, she thought. *The way Anna helped me.*

Her mind quickly worked, playing forward the different ways that she could repay Anna's kindness and devotion toward her over the years. After all, Anna had taught her how to properly balance being a godly woman with her commitment to helping the community. *It is more blessed to give than receive,* had been the way that Emma was raised. After the fifteen years of sacrifice that Anna had made, raising her *onkel's kinner* rather than her own, Emma had taken great satisfaction in seeing her happily married at last.

Now this newcomer to their community, obviously from a smaller and less cosmopolitan settlement of Amish, could benefit from Emma's friendship and guidance. Emma could help Hannah adapt to the ways of the Lancaster

County Amish as well as possibly finding her too a suitable match...just as she had done with Anna!

With a new sense of purpose, Emma leaned forward and paid extra attention to every word that Hannah spoke and to her every interaction. She also observed how her guests interacted with the young woman, especially Paul Esh. The more Emma watched, the more convinced she was that her role in assimilating this newcomer into the community in order to ensure that Hannah was properly acclimated and accepted, and possibly even married, was meant to be.

Now that Anna was happily settled into her new life with Samuel, it was time for Emma to guide another young woman to a long life of wedded bliss. And by the end of the evening she was convinced that Hannah was the one that God intended for her to guide.

✦ Chapter Two ✦

EMMA PULLED BACK on the reins, a soft "whooooa" on her lips as she waited for the horse to slow down and stop in front of Gladys's small ranch house. It was only a mile from the home she shared with her *daed*, but it was located on a much busier street. She waited patiently for Hannah to emerge from the front entrance, pausing to ensure that the door shut properly behind her before she crossed the small patch of grass and opened the buggy door.

"*Gut mariye*, Emma!" Hannah practically sang as she climbed into the buggy.

In her pink dress and odd-shaped prayer *kapp* the young Amish woman from Ohio was, indeed, fair enough. There was an amusing spring to the seventeen-year-old's step that spoke of youth on the verge of womanhood. Her dark eyes sparkled and her ruddy cheeks hinted at plenty of time spent outdoors. Emma wondered whether her new friend had worked on a farm in Ohio and made a mental note to inquire further about her life back home.

"All is *vell* today, *ja?*" Emma replied as she tugged gently at the reins for the horse to back up so that she could pull out of the horseshoe-shaped driveway.

"Right as rain, *ja!*"

There was something jovial about Hannah which confirmed Emma's initial opinion of the young woman. Despite the four-year age difference between them and Hannah's particular mannerisms, she would certainly do well as a replacement companion for Anna. Furthermore, Emma knew that her idea for arranging a match between Hannah and Paul would certainly cement her unofficial role as matchmaker in the *g'may*. The image of Gideon's face when she, once again, could boast her success brought her much inner delight.

"I understand that you grew up in Ohio," Emma began probing cautiously. "You must be missing your parents, *ja?*"

"Oh." The simple word came out as a gasp and Hannah glanced away. She seemed to hesitate and clear her throat, reluctant to discuss the matter.

"Is something wrong?"

"*Ja vell,*" Hannah began to reply, squirming ever so slightly in the buggy beside Emma. "I was raised by my *aendi*. Or, at least, I call her my *aendi*." When she paused from speaking, Hannah glanced at Emma and saw that her new friend was frowning. "I never knew my parents," she offered as an explanation.

Emma fought the urge to gasp at this news. How could anyone not know his or her parents? Despite the fact that her own *maem* had passed away to join Jesus in heaven while Emma was still a small girl, she at least had the memories of her *maem* from the first part of her youth. With her *daed* being so much older than her *maem*, she prayed her thanks to the Lord every morning and every evening for having permitted him to stay with her for as long as he already had.

"I see," she finally managed to say, wondering whether they had died from disease or accident. The thought of any other possibility never crossed her mind. "Most unusual circumstances, I imagine."

Hannah shrugged her shoulders, obviously not as uncomfortable as Emma about her family background. Of course, having grown up under such a situation, it would not make her uncomfortable, at least not uncomfortable enough to provide further explanation to Emma.

"And your *aendi*?"

"Oh, she was a lovely woman." A smile spread across Hannah's face and she seemed to come to life. "I helped her serve dinner to guests and worked at market. We always met the most interesting people at her dinners. *Englische* women, mostly." She laughed. "They so loved to have a true Amish meal. Isn't that something? What we take for granted they seem to covet so!"

Emma laughed with her new friend. "We see the same curiosity among the tourists here too. I see there is not much difference between Holmes County and Lancaster County after all!"

"Oh, it's different," Hannah admitted. "I feel it is much more ..." She sought for the right word. "Proper."

"Here?" The word squeaked out and Emma could barely contain herself. "Proper? In what way?"

Hannah shrugged. "It's hard to say exactly." Then, as if fearing she may have offended her new friend, she quickly added, "But I don't mean it in a negative way."

"Of course not." Emma slowed the horse down at a stop sign, looking both ways before she crossed the intersection. Another buggy passed, going the opposite direction, and the driver, an older man, lifted his hand in greeting to the two young women.

"My *aendi* fell ill last spring. Now she's in a nursing home where she can be better cared for. That was why I came to Gladys's. They were right *gut* friends, Gladys is almost like another *aendi* to me. So when she offered for me to stay here, I thought a change might be nice."

"But you like Lancaster, then?"

Hannah smiled as she nodded her head. "Oh, *ja*! Very much. However..." Her voice trailed off and the smile faded just a touch. "Besides you and Gladys, the only other people I know here are the Martins. Do you know them? They live on the south side of Route Thirty, you know. Near Strasburg."

Strasburg? To Emma, that seemed so far away from where she lived in Lititz. "*Nee*, I don't seem to know the family name."

"They were originally from Ohio, you see. But moved here a few years back. When Elizabeth Martin heard that I was to come here, she invited me to stay at their farm for a few weeks. To visit, you know."

Emma turned the buggy into the parking lot of the fabric store, located next to the Kitchen Kettle in the town of Intercourse. While the tourists tended to visit the cluttered stores of the shopping village, few ventured to the hidden treasure of the dry goods store next door. It was hidden by the hardware store and a well-kept secret among the Amish. "I'm sure that was nice to visit with an old friend. A great way to start your new life in Lancaster County."

For the next hour they browsed through the rows of bolts of fabric, discussing the different colors and patterns while rubbing the cloth through their fingers to check the quality of the material. They ignored the few *Englische* tourists who walked past them, staring at the two Amish women while they shopped. To further isolate themselves, Emma began speaking Pennsylvania Dutch so that the outsiders could not eavesdrop on their conversation. Hannah suppressed a giggle when Emma did that, and both of them had a laugh about it when they finally left the dry goods store, their arms laden with wrapped cloth.

"Do you mind if I run to the hardware store, Hannah?" Emma was putting the packages into the back of the buggy as she spoke to her friend. "My *daed* needs a new hinge for the stall door. I promised I'd pick it up today as Paul Esh volunteered to stop by later and fix it for us. The old one is barely hanging on!"

"Of course!"

Emma smiled at her friend. "He's such a *gut* man, Paul Esh," she started. "That was thoughtful of him to offer to fix the hinge. My *daed's* hands don't work so well anymore, you see."

Hannah nodded her head in agreement. "He seemed most pleasant the other day at your *haus*."

Together they crossed through the parking lot and entered the hardware store's back door, avoiding the foot traffic along the main street of the town. "And a godly man, at that," Emma was quick to add. "Why, I was visiting a sick elderly woman just a few weeks back, and just as I was about to leave, he showed up with a box full of canned peaches! Very thoughtful of him, ain't so?"

"*Ja, ja!*" This time Hannah seemed a bit more enthusiastic as she responded.

No sooner had they started walking down the center aisle than a young man almost bumped into them. He was a tall Amish man who wore dirty black pants and a white shirt that was missing one button. Emma had never seen him before so she was quite surprised when Hannah greeted him with a smile.

"Ralph Martin! Whatever are you doing here?"

"Why, Hannah Souder!" He grinned in response to her greeting. "I thought you were staying in Lititz with Gladys! A pleasant surprise bumping into you, I must say."

A hint of a giggle escaped Hannah's lips and she blushed. "We only just came to town for quilting supplies."

Emma frowned, looking first at her friend before turning her gaze to the man standing before them. He looked to be not much older than she was, but there was a weathered look to his face. Certainly he was a man who worked outdoors, and that most likely meant that he was a farmer. Yet she could not understand his disheveled appearance. To come to town in such a filthy outfit, she thought!

His eyes flickered toward Emma.

"Forgive me," Hannah gushed. "Ralph, this is my friend Emma."

He nodded his head in acknowledgment but paid no further attention to Emma. His eyes were large and wide, seeing only Hannah.

"Elizabeth will most certainly tell me to send her regards," he said. "She has missed your company."

"*Danke*," Hannah replied, her cheeks flushing under his constant stare, the change in color not going unnoticed by Emma.

"You are staying in the area then?"

The question was directed to Hannah, and Emma was beginning to realize that she was not a part of this conversation. Indeed, she felt like a voyeur, watching a scene unfold before her and, with it, the image vanished of Gideon's smiling face approving Emma's match between Hannah and Paul.

She listened to the banter between Hannah and Ralph, a frown on her face as she saw the telltale signs on Hannah's. Indeed, there was a connection between her friend and this young man, a connection that was not one sided but reciprocated by each. Politely Emma excused herself to hurry down the aisle, searching for the hinge that her *daed* needed. Her mind reeled as she realized that her plans for helping Hannah find favorable appeal in the eyes of Paul Esh might be compromised by this one chance meeting in the hardware store.

Only after she had paid for the hinge and returned to Hannah's side did she realize the extent of her friend's interest in Ralph Martin. They were discussing an article in the latest *Blackboard Bulletin* and laughing about the writer's interpretation of a particular Scripture. Emma cleared her throat and forced a smile.

"We really must get going," she whispered to Hannah, eager to leave the store. "We need to stop over at Anna's for help with the pattern, and I need to be certain to return home by dinnertime."

"I've kept you long enough, then," Ralph said, obviously overhearing what Emma had whispered, just as she had intended. "It was right *gut* to see you again, Hannah." He lifted his hand to wave at Emma before turning around and heading down the next aisle.

Emma's eyes trailed after him, and she noticed that he looked up not once but twice to watch as Hannah left the store. Emma quickly decided that she needed to know more about this Ralph Martin and to understand what, exactly, was the extent of the relationship between him and Hannah.

"How well do you know Ralph Martin?" she asked as they walked down the sidewalk toward the horse and buggy tied to the hitching post.

Hannah giggled and blushed for the second time. "When I first came out here, I stayed a week at their house. I met his sister, Elizabeth, in Ohio when she came out last year for a cousin's wedding."

Emma's red flag went up even further. "And what does Ralph do for a living?"

"He raises pigs," Hannah replied.

Immediately Emma's feet stopped walking and she turned to stare at her friend. "You mean he's a pig farmer?" Despite her best intentions, Emma couldn't hide the tone in her voice, a tone that bespoke her displeasure at this occupation. After all, everyone knew that being a pig farmer was one of the most distasteful careers for an Amish man. It was, indeed, a dirty business, with a smell that lingered on the skin no matter how often one showered. "And you stayed at their farm for...an entire week?"

Hannah nodded, too wrapped up in her thoughts to notice Emma's tone. "They rent it, you know. From your friend Gideon, I believe."

This was news indeed. Emma frowned. She had never inquired too much about Gideon's private business. Most of the times when he visited, his attention was directed at her *daed*. Of course, as the years had passed and the acquaintance become more familiar, she knew that he owned a large property where storage sheds were built for the *Englische*. He had upwards of twelve Amish men who worked for him, building the structures, a fact that freed up quite a bit of his time to permit, among other things, his weekly visits to her *daed*.

"Why, I had no idea! Gideon never mentioned that he rented out a farm. And all the way in Strasburg?" She made a mental note to inquire about this tidbit of news from her *daed*. "With all the time that he spends visiting, I should think I would know him better than most!"

"It's a small farm," Hannah said. "I believe he inherited it." She was quiet as she searched her memory. "*Nee*, that's not it. He bought it when he was younger and intended to farm. However, he's been letting it out to the Martins for almost twelve years. That's what Ralph told me."

This news surprised Emma. She didn't like being caught off guard. "Regardless, I'm quite certain that I have never met your friend before today!"

"What did you think of him?" Hannah asked, a soft smile on her lips—one that Emma didn't care for at all. She could read the message behind that smile. It was a smile that spoke of buggy rides home from singings and whispered promises in the dark. "He's a rather kind-looking man, *ja?*"

Emma hesitated before responding, trying to carefully figure out her words before speaking. She certainly did not want to insult this man. Still, she was perplexed as to how she could point out the obvious flaw to her friend. "I think most people are, ain't so?" she finally stammered. "There is certainly nothing unkind in his face."

The hesitant manner of Emma's speech caused Hannah to pause and ponder her words. "Is there something wrong with Ralph, Emma?"

"*Nee, nee*," she responded quickly...too quickly...as she resumed walking toward the buggy. She lifted her hand and waved to an older woman who walked down the sidewalk toward the store they had just left. "I've always admired farmers for their gentle mannerisms and simple ways."

"He is gentle," Hannah admitted.

"I suppose he doesn't leave the farm very often," Emma added. "It must be a lonely life, living on a farm. Most girls today work at market or clean unless they were raised on a farm. I'm rather thankful that my *daed* wasn't a farmer."

"It is hard work," Hannah agreed.

"Ja vell," Emma smiled. "I'm sure he'll be a right *gut* man for some woman who doesn't mind the occupation that comes with him."

"You mean because he raises pigs?"

Emma glanced at Hannah. "I had an *onkel* who raised a pig once and I could scarce stand the stench. I wonder how many pigs Ralph keeps?"

A forlorn look of understanding crossed Hannah's face. "He gets them on contract. There weren't any there when I stayed with Elizabeth, but she told me he gets over a hundred at a time."

"A hundred!" Emma gasped at the number. "Why! You must thank the good Lord that you were there in between contracts! The smell of a hundred hogs would never have left your clothing!"

Hannah wrinkled her nose. "I suppose there was a mild odor to the farm, I do reckon."

"Certainly nothing like a dairy farm or a home with a man of trade," Emma added casually. "I'm more familiar with men like Gideon King and Paul Esh! Why, I'm sure that Paul Esh's house never smells like pig!" She laughed lightly and was pleased that Hannah joined her. "And I can scarce imagine a pig farmer ever being nominated to lead the church! That's such a great honor, you know," she whispered before she opened the buggy door and placed her foot on the metal step. "A true godly man leads the church, nominated by the people and chosen by God."

Hannah didn't respond.

"Consider how different your Ralph is when compared to Gideon or…" She glanced at Hannah. "Paul." She smiled. "Why, Paul was most delightful company the other night, and he's a godly man, don't you think?"

"Paul did seem rather righteous the other evening," Hannah said slowly. "In a good way, of course."

"Of course." Emma pulled herself into the buggy and moved over, giving Hannah room to join her on the cloth-covered seat. "After all, Paul is the son of the bishop. I would expect nothing less than for him to be a role model of righteousness for the rest of us to emulate. Why, I wouldn't be surprised if he was nominated to lead the church one day too!" She smiled at Hannah, who was now sitting beside her. "After he's married, that is."

Without another word Emma released the brake to the buggy and urged the horse to back up a few steps before pulling lightly on the right rein in order to leave the parking lot of the general store. There was no further discussion about Paul Esh or Ralph Martin as they drove the back roads toward the Wagler home. Instead, the two young women began to talk about the quilt that they intended to make and how exciting it would be to have it finished in time for the October auction.

The Wagler home was small and quaint. As farm land fell prey to development, the Amish community continued to expand, forcing more and more families to live in contemporary homes. It was easy to convert them to accommodate the Amish lifestyle, simply by removing the electric lines and modern conveniences. The Wagler home was one of them.

However, it sat on a nice-size lot, and most would consider it a farmette despite the fact that most of the property seemed to be simple pasture.

As Emma pulled the buggy into the driveway, she looked around at her friend's new home with a sense of comfort. Samuel Wagler may have been alone for many years, but it was clear that he had a fine sense of care when it came to his property. Not a weed grew among the landscaping, and the bushes were all properly trimmed. It spoke well of his character, and once again Emma was pleased for her cousin in marrying such a fine man.

"*Wilkum*, girls!" Anna Wagler stood at the front door and smiled at the two young women as they made their way to the house, their arms laden with cloth for the quilt they were going to make. "I was wondering when you might arrive! Come in, come in!"

Despite being older, Anna still had the physique of a young woman, tall and willowy instead of the typical stoutness found in Amish women her age. Her brown hair, pulled back under the white heart-shaped prayer *kapp*, lacked any gray, and her dark eyes sparkled at her two visitors. Clearly Anna was happy in her new home and eager to entertain her former ward and her friend.

The kitchen was smaller than the one at Emma's home, and it took her a moment to get oriented to the differences between the two. There was a small, plain pine table with a pretty green-and-white checkered tablecloth covering it. Anna had already set out a pitcher of meadow tea and a basket of freshly baked cookies. After the proper greetings were exchanged, Anna encouraged the girls to partake of the refreshments. While Emma merely took one cookie to nibble at, Hannah was more than happy to have two.

"So which pattern will you do then?" Anna asked as she fingered the material. "You sure picked out beautiful colors."

And they had. Emma loved the color blue and had picked different variations and patterns in that color. Against a white backdrop, the quilt would be lovely on any bed. "For the center panel," she responded, her fingers brushing against one bolt of the fabric. "Something simple like the shoofly pattern, I reckon. But I'm thinking to leave a wider border and do some more detailed quilting patterns there."

"Why, that will be quite lovely!" Anna exclaimed.

"And we'll be donating it to the Mennonite Central Committee to raise money for the poor," Emma added with a smile. Her face lit up at the mention of helping others. She had first started donating her work when she was fourteen. Her older sister, Irene, had helped with her first quilt, a simple twin-size quilt in greens and brown cloth. While not a very intricate piecing design, the quilting itself had been labored over during the late summer and early autumn months. When she had finally finished it, everyone had been surprised at her proclamation that she was donating it, rather than putting it into her own hope chest.

Over the years Anna had helped Emma with the piecing and quilting for at least five quilts. It saddened both of their hearts that, because of her marriage, she would not be able to work on this new quilt with Emma. In times past they enjoyed many a quiet afternoon seated in front of the old wooden quilting frame set up in the living room of the Weaver household. There was something about quilting that created a bond between women.

"And Hannah," Anna began, shifting her attention from Emma to the younger woman. "Have you made many quilts then?"

"Nee." Hannah shook her head in response. "This will be my first."

"Your first quilt?" The question came out more as an expression of disbelief. Anna looked from Hannah to Emma then back to Hannah. Emma didn't need for Anna to say what was on her mind. It was almost impossible to believe that any Amish woman had never made a quilt. *"Ja vell,* then," Anna stammered, searching for the right words. "It's right *gut* that Emma shows you how, I reckon. She has a lovely stitch."

"It's no finer than yours, I reckon," Emma countered demurely, but her eyes glowed at the compliment. "After all, it was you who taught me."

For the next hour the three women sketched out on paper the pattern for the quilt, deciding the order of the different fabric for each of the individual squares used to make up the quilt. Most of the discussion was between Emma and Anna, Hannah being a mere observer who watched the conversation as if she were at a volleyball game. Her eyes traveled from Emma to Anna and back to Emma again as the two women laid out their plan on paper, obvious experts in a field that Hannah knew nothing about and to which she could contribute nothing more than her enthusiasm for learning.

It was close to eleven when they heard the sound of men's footsteps on the porch. Emma lifted her head from the paper where she had been sketching the final design and glanced at Anna, an unspoken question lingering in the air. It didn't need to be answered as Samuel appeared in the doorway with a familiar face by his side.

"Why, Gideon King!" Emma exclaimed. "Whatever brings you here?"

He laughed at her reaction. "Helping Samuel with some new equipment he bought at the auction. You shouldn't sound so surprised, Emma. I do have other friends beside your *daed.*"

She made a face at his teasing statement but did not respond. She was too used to Gideon being a fixture at their own house, a regular companion to her *daed*, welcomed even more now that Anna had married and moved to her own house with her new husband.

"Equipment?" Anna smiled and glanced over Gideon's shoulder at her husband. "Did you purchase something then?"

"Ja, ja, I did." He set his straw hat on the counter and ran his fingers through his graying hair. The age difference between Samuel and Anna disappeared whenever he set his eyes upon his young wife. The sparkle that lit up his face made it more than clear how he felt about her. "It's only a small farmette, but we can have a right nice garden and I can set up my shop in the outer building."

Emma raised an eyebrow and glanced at Anna. "You'll be gardening?"

"Oh, *ja!* A right big garden with corn, brussels sprouts, asparagus, and peppers, as well as the usual things we planted at your home."

The way Anna nodded her head and smiled surprised Emma, for while Anna had been the main gardener at the Weaver home for all of those years, she had never expressed such enthusiasm for the chore. Granted, the Weaver property was small, not even two full acres, and the garden had only consisted of simple things, such as herbs, tomatoes, beans, and cucumbers. For the rest of their needs they had chosen to buy their vegetables and canned goods from neighbors and friends. They had kept far too busy with quilting and visiting and tending to the care of the house and *Daed*, especially after he retired from his work repairing buggies.

"I never knew you to be one to garden, Anna!" Emma laughed lightly as she said it. "I may have to learn one or two more things from you yet!"

"I don't think I taught you all of my tricks," Anna teased back. "We are also going to raise chickens and sell eggs!"

At this announcement, Emma's mouth dropped open and she found herself rendered speechless.

It was Gideon who laughed this time, only not at Anna's announcement. "Well played, Anna. Anyone who can steal the words from our dear Emma has my admiration. Lord knows that I've been trying to do it for years." He winked at Hannah. "And not often able to succeed, might I admit."

"I gardened in Ohio and found it most relaxing," Hannah declared.

Surprised, Emma turned her eyes to look upon her friend. "Did you, then? Why, you are a gardener but not a quilter! I think today is a day of surprises for me...from my cousin Anna and my new friend Hannah!"

Everyone laughed at Emma's innocent remark and she too joined them, always being agreeable to laughing at herself when the situation warranted it.

The clock on the wall began to chime. Emma turned to look at it and gasped when she saw the time. "Oh, help!" She began to gather the items on the table, stacking the papers in a neat pile and placing them on top of the folded piles of cloth. "We best get going," she said to Hannah. "*Daed* will need his dinner!" Everyone knew that Henry Weaver was a creature of habit as well as one of worry. If Emma was late to return, her *daed* would not only worry about his *dochder*, he would also be forced to wait for his noon meal. The combination of both would create havoc for all to experience for several days, for he'd be certain to inform everyone of the matter and the reason for it.

Still, the blame did not rest entirely on Henry's shoulders. Emma was only too willing to ensure that her *daed* wanted for nothing. While her compassion for others was well known in the *g'may*, being one of the traits that made her the go-to person during a time of need, her coddling of her aging father was another matter entirely. Some of the *g'may* members thought it was *wunderbaar gut* that a *dochder* took such doting care of her *daed*, while others disapproved of the fact that she could have no private life of her own while tending to his. Despite having taken the kneeling vow several years prior, the bottom line was that Emma Weaver had refused to court any young man in the *g'may* and gave no indication that she'd ever settle down, not if it meant leaving her *daed* on his own.

Gideon stood on the porch, watching as the two young women hurried to the waiting buggy, eager to return to the Weaver home in order to start cutting the pieces for their quilt top. He smiled at their enthusiasm but there was something else, something wistful and distant in his gaze.

When the buggy pulled away, he turned to Anna. "I'm not quite certain about this friendship between the two girls," he mumbled.

"Is that so? I do wonder that!" Anna sounded genuinely surprised at his statement.

Gideon shrugged. "Hannah seems quite innocent and different from our Emma. Certainly not as mature. I fear Emma is placing a replacement *kapp* upon her new friend's head in order to fill a void from your departure."

Anna glanced toward the road as if she could still see the two women. But the porch was empty and the road long deserted by the buggy. "Hannah might be a breath of fresh air for Emma," she countered. "After all, Emma has a lot she can teach her. She is wise beyond her years."

At that, Gideon smiled. "Wise indeed. She learned from the best, I reckon." The look in his eyes indicated that he was referring specifically to Anna's influence on Emma.

"No better than any other woman in the *g'may*." While her words spoke of modesty, the flush on her cheeks, however, said otherwise.

"Well, at least they are spending their time doing something for the good of others." There was an approving tone in his voice, at last.

❧ *Chapter Three* ❧

THE QUILT TOP was rolled in the large wooden frame next to the living room windows. Emma preferred that location for the afternoon sun, the natural light warm and welcoming for the hours she would spend seated in her chair, her head bent over the quilting frame as she worked. Years ago her *daed* had found her a special chair just for her quilting: old with a cracked leather seat and resting on wheels so that she could slide down beside the frame as she quilted. When others came by to help her quilt, she always offered them her chair, but they would decline, knowing that Emma's quick stitches were better suited for the rolling chair while they could make do with folding chairs.

For the past week she had worked diligently on the quilt. With the help of Anna, the two women managed to piece the quilt top in only two days. Both Hannah and Emma spent almost a full day working on it the previous Saturday, even beginning to quilt the pattern with Anna joining them for the early part of the afternoon. With Emma's love of quilting, she often spent additional hours in the evening after Hannah returned home, the silence of the room broken only by the gentle hissing of the propane lantern beside the quilting frame.

The only day she did not quilt was Sunday, a day when such pleasures were forbidden by Bishop Esh. It didn't matter to Emma. She always enjoyed a day of worship, relaxation, and visiting with friends and neighbors.

On that particular Sunday she attended the worship service with her *daed* at the Yoders', who owned a nearby farm. The three-hour service, followed by an hour of fellowship, took up the first half of the day. Then, as usual, Emma invited the Widow and Maedel Blank, Paul Esh, Gideon, Gladys, and Hannah for supper. The Waglers were still busy visiting family on the weekends, something that newly married couples did for the first few months of their marriage.

It was a lively gathering, with Hetty Blank's constant chatter and habit of repeating herself to her *maem*, keeping the noise level energized. And then there was Henry with his fretting over the types of food the people in the *g'may* were eating, worrying that nonorganic food was causing sickness. Both Gladys and Gideon seemed to listen with the utmost respect. At one point Emma thought she heard Gideon promise to help plow the garden in the back so that the Weavers could continue growing their own food next spring. *And who would tend this garden?* Emma wondered. Personally she did not relish the chore.

But it was the interactions between Paul and Hannah that Emma paid the most attention to. She thought herself most clever in seating Paul next to Hannah, pleased to see that the conversation between the two flowed naturally and with intimate ease. Hannah seemed to hang on to his every word, and on the few occasions that she spoke, he seemed to do the same. Inwardly Emma hugged herself in delight at the knowledge that once again she may have made a *wunderbaar gut* match!

In the evening Paul even offered to pick up both Hannah and Emma and take them to the Sunday evening youth singing that was to be held in the Yoders' barn. Emma was quick to agree, knowing that Paul would certainly offer to bring them home as well. With Gladys's home located farther away than the Weavers, Emma asked if Paul could drop her off first, claiming the onset of a sudden headache which had not been *entirely* untrue. However, the primary reason for the request was to enable him plenty of time to spend alone with Hannah as they rode the buggy through the dark back roads of Lititz.

The following day, Hannah came quilting. With great delight, she meted out the details of the buggy ride home and the conversations that she had shared with Paul.

"He loves to garden, Emma! Did you know that?" she asked as they sat around the quilting frame. "And he had *wunderbaar* advice about planting medical herbs. You know how I love to garden so!"

Emma merely smiled, replying with a nod of her head as well as the occasional "*Ja*" and "Oh help!" in response to the surprising stories that Hannah shared with her.

On Tuesday Anna and Hetty joined them for quilting. It wasn't as peaceful as the previous day. As was to be expected, Hetty spent most of the time talking about her niece, Jane, who lived in Holmes County, Ohio, with her parents. They had moved there years before when land was too scarce for her *daed* to continue farming. Because Jane's family was tied down to the land and animals they raised, the only time that Hetty and her *maem* managed to see their favorite niece was on the infrequent trips that they managed to take to

Ohio. The last trip had been over three years prior, a fact that Hetty lamented quite frequently.

Usually when Emma visited Hetty and her *maem*, Hetty insisted upon reading the latest letter from Jane, sometimes not just once but twice. On Tuesday Hetty brought along the latest missive, one that had arrived that very morning. Emma, taking a deep breath, had said a silent prayer for God to grant her patience, and focused more on the quilting than on Hetty's words.

So today she was quite grateful that no one was planning to visit. Anna and Hetty had their own commitments, and Hannah had asked to be excused from assisting with the quilt as she needed to help Gladys with some chores around the house.

Indeed, Emma was quite content with that arrangement. She loved nothing more than to sit there, in her special wooden chair on wheels, and reflect on Scripture while quilting. Besides, she reasoned, she could quilt ever so much faster when she wasn't engaged in conversation anyway. The progress of the quilt was apparent; it was coming along nicely, and they were well ahead of the schedule Emma had sketched out in her diary.

So it surprised her when, shortly before noon, Hannah rushed through the kitchen door and hurried toward the living room area. Her face was beaming and she held a small envelope in her hand. The glow in her eyes clearly indicated that she came along with wonderful news. Still, it took a moment for Emma to calm her nerves from the unexpected intrusion.

"My word, Hannah!" Emma set down her thimble and needle and spun around in the chair. She lifted her hand to her chest, placing it over her heart. "You startled me! I didn't expect you today."

"My apologies!" Hannah's eyes twinkled and she smiled brightly, pushing at a stray strand of her ginger red hair that had fallen free from her *kapp*. "I could scarce wait to tell you the news. I nearly ran the entire way here! I can hardly believe it myself."

"Ran? Why, that's close to a mile! Whatever could have happened? Do tell!"

Hannah giggled and thrust the envelope at her friend. "You must read it for yourself. I don't think I am capable right now of speaking of it!"

Hesitantly Emma reached for the envelope, taking it from Hannah's outstretched hand. She withdrew the letter and unfolded it, too aware of Hannah's glow of happiness. Quickly her eyes scanned the neatly written words on the paper... not once, but twice. The shock of the words almost caused her to catch her breath, but she made certain to be extra careful to moderate her reaction. It would do no good to speak her mind on this matter.

"Can you believe it?" Hannah clasped her hands together and gave a little bounce of delight. Another giggle escaped her lips and she spun around, the skirt of her dress flaring out. "Ralph Martin wants to court me!"

"I...I see that," Emma said as she neatly folded the letter and carefully slid it back into the envelope. An official request for courting, especially at this time of the year with the wedding season just months away, meant only one thing: an imminent proposal for marriage. Since he lived in a different church district, Ralph was clearly asking for her permission, with that on his mind. It made no sense to travel all the way to Lititz from Strasburg if Hannah had no interest in seeing him.

"What do you think?" Hannah reached for the letter, holding it in her hands as if it were the most precious item on earth. She stared at it, her eyes taking in the neat handwriting on the outside of the envelope. "It's a fine letter, isn't it?"

"Indeed." Emma took a deep breath. "So fine a letter that it lends me to wonder if his *schwester* helped him write it. I can hardly imagine the man I met last week capable of expressing himself so well, never mind this impressive penmanship!"

Hannah giggled again and pressed the missive to her chest. "Can you imagine?"

"*Nee*." Emma pursed her lips. "*Nee*, I really cannot."

As if sensing that Emma did not quite share her joy, Hannah stopped and looked at her friend. "What shall I do?"

Emma frowned. "In regard to the letter?"

"Of course!" Hannah replied, her tone slightly exasperated. "Shall I write back right away then?"

"*Ja*, I think so," Emma concurred.

Hannah sighed and plopped down into the recliner near the window. She tapped her fingers impatiently on the arm of the chair. "But what must I say? I'm not nearly as eloquent as you are, Emma. I do need your help, please."

For a moment Emma pondered her words carefully. "I think it should be drafted in your own words, Hannah. Show your gratitude and flattery while expressing your own disappointment as you refuse him gently but quickly and with kindness."

Emma's words stopped Hannah, causing her hands to fall to her side, the letter still held in her left hand. "Refuse him?" Her mouth fell open, and the shock that she felt at Emma's words was apparent on her expression. "You think I should *refuse* him?"

"Oh, help and bother!" Emma covered her mouth and looked away. She felt the heat rise to her cheeks as she realized her blunder. *A time to keep silence, and a time to speak,* she thought to herself. "I'm so sorry, Hannah! I misunderstood you. I didn't suspect that you were actually considering a favorable reply!" She reached out and clutched her friend's hand, staring into her face. "Please forgive me."

"Forgive you?" Hannah asked, a confused look on her face.

"Just never you mind my words, Hannah. I wouldn't dream of telling you what to do! Courtship is, after all, a very private matter."

But the seed was clearly planted.

"You...you think I should turn him away?" The tone in Hannah's voice was a mixture of surprise, indecision, and concern. Clearly she cared about Emma's opinion and what Emma thought about her possible suitor. "I hadn't realized he cared so much for me," she began, speaking aloud more for her own benefit than Emma's.

"Marriage is forever," Emma pointed out. "How long did you stay at their farm? A week? How well could you get to know someone in such a short period of time?"

"I suppose not very well."

"And I imagine it was short visits with his *schwesters* around, *ja*? Just short, friendly exchanges?"

Hannah nodded her head. "He was friendly, true. But to want to officially court me? I reckon it is rather...surprising," she said, although it sounded as though she was trying to convince herself more than Emma.

"Seems to me that, *mayhaps*, you have your own doubts,

ja?" Emma smiled softly as she returned her attention to her quilting. "Anna always told Irene and me that when a woman has doubts, she has no choice but to refuse. When one hesitates to say *ja*, then one must say *nee* immediately!"

There was a moment of silence, as Hannah contemplated Emma's words.

Emma took advantage of the pause to continue. "Of course, if you think Ralph is the most interesting and godly of men and wish to spend your life with him without any second thoughts about your future..." She let her voice trail off, the sentence unfinished as she pushed the needle into the quilt top once again. The silence that ensued reassured Emma that she had hit her mark and that Hannah was considering her words.

"I suppose it *is* rather sudden," Hannah admitted.

"And to spend your days as the wife of a pig farmer," Emma added, a disapproving look on her face. "I dare not think about how long and tedious your days would be. Why, we'd never get to see one another, I'm sure and certain! You'd be married to the farm as much as to Ralph!"

At this, Hannah gasped. "Never see you? I never thought about that! Oh, Emma! I can't imagine not being able to visit you on a regular basis!" She took a deep breath and tilted her chin, a fresh look of resolve on her face. "You are so right, Emma. I had not thought this through. I have no choice but to refuse his offer."

Setting down the needle, Emma smiled at her friend. "Well then, I reckon you should reply to him straight away, *ja?* Best tell him immediately what your response is to his proposition." Without waiting for an answer, she stood up and hurried over to the kitchen cabinet next to the refrigerator. She opened the drawer and withdrew a small, flat box.

"I have stationery here, Hannah. You can sit at the table to write the letter, if that helps."

To Emma's surprise, the color suddenly drained from Hannah's face. "Please help me, Emma. I have no idea what words to use!"

"Now, now," Emma soothed. "As I already said, just be kind and gentle yet firm in giving your refusal. I suppose it shouldn't be too long of a letter for fear that he will consider that a tease. You certainly have no need to fear your selection of words, Hannah. You are, after all, an intelligent creature."

Feeling more confident, Hannah nodded, an expression of determination on her face. She took the paper and a pen from Emma before bending her head down to begin drafting the letter to Ralph Martin, informing him that he dare not come courting her at Gladys's house after all.

After the letter was completed, carefully worded to avoid hurt feelings, or at least to lessen the blow, Emma inquired if she needed to return directly to Gladys's home. When Hannah shook her head, stating that she had managed to complete all of the necessary chores, Emma was quick to suggest that they return to the living room to quilt. A distraction would do her friend good, and Emma knew that sewing could do just that.

They sat by the quilting frame, the silence allowing time for meditation and reflection. Emma loved the sound of the thread poking through the fabric and sliding, ever so gracefully and smoothly, as she pulled it up from beneath the material. She could quilt for hours, she reckoned, but after a while her back would begin to ache just enough that she would have to set down the needle and thimble to take a moment to stretch her back. Blinking as she stood before the window, she felt a slow burning beneath her eyelids. *It won't be long,* she realized, *before I'll be needing glasses.*

"How long until we are finished, you reckon, Emma?"

Emma glanced over her shoulder at the quilt. In just a week, they had managed to quilt almost half of the quilt top. "Why, no more than two weeks if we continue to work at the same pace. Even less if we work harder. *Mayhaps* Anna might come visiting again to help a spell. Many hands make light the work." The adage was core to the Amish belief system. When people volunteered their assistance, tasks were always completed faster, and the fellowship of working alongside others always made the work more enjoyable.

"I was thinking," Emma said cautiously, breaking the light silence that had befallen them. "I'm sure that you'd like to meet more people in Lititz, and I had an idea about how to do so."

"Oh?" To say that Hannah was intrigued was putting it mildly. She set down her needle and stared at her friend. "Please share it with me. I'd love to hear it."

"Well," Emma started, her head dipped down as she pushed the needle through the quilt top. "You know I go visiting on Thursday mornings. I like to stop in at the homes of the widows in our district. Those are usually the days that their caretakers and family are busy at market, you see."

Hannah nodded, hanging onto every word that Emma spoke. Emma was pleased that her friend showed such interest, glad to create a diversion for Hannah after such an emotional morning in regard to Ralph Martin's letter.

"Ja vell," she continued. "If we were to ask members of the *g'may* to give us their favorite adages and Bible verses, we could compile them into a nice little booklet to copy and distribute to the widows for Christmas." She looked up, her

eyes glowing. "I do believe those women would love that, don't you think?"

A smile crossed Hannah's face as she gazed at Emma. "That is such a lovely idea, Emma. It almost brings tears to my eyes at how thoughtful and kindhearted you are."

"No more so than anyone else, I imagine," Emma responded modestly. "Although I do confess that it serves the additional purpose of better acquainting you with more people in the *g'may*."

The opening of a door interrupted their concentration. Emma glanced over her shoulder as her *daed* walked into the room, Paul Esh following close behind. At the sight of Paul, Emma smiled and immediately set down her needle and thimble.

"*Gut mariye*, Emma." Paul nodded in her direction. "And to you too, Hannah. I'd say that I'm surprised to see you here, but I heard from your *daed* that you are busy working on a new quilt for the auction."

"Hannah is helping mc, indeed."

"How very good of you, Hannah. It will certainly raise money that is much needed to help those less fortunate." Paul paused, his eyes drifting over the quilt that was spread taut in the frame.

At last Hannah stepped outside of her tendency toward shyness, as she replied, "Emma has arranged to donate the quilt to the Mennonite Central Committee. I have never quilted before so this has been a fun, new adventure for me. Emma has taught me so much!"

"I can only imagine," Paul said approvingly. "She is known for her many talents. And I'm sure she must certainly be a great teacher."

"Oh, *ja*, the best," Hannah gushed. "She knows so much about quilting. I have found a new passion, indeed!"

"A woman who quilts has admirable talents in my eyes. Such creativity and patience. I always said a quilting woman would be the one who steals my heart." He paused and glanced at the two women. "If that is God's will, of course."

Emma watched the exchange between the two, the smile still on her lips as she recognized a sparkle in Hannah's eyes that mirrored itself in Paul's. With a delightful skip of her heart she realized that a courtship would most certainly ensue between the two of them. And she was more than certain that Paul, while vastly different and much more acceptable in her eyes than Ralph Martin, shared one thing in common with the man: marriage on the mind.

"And what brings you to visit today?" she ventured to ask when a small lull of silence fell over the small group.

Removing his hat, Paul stood between the two women. His brown hair, cut in a typical Amish style of flat across the forehead and angled by his ears, was flattened on his head, and he quickly ran his fingers through it. "Figured it was time to make good on my promise to your *daed* and fix that hinge on the barn door. And none too soon, I might add. The old rusty one was more than ready to retire, I do believe."

Both Hannah and Emma laughed at his joke.

"*Danke*, Paul. His hands aren't as strong as they used to be."

"My pleasure," he replied with a beaming smile on his face.

Henry, however, grumbled under his breath at her comment. "Hands are just fine. It's my eyes that aren't so good. Need to eat more carrots, I tell you."

Ignoring her *daed's* complaints, Emma got up from her

chair and started toward the kitchen. "I made some fresh bread this morning," she said. "Let me package some for you to take home. To thank you for your help." Before Paul could counter her offer, she rested her hand on his arm. "We insist, don't we, *Daed*?"

"It's not that white bread, is it?" Henry called over his shoulder before turning his attention back to Paul. "Wheat bread, that's the only kind to have. Read it in a book about avoiding that cancer. Wheat works wonders. Any other is not healthy for the body. Wheat, I tell you."

With a quick lift of her eyes, Emma hurried past the men and into the kitchen. "*Ja, Daed*, it's wheat bread. I'd think no more of baking you white bread than I'd consider baking you a cake!"

Henry caught his breath and shook his head. "Cake! Why, that's just as bad as the white bread. All that sugar is bad for the body." He turned to Paul. "We need to eat healthier, honor God's temple in our bodies, and not poison it with sugar and processed food. Those *Englische* folk…why, just look at how they poison themselves and all the diseases they get as a result! You must tell your *daed* to preach about the benefits of wholesome food and whole-wheat bread made with flaxseed oil, as well! And when Irene visits next week, we must caution her to limit the sweets she gives to her *kinner*!"

Glancing over her shoulder, Emma noticed that Paul nodded his head in response to her father's ranting. She barely suppressed a smile and went about the task of wrapping the freshly made loaf of whole wheat bread in plastic for Paul's journey home. She took longer than usual, working slowly so that Hannah had no choice but to engage in conversation with Paul. He was quick to admire the progress of their quilting.

"I can't believe how much you have accomplished so far!" he exclaimed, a genuine look of admiration on his face. "I do believe you will be ready for binding the edges within the next week!"

Hannah looked over at Emma, not certain how to respond.

"Oh, the binding!" Emma returned to the room and handed Paul the wrapped loaf of bread. "We must send that out to be done. I must confess that binding is not one of my strengths."

At this comment, Paul shook his head. "I find that hard to believe, Emma. You make so many beautiful quilts. Binding should come quite naturally to someone with your talents!"

His compliment did not go unnoticed and she was quick to deflect it. "*Nee*, it is one of my weaknesses, indeed. I usually send my quilts to the Hostetler sisters in Bird-in-Hand. They truly do the most beautiful work when it comes to binding the edges."

"The Hostetler sisters?" He looked first at Emma then at Hannah. "They are well known for their work, I admit. I imagine they would do great justice to this quilt. I would be honored to take the quilt to them when the time comes for it to be bound." He returned his gaze to Emma. "Consider it my contribution to your generous donation."

"That is more generous than necessary, Paul."

"I insist!" He looked back at Hannah, a smile on his lips. "Don't you agree, Hannah? I should be allowed to contribute?"

And so it was settled that Paul would come back the next weekend to collect the quilt and take it to Bird-in-Hand. Emma watched the exchange between Hannah and Paul with great delight, approving of her friend's gracious acceptance and Paul's gentle fending off of her compliments. A new suitor would certainly help ease Hannah's potential second thoughts at having rejected Ralph's proposal, she thought.

❧ Chapter Four ❧

I T WAS SATURDAY afternoon at the Weaver house. The windows were open and a light breeze stirred the air just enough to keep it comfortable inside, despite the unusually warm September weather. Outside the birds swarmed the bird feeder that hung from the black shepherd's hook among the front bushes. The noise of their chatter floated into the room, a welcome song of mirth and happiness that kept Emma company. Occasionally a car drove by the house, its engine disturbing the peacefulness of the surroundings. Otherwise it was a lazy, relaxing day, just perfect for Emma to focus on her quilting.

Earlier that morning Emma had visited with the Blanks. While she normally visited on Thursdays, she had promised Hetty's *maem* to drop off a schnitzel pie. She liked to bake pies early in the morning on Saturdays, the room still cool from the night air and the smell lingering in the kitchen for most of the day. But to spend the time making only one pie made little sense to Emma. So when she did bake pies, she always made extra ones to give to neighbors and friends.

Given that she had already spent time visiting on Thursday, her stop at the Blanks' house that morning was shorter than usual. She used the excuse of wanting to return home in order to work on the quilt so that neither woman's feelings would be hurt that she didn't stay longer. However, once she left their house, she took her time walking home, enjoying the heat of the sun on the nape of her neck. As she wandered down back roads, she paused to admire the green fields of the neighboring farms. It wouldn't be long before the corn stalks turned brown and were cut for fodder, leaving bare fields to greet the winter months.

By the time she returned home, it was almost noon. She had to hurry to make a light meal for her *daed*. Boiled potatoes and carrots accompanied the meatloaf that she had cooked earlier in the day. The two of them ate at the table, little conversation between them with the exception of Emma updating her *daed* about Hetty's appreciation for the schnitzel pie.

For the most part, it was a quiet sort of afternoon. The usual flurry of visitors was not expected at the house since Hannah had plans to join Gladys at a neighbor's home for supper. Emma had hoped to see Anna, but learned earlier in the week that Samuel was intent upon visiting his cousin's farm with his new wife. Without her favorite people around to entertain, Emma was quite content to sit in her chair by the quilting frame, putting the finishing touches upon the outer border while she half listened to her *daed* snore as he napped in his recliner chair.

The clock had just struck two o'clock when she heard the sound of horse hooves and buggy wheels pulling into their driveway. Setting down the needle, she glanced out the window, but from her vantage point she was unable to see who had just arrived.

"Are you expecting someone, *Daed*?" she asked softly, turning to look at him.

Jolted from his sleep, Henry grumbled for a moment as he gained his senses. He rubbed his face and sat up straight in the recliner. "What did you say, Emma?"

"I asked if you are expecting someone, then? I hear a buggy in the driveway." When he didn't respond, still dazed from his slumber, she frowned and stood up in order to walk into the kitchen for a better view from the front window.

"Who is it?" her *daed* called.

She didn't have to answer as the door suddenly opened and Gideon entered, removing his hat and placing it on the hook near the door. He grinned at Emma and called out a greeting to Henry.

Immediately upon hearing Gideon's voice, Henry brightened and shifted his weight in the recliner. "How right *gut* to see you, Gideon!"

Emma remained speechless. She quickly glanced around the kitchen, saying a prayer of thanks that everything was neat and tidy. It would never do to have a visitor see anything less than a pristine kitchen. "We weren't expecting you," she managed to say.

Ignoring Emma's comment, Gideon crossed the room and properly shook Henry's hand. "I was visiting friends down the road and thought to stop by for a Saturday afternoon visit." He glanced at Emma. "If that pleases you, of course," he added with a light-hearted tone to his words.

"Always a pleasure," Henry countered, the expression on his weathered face speaking of the genuine delight he felt at his friend's surprise appearance. He gestured toward the sofa. "Sit for a spell, *ja?*"

"Don't mind if I do." Gideon took his seat and sighed as he leaned back. "God has graced us with a beautiful day, *ja?* I'm surprised that you are inside when it is so lovely outdoors."

"Avoid the midday sunlight. The doctors say so, nowadays. It's a wonder that the farmers of olden days didn't all just drop from skin cancer!"

Gideon laughed.

"As for you, you must stay for supper. We insist!" He turned to look at his *dochder.* "Don't we, Emma?"

"But of course!" Quickly she began to hurry about the kitchen, opening cabinets and trying to determine what she would serve for supper. She knew that Gideon lived alone and was certain that he was most likely lonely, which explained his frequent visits to the Weaver household. However, she had not been expecting anyone and therefore had not planned a proper Saturday supper.

"Don't go to any trouble on my behalf, Emma," Gideon said as if reading her mind. "It is the company I seek, not the food."

She spun around and put a hand on her hip, giving him what could only be described as *a look.* "Now Gideon, if there is one thing you must know, we will never let anyone leave our home with anything less than a full stomach!"

He shook his head, laughing under his breath. "You fuss too much, Emma. But if there is one thing I have learned over the years, it is best to not argue with you on the small things. I save *those* types of discussion for items of much greater importance."

With a quick puff of air she scoffed at him. "Seems you enjoy arguing with me as much as you enjoy *Daed*'s conversation!" She put her hands on her hips and stared at him. "Come to think of it, I'm not certain which you might enjoy more!"

"Now, Emma," her *daed* chastised gently. "You know that Gideon is only looking out for your best interest. We all are. Such a special young woman is bound to need guidance from time to time." Then without another word in reference to Emma, Henry began to share some of the local stories he had heard just the previous day when he went into town to replenish feed for the horse.

Shortly before four o'clock Henry announced that he was going to take a walk down the street and back. The doctor had told him to exercise more and take in the fresh air whenever possible. Since then he had taken to a late afternoon stroll in order to enjoy the sun without worrying about the harm of its rays. Often he would pause to visit with the neighbors when they were outside. His walks usually took a good forty-five minutes, sometimes a bit longer if he happened to reach the farm at the end of the lane. Emma knew that he enjoyed leaning against the fence and watching the cows in the field as they walked, single file, along a trodden path toward the barn for the early evening milking.

Without Henry's presence the house was deathly silent except for the ticking of the clock that hung on the wall. Every five minutes or so Emma heard the familiar crinkling sound of the paper as Gideon turned the pages of *The Budget*, the weekly newspaper with news of Amish communities across the country. It was a comforting sound, one of peaceful belonging. She felt much less alone with Gideon's presence in the kitchen.

After the fourth time hearing the page turn, she smiled to herself as she poked the needle through the fabric of the quilt, her stitches neat and small on the fabric. "I never can understand how a man can spend so much time reading that paper." She lifted the needle from the underside, pulling the white thread through the quilt top. "With the bishop so adamant about gossip, I don't see where *The Budget* is not much more than a step above that!"

"Gossip, you say!" Gideon gave a soft chuckle and put the paper down. "I bet if I told you that I have my own bit of gossip today, you'd find that most interesting, Emma, and wouldn't complain one bit."

She laughed, knowing that Gideon knew her too well. Still, she tried to act nonplussed, aware that denial was the proper response for a godly woman. "I have no interest in gossip, Gideon King! The bishop preached about it quite sharply just two services ago!"

Leaning forward, he met her gaze when she glanced over her shoulder, and he tried to hide his smile. She frowned and turned back to her quilting as he spoke. "Even if I told you this gossip is about a good friend of yours and what seems to be an upcoming proposal of marriage?"

Her fingers stopped moving, lingering over the fabric as she felt her heart beat inside of her chest. Was it possible that Paul Esh had moved so quickly? Had her matchmaking skills proven so powerfully insightful that she had another success already? *How fortunate for Hannah*, she thought. *Two proposals in one week!* Emma spun around on her chair and stared at Gideon. "Why would Paul confide in you, Gideon? I don't see where you are in his confidence for such private matters!"

"Paul?" He seemed genuinely confused as he repeated the name as if to make certain he had heard her properly. "Paul Esh?"

"That is who you are speaking of, *ja*?"

At that comment, the realization struck him and he stood up, walking toward her. "Oh, Emma," he laughed. "I do not speak of Paul, but I do indeed speak of Hannah! A tenant of mine, Ralph Martin, came to speak to me earlier this week about renting the *grossdaadihaus* on the farm that he lets from me, the one in Strasburg. Seems he's interested in it for him to bring home his new *fraa*. When I inquired as to who the lucky woman is, imagine my surprise to hear *your* friend's name slip through his lips!"

Her shoulders stiffened and she pressed her lips together at his words. She lifted an eyebrow and spun her chair back around, pretending to turn her attention to the quilt. She had forgotten that there was a connection between Ralph and Gideon. "I see," was her only retort.

It was Gideon's turn to frown. "Emma! Surely you must be happy for your friend, even if the match is not with your approved Paul Esh."

She made a soft huffing sound and glanced at him over her shoulder. "You mock me, Gideon!"

"I assure you that I do not," he retorted playfully, his hands on his hips and a feigned look of innocence on his face.

"Well, your secret is not so secret anyway," she countered, not buying into his teasing. "I already knew of this proposal."

Gideon leaned over her shoulder to look at the quilting. He paused to point out that she had missed a small section in one of the leaves that she was stitching. She swatted at his hand, but her cheeks colored at the error that he had pointed out.

"So she took you in her confidence, did she?" When Emma did not respond, he paused, and as the realization of the full meaning of her statement hit him, he stood up straight, his eyes scanning the horizon through the window. "Of course she did and she must have said no," he said, more to himself than to her. "Otherwise, you would not have thought of Paul Esh when I first mentioned the matter." He took a deep breath and placed his hands on her shoulders, spinning her around so that she faced him. "Emma, what did you do?"

"I did nothing," she started, but the words sounded meek. It was clear that she was not telling the entire truth, even to herself.

"Emma…"

She shrugged her shoulders so that his hands fell back to his side. She did not like the scowl on his face nor the tone of his voice. His constant disapproval was grating on her nerves. Despite his being a part of the family, Gideon King sometimes took his self-appointed role as her big *bruder* a step too far. "*Ja vell*, I did nothing more than a true sister would do."

"A true sister?" He stared down at her and shook his head. "That would have been a *wunderbaar* match, Emma, even if it did not fit your plans."

"*Wunderbaar* for Ralph Martin, I'm sure." She tried to spin her chair back to continue quilting, but the way that Gideon was standing blocked her way.

"I admit that you have helped her tremendously, Emma, but I am not so sure that your presumption about Ralph Martin is fair. She is a young woman with a questionable family background and upbringing." Emma gasped at his words, but he did not let her interrupt him. "As for Ralph, he's a godly man with a spotless reputation and a lot to offer your friend."

"He's a pig farmer."

Gideon tilted his head and blinked his eyes just once. There was a look of complete disbelief on his face that made her feel uncomfortable, and she tried to look away. "What does being a pig farmer have to do with his being a fine match for your friend? He's a hard worker, honest, and kind!

Aren't those the most important things, besides that she finds a man who honors God and his community? And lest you forget, he seems to be quite taken with her."

To this statement she did not reply.

"Why, Emma Weaver! This has nothing to do with Ralph Martin or his occupation, which you find so distasteful for some unknown reason! It has everything to do with your fixation on Paul Esh marrying her instead!" He laughed, but there was no mirth to his laughter. "That is most ridiculous. You know that, don't you?"

"I'm sure I do not know what you mean!"

He placed his hand under her chin and made her look at him. "You should know better than to meddle, Emma. Ralph Martin may be a pig farmer, but he is a right *gut* man and is well thought of in his *g'may*. I think highly of him and know that he would make your friend a fine husband. She would have a *gut* future with Ralph, and that is what you should be focused on."

Placing the needle on top of the quilt, Emma stood up and moved away from Gideon. His brotherly advice was getting on her nerves today, and she was having a hard time holding her tongue. "A girl like Hannah would do far better with someone like Paul," she proclaimed. "She is not farm girl material, Gideon. Certainly she is more familiar with labor in a store than a field."

"Not farm girl material?" He ran his fingers through his hair, his eyes wide and full of disbelief at her statement. "Since when have you become so very proud, Emma Weaver? I am disappointed in your hand in this matter." He didn't wait for her answer. "There is so much advantage for Hannah in this match, one that is before her and not one that you dream of! Even I would think that you would see that!"

"Then you must think very little of me!"

"What I think of you right now, I prefer not to say," he admitted rather harshly. "The goodness and godliness of Ralph Martin is unquestionable. Despite your desire to seek better for your friend, I do fear that you will not find it, Emma. I only hope that Ralph will be able to move on and maintain his godly spirit that you so quickly dismiss because of his occupation." He turned his back to her and stared out the window. "And for what? A hopeless dream that Paul Esh will fulfill your need to meddle and matchmake? *Ja vell*, Emma, I dare say that Paul will think more rationally than you. His desire is to marry a woman who is suited to be part of a bishop's family. Despite your protests, Hannah is not that woman!"

Emma caught herself from gasping at Gideon's words. Lifting her chin, she narrowed her eyes and looked at him. "You criticize me for thinking Ralph is not good enough for Hannah, and then declare that Hannah is not good enough for Paul."

"Indeed it appears that I did," Gideon shot back, leveling his gaze at her as if speaking to a child. His condescending tone did not go unnoticed by Emma, and she fought the urge to squirm under his rebuke. "Apparently I have a much more mature awareness of what matches are suitable as well as realistic."

Emma tried to hide her discomfort and hurried over to the kitchen, wishing that her *daed* would return from his walk. While Gideon always tended to be on the critical side when it came to Emma, he had never spoken so harshly to her. She felt tears stinging the corner of her eyes, but blinking rapidly, she willed them away. When she had control of her emotions, she forced a smile and turned back to look at him. "If I had hopes of Paul with Hannah, that is not the motivation, I can assure you," she finally said. "I only hoped to keep Hannah from making too rapid a decision, Gideon, and an unwise one at that."

To her surprise, Gideon made a groaning noise, one that spoke of vexation and frustration. He spun around on his heels. "Please beg forgiveness of my departure from your *daed*," he snapped. "I have suddenly lost my appetite for conversation, never mind fellowship over a meal." Without another word, he stormed out of the kitchen. Within minutes Emma heard the familiar clip-clop of horse hooves and the gentle humming of buggy wheels, an indication that Gideon had left to return home.

❧ Chapter Five ❧

THE TWO YOUNG Amish friends were walking at a brisk pace down the street, Emma in a freshly laundered and crisply ironed pale green dress, which contrasted sharply against Hannah's faded pink one with the torn hem and the hole in her skirt. Both were carrying a basket filled to the rim with fresh vegetables and canned fruit. Emma smiled as they walked toward the row of ranch houses along the main thoroughfare, her face turned toward the sun as if drinking in the wholesome goodness that shone down upon them. Besides quilting and entertaining visitors, there was nothing Emma enjoyed more than her weekly visits on Thursday to the elderly widows who lived near her home. That pleasure was now showing on her face. As for Hannah, she was happy to spend time with her good friend Emma.

While most of the widows and widowers lived with their grown *kinner* on the family farms, usually in the *grossdaddihaus*, there were just as many of them, mostly women, who lived in the smaller portion of the more contemporary homes scattered in the community, houses that were occupied by their older children who worked at market or at local stores. Several years back Emma had taken it upon herself to visit with these elderly women each and every week. Anna had often accompanied her, but today it was Hannah who walked beside her.

"It's so nice of you to visit with the widows," Hannah gushed. "I'm sure they truly appreciate it."

Emma glanced at Hannah. "I suppose I appreciate the visit as much as they do." She sighed after she spoke and gestured toward the first house so that Hannah knew to cross the street with her. "It's right rewarding to bring sunshine into their lives, I reckon. And, in turn, they give it back tenfold." It was indeed something that Emma truly enjoyed doing for her community, but little did people know that she found as much enjoyment in the deed as the recipients. For Emma, this was a way to stay abreast of what was happening in the *g'may*, who was getting married and who was not, who was expecting a new *boppli*, who was moving and where to...all little tidbits of information that she could not possibly glean while staying home, taking care of her *daed.*

Their first visit was to Mary Yoder, an older woman who could not walk very well without the help of a cane. Way back when Mary had been considered a pillar of strength in the community. All the women had known her quite well and she too knew most of them, for Mary had been the only midwife within a thirty-mile radius. There was scarcely a day when her services were not required to assist in childbirth, for which *Englische* doctors were rarely consulted. Mary had a Mennonite acquaintance, John Bucher, a pious and righteous man who drove her at any time of the day or night, as emergencies arose. She was the only Amish woman in the *g'may* authorized by Bishop Zook to keep a telephone in her kitchen, but only for such emergencies.

Now these days were long gone, and Mary was no longer

helping anyone in her community. But some of the elders, when reminiscing about the past, never failed to mention how many dangerous complications Mary had been able to overcome, sometimes even saving a mother in the process.

Emma always stopped to visit with her first in case Mary needed anything before her *dochder* returned from cleaning houses, at eleven o'clock. In fact, Emma timed her visits with all of the women to make certain she was there when others were not, in case they needed any assistance while alone.

"*Gut mariye*, Mary!" Emma called out from the front step, her voice louder than usual since Mary was hard of hearing. The elderly woman sat on the porch and looked up when she heard Emma's voice. Emma waved and stepped forward to join her. "I brought a friend with me today!"

"Anna?"

"*Nee*, Mary. You know that she was married to Samuel Wagler just last month." Emma reminded her. "She lives farther away now and couldn't visit." There was a look of disappointment on Mary Yoder's face. "But I have someone new for you to meet today! I've brought my new friend, Hannah Souder, with me. She's just moved here from Ohio. Wasn't that nice that she came along, Mary?"

When Emma glanced at Hannah, she was surprised to see her hanging back at the gate, seemingly reluctant to greet the aging woman. Mary sat in her rocking chair, her left eye clouded over with white from a cataract which would keep growing until the day when she would be called back to her Creator. Her skin, leathered and wrinkled, drooped with old age. Her smile showed that she barely had any teeth left. But there was a joy in her face as she turned her head in the direction of Emma's voice.

"We brought you some freshly canned peaches, dear Mary. Hannah and I canned them just last week. Shall I get you a bowl and spoon for you to enjoy some right away, or would you prefer to save them for later?"

Reaching out a wrinkled and trembling hand, Mary patted Emma's arm. "Such a good girl," she replied. "So thoughtful and kind. I'll save them for later. I don't have much appetite these days. *Danke*, Emma."

Hannah finally inched forward for proper introductions. Her shyness amused Emma, who thought it rather charming despite being unusual. It wasn't as if Hannah hadn't been meeting people since having moved to Lancaster!

For the next fifteen minutes Emma sat in the chair next to Mary, talking with her about the quilt that she and Hannah were making for the Mennonite Central Committee's upcoming auction. In great detail she explained the pattern and colors, taking special delight in Mary's reaction to the description of the different fabrics being used. For a woman in her nineties, Mary still had some interesting anecdotes to contribute to the subject. At one point the two younger women laughed out loud when Mary admitted how she despised quilting so much that, whenever she was invited to a quilting bee, she made sure to use her right hand—she was a leftie. Her stitching was so horrible that soon enough the invitations ceased to come her way. "What a relief!" she exclaimed. "But don't let anybody know now." She ended the story with a twinkle in her eye.

"That was a lovely visit indeed, wasn't it?" Emma commented as she swung the basket in her arm and continued walking down the road toward the next stop: Katie Miller. But she most looked forward to their second-to-last stop of the day: Sarah Esh. Sarah was the great aunt of Paul Esh, and Emma was eager to get to her house because sometimes Paul visited with her too. Only last week hadn't Paul been sitting there when Emma arrived? While he had acted somewhat surprised, Emma suspected that he had known she would visit his great aunt and surely had hoped that Hannah would be accompanying her. Today if Paul was there, he would not be disappointed.

"Such a charming home Mary has," Hannah said as they walked. "I thought her display of pink china pieces and ceramics was lovely, didn't you?"

Indeed, Mary's small abode was decorated as plain as possible, but still her personality came through in her collection of tea cups, vases, and plates, all in her favorite color: pink.

"She will be one to enjoy the Christmas gift we are planning, for sure and certain," Emma pointed out.

"Oh, it's such a sad state," Hannah sighed. "Aging and being all alone. I'm sure she must miss her husband very much. But at least she was married and has children to see to her needs. I'd so hate to be alone and never marry."

There was something wistful in Hannah's words, and Emma immediately worried that she was thinking of Ralph Martin's letter. Why was she in such a hurry to wed? Was hope of marriage the real reason she left Ohio for Lancaster county? Not knowing what to say, Emma chose to maintain her silence as they continued down the road. A buggy passed nearby. The driver waved at them and Emma lifted her left hand in greeting to the driver, despite not immediately recognizing who it was. But she could have been recognized, and it would be considered unfriendly not to return the acknowledgment.

After a few moments of silence Hannah turned to Emma and surprised her by saying, "Forgive me if I seem to pry, but it's a wonder, Emma, that you have not married as of yet. You are so well thought of in the *g'may*; nary a person has anything but the highest praise for your devotion to God and the community. And, if I may be so bold, you are beautiful, talented, and charming. Why, I'd think you'd have plenty of suitors asking to take you for a buggy ride home after the singings on Sundays, that's for sure and certain!"

Emma's response was a simple laugh.

"It's true!" Hannah cried out in alarm. "I don't see cause for laughing! I did not intend to make fun!"

"Dear Hannah," Emma began, her voice patient and gentle. "Don't worry. I did not take it the wrong way and you are definitely not prying. Your praise is flattering, but I don't believe it is warranted. Even so, the issue isn't whether I am beautiful, talented, or charming; the issue is whether or not I can find someone else who shares those same traits! Quite frankly, in the absence of such a man at this point in my life, it might come as a surprise to you to learn that I have no intention of ever marrying!"

The confidence in her announcement and the firmness in her voice made Hannah stop walking and reach out to touch Emma's arm. "Why, Emma! I don't believe you *really* mean that."

She smiled. "But I do."

Hannah frowned. "That would be such a sad thing, for I think you'd make a wonderful *fraa*, and I cannot believe that my opinion is not shared by many young men in this community!"

Casually Emma shrugged. "*Mayhaps*, but I shall not find out! I'm perfectly content to remain an old *maedel*. Being on your own does have its advantages!"

At this statement, Hannah gasped. "Emma! That would

be so very lonely, don't you think? No *kinner*. Whom would you be tending to?"

A light laugh escaped Emma's lips and she batted a hand in Hannah's direction. "*Nee*, not so lonely at all. I have my *daed* to tend to, Hannah. And a wide circle of right *gut* friends. I prefer my independence too much, I reckon. I'm not like my *schwester*. Indeed, Irene's perfectly content to stay at home and tend to her *boppli* and the other *kinner*."

"But when you become elderly, Emma, who will take care of you? Are you looking forward to being a poor old *maedel*?"

"My dear Hannah, tell me: is it the *being poor* or the *being old* that bothers you the most?" She didn't wait for her friend to respond before she continued. "Thanks to *Daed* selling his business, I am fortunate that I shall never be the former, and despite our deepest desires, none of us can avoid being the latter."

The reaction on Hannah's face spoke of her surprise at Emma's words. For a long moment both women remained silent. Hannah seemed to be trying to collect herself after hearing Emma's short speech about marriage. "If you are so against marriage," she finally said, "it's a wonder why you would push such unions on others."

"Do you think that I push them?" Emma replied at once. The thought of being perceived in such a light struck Emma with a degree of dread and dismay. While she had encouraged Anna and Samuel's courtship with that initial invitation for supper, she had never considered herself as pushing marriage on anyone.

"I don't mean to, Hannah. In fact, I think we just had a discussion recently against such a union."

"You mean Ralph Martin then?"

"Exactly!" Emma looked pleased that Hannah was

following her train of thought. "If I simply pushed unions, to use your exact words, I would have persuaded you to accept his call for courtship."

"That is true," Hannah reluctantly agreed, breaking eye contact for an instant.

"You, however," Emma went on, encouraged by her friend's body language, "were asking me about my intentions for my own marriage. And while I know that many young women marry for the sake of convenience, to work alongside a companion and to create a comfortable future for themselves, I have no need for such comfort. My *daed* does not need me to work outside of the house. My quilting brings in a fair amount of extra income, which, by the way, I do not really have a need for but enjoy using for helping others. And I will be well tended to in my old age as I intend to stay at our little house. Unless I were to fall in love, there really is no need for me to marry, now, is there?"

After such an assertive proclamation, there was little left for Hannah to offer by way of an argument, but she had a hard time letting go of the most pressing question in her mind.

"But to be so alone, like Mary Yoder? Or a *maedel*, like Hetty Blank?" The expression in Hannah's voice conveyed her disbelief in what Emma had just said. While it was not unusual for Amish women to remain single, Emma's admission seemed to strike Hannah as being contrary to her new friend's disposition.

Emma shook her head at this last statement from Hannah. "*Ja vell*, I think I'm a bit better suited to conform to society than Hetty Blank. I'm certainly a bit more capable of maintaining my independence without a need for assistance from the *g'may*. Our church district members can focus on the needs of the disadvantaged widows rather than mine." The noise of a horse and buggy approaching from behind interrupted her train of thought, and Emma glanced over her shoulder to see who it was. An older man with a long white beard lifted his hand to wave to her, and with a broad smile Emma waved back. "And I too have nieces and nephews that will help me, if needed, as I age," she added.

They were approaching the next stop on their tour of the neighborhood, and as a matter of good form, Emma quickly changed the topic.

"Now, here is a lovely woman," she said as she gestured toward the front gate. "Katie Miller. But she's been feeling poorly these past few weeks. I brought her some homemade chicken soup." Emma smiled brightly. "Anna always made me chicken soup when I was not well. Nothing like good, wholesome chicken and vegetable soup to make anyone feel better, don't you think?"

Katie Miller lived in the converted two-car garage of a more modern home. She rented it from another Amish family who had bought it several years ago from a Mennonite neighbor. A widow, Katie had tragically survived all of her own *kinner* but one, and that son had not joined the Amish church. That left Katie Miller no other option than to live alone, in the rented section of a fellow church member's house instead of with her own family. And, with poor health, she looked forward to Emma's visit each week.

The visit was short, only thirty minutes in duration. Emma fluttered about the small house, making certain to heat up the large bowl of soup for Katie Miller—certainly her only hot meal for the day—and serving it to her when it was just shy of being too hot. While the older woman ate her soup, Emma sat perched upon her chair and chattered away about the different happenings among the families in their *g'may*. She laughed often and would pause to ask questions of Katie, a way to keep the woman involved in the conversation despite her days spent living alone in the small apartment.

All too soon it was time to leave. Emma quickly washed and dried the dishes and utensils that she had used, so that Katie wouldn't have any mess to tend. Before leaving, she made certain that everything was in order and Katie was content in her recliner chair, her Bible nearby so that she could read while the light was still streaming through the windows in the room where she sat, alone with her memories.

No sooner had they shut the screen door behind them than Emma heard someone call out her name. It was Paul Esh, riding down the road in an open carriage. She almost gasped. What good fortune and how timely, she thought as she nudged Hannah's arm with a little too much enthusiasm.

"Look!" she whispered hoarsely, nodding her head toward the approaching carriage. "I wouldn't be surprised if he stops to offer us a ride!"

Both women waved to him, and sure enough, Paul stopped the horse in front of Katie Miller's driveway. With a broad smile, he gestured for the two women to come and join him in the carriage.

"If I know anything, Emma Weaver," he laughed, "you are making your rounds and your next stop is at my *aendi*'s house and then off to spend time with the Blanks, ain't so! Let me take you both. It will be faster and I could certainly use the good company, I reckon."

Without hesitation, Emma accepted the kind offer and hurried to the side of the carriage. She placed her basket in the back section, making certain that it was properly secured.

The slight delay permitted Hannah to climb first into the wagon so that she was seated next to Paul. With a smile, Emma joined her.

When the horse was finally moving again Paul leaned forward and peered at Emma first and then Hannah. "I see you have company today on your weekly rounds," he said cheerfully. "That's right *gut* to see you bringing your new friend with you to visit the women. I'm sure they are most appreciative, ain't so?"

With the slightest of movements, Emma tried to nudge Hannah to respond, but no words escaped her friend's lips. When it became clear that Hannah was not about to speak, Emma did so for her. "I'm not certain who enjoyed meeting Hannah more," she started, "Mary Yoder or Katie Miller! And Hannah made the most delicious soup for Katie Miller!" Emma couldn't ignore the sharp look that Hannah gave her. "Well, she helped heat it up, anyway."

"Without doubt, the women appreciate any and all kindness shown to them. I find I learn so much from spending time with them as well. Such wisdom they carry upon their shoulders, if only the youth would pause to listen." Paul had a way of speaking that made everything sound noble and good. His eyes sparkled as he talked, and Emma was pleased to notice that he was looking at Hannah every bit as much as he was looking at her. "Putting others' needs before our own is just one way that we can walk with Jesus," he added.

When Hannah did not respond, Emma, once again, took the opportunity to do so. "Perhaps you have heard that Hannah is helping me collect Bible verses to put together special books to give to the elderly this Christmas. With our quilt almost finished, we've begun working on this new project, and it's coming along quite nicely. She's going to organize the verses and rewrite them for the different books to give as gifts!"

"Are you then?" He seemed genuinely impressed. "And what are these verses about, I might ask?"

Hannah lifted her eyes to look at Emma for a moment, as if silently begging Emma to respond. When Emma remained silent, Hannah had no choice but to answer. "Well," she began, "we are asking for people to write their favorite Bible verses, so there is no particular subject. It could be any topic of interest to them."

"We should have our final verses this weekend," Emma added. "My *schwester*, Irene, and her family are to visit. I just know that she'll want to contribute to this project. She grew up and worshipped with these women too."

Paul tilted back the straw hat he was wearing and nodded his head in approval. "Why, I know you have not asked me, but I should like to contribute my own favorite Bible verse to your collection as well!"

Emma watched as the color rose to Hannah's cheeks. Despite her plainness, there was a demure beauty to the young woman, and it was clear to Emma that Paul had noticed it. If only they had some more time alone, she thought. And then she realized exactly how to arrange that.

"Oh, help!"

Paul turned to look at Emma. "What is it, Emma?"

She waved her hand toward him and shook her head. "Silly me. I left my sampler at Katie Miller's."

He pulled back on the reins, stopping the horse. "I shall happily turn around so that you can fetch it. It won't take but five minutes."

Emma was quick to cut him off. "*Danke*, Paul. That's a right nice offer. But I don't mind walking by myself to retrieve it. *Mayhaps* it's more helpful if you took Hannah to your *aendi*'s house. She'll be waiting for her visitors. I can meet up with the both of you at the Blanks. I'd feel rather poorly if your *aendi* missed out on visiting with you. She dare not suffer because of my silly forgetfulness!"

Reluctantly Paul agreed, but only after Emma insisted again, and without waiting for another word, jumped out of the carriage. She waved good-bye to them both and hurried down the road in the direction they had just come. She glanced over her shoulder only once, smiling when she saw Paul continue driving the horse along the road to his aunt Sarah's house.

A little time alone, Emma pondered, *will do the two much-needed good*. The time spent walking alone did not bother her in the least. She would appreciate the exercise anyway. Indeed, she rather enjoyed it, for a warm feeling of delight washed over her as she dreamed of an upcoming wedding of Hannah Souder to Paul Esh.

As she was walking toward Katie Miller's house, Emma thought of Hannah's previous words: "If you are so against marriage it's a wonder why you would push such unions on others." And then it struck her: if she had so vehemently refuted her friend's allegations, she pondered, why would Hannah's potential nuptials with Paul Esh so vividly permeate her imagination? Why did she enjoy the idea of others being wed, while she would not even entertain the thought of putting herself in a similar situation?

Was she becoming, after all, a matchmaker? In her culture these things were better left to the Almighty. Overt matchmaking was *not* the way of the Amish, but certainly nudges here or there in the right direction couldn't hurt.

❧ *Chapter Six* ❧

WITH THE *KINNER* running through the house, and run they could, the noise level was greater than normal. Emma, having a hard time keeping her countenance, found herself more than once laughing at the antics of her young nieces and nephews. Her usually quiet kitchen had become a lively playground this Saturday morning, chock-full of little voices, rowdy laughter, and the sounds of bare feet padding across the freshly washed and waxed linoleum floor. There was a warmth in the air that didn't come from the outdoors but from within the heart.

"May I hold the baby again, if you don't mind?"

Her older sister gratefully handed her infant son to Emma. While she didn't say so, she clearly looked relieved to have a break from holding the baby. "He's still sleeping, but if you hold him, I can see to the bread."

"You always did make the best wheat bread," Emma complimented her sister as she carefully took baby George in her arms. "*Daed* still compares my loaves to yours, can you believe!" She laughed, nonplussed that her own baking skills did not measure up to Irene's. "He'll be ever so glad to have yours on hand for a while. I'm both grateful and eager to be able to freeze a few loaves to hold him over."

With the oven door open, the enticing fragrance of warm dough permeated the room. To Emma, freshly baked bread was the most welcoming smell in any Amish kitchen. Irene poked at the loaves. Deciding that they were finished, she reached for a potholder and began to pull out the pans.

"Is he still on that whole-wheat kick, then?" she asked, setting the metal bread pans on a rusty cooling rack.

"Oh, that and more!" her sister replied. She pretended to scowl as she teased, "Don't dare mention a word about cookies or cake in his presence. You'll get an earful of rantings, for sure and certain, about the evils of sugar!" Still laughing, Emma cradled the baby gently in her arms. She leaned down and placed a soft kiss on his forehead. A whiff of lavender caressed her nose and she smiled. "I just love how babies smell, don't you?"

Irene didn't have a chance to answer as her two older sons ran down the stairs, pushing and shoving at each other to see who could beat the other to the kitchen. "Henry and John Junior!" she scolded. "No running in the house!"

Neither boy seemed to hear her as they raced through the kitchen, almost knocking over their younger sisters who were playing with some blocks on the kitchen floor.

"Such energy," Emma laughed as the boys burst through the door and bounced down the steps to play in the front yard.

Irene smoothed down the front of her black apron and sighed. To Emma, her older sister looked worn out and tired. With dark circles under her eyes and graying hair, she had aged tremendously since giving birth to her fifth child just four months prior. "Energy that is wasted on the young, I fear."

"Oh, Irene!" Emma frowned at her sister's lament. While

Emma always tended to err on the side of positive thinking and rainbows, her older sister, like their father, had always been one to look at the dark side of things. During their growing-up years Emma had excused the difference in their perspectives with the fact that Irene had felt the loss of their *maem* more than she had. But if Emma had hoped that marriage and a family of her own would replace her sister's clouds with sunshine, she had been sorely mistaken. "You just need the baby to be a little more independent and then you'll regain your energy, I'm sure."

Irene responded with a simple shrug of her shoulders. "*Mayhaps*. Or *mayhaps* I need Lizzie and little Emma to be older to help more. They're too young still to do much more than get underfoot." Using mismatched potholders, Irene began to remove the still-hot bread from their pans. She lined them up on the rack and set the pans in the sink to be washed later. Satisfied, she admired the six loaves. "Just about perfect," she whispered. "John will be most pleased."

"Where are the men anyway?"

Irene and her husband, John, had arrived earlier in the day, eager to visit with Emma and *Daed* before heading back to their own farm. Yet, upon arriving at the Weavers' house, John had disappeared with his father-in-law outside and they had yet to return. Neither woman minded, for it had provided them time to catch up and visit before the other guests arrived.

It was close to eleven o'clock when a buggy pulled into the driveway. Glancing out the window, Irene peered around the property before spotting the men standing on the far side of the small horse barn. "Gideon's arrived."

Emma remained unusually silent.

"I think he's brought your friend with him," Irene said, turning back to look at Emma.

This brightened Emma's mood. She had asked Hannah to join the Weaver gathering, despite Henry's private grumbling about not wanting to share his precious, limited time with Irene with anyone outside of the family.

When Hannah entered the kitchen, Emma was quick to properly introduce her friend to her sister before inquiring about the circumstances of her arrival in Gideon's buggy.

"Oh, that?" Hannah laughed. "He came upon me walking the road and stopped to offer a ride. I must admit that it was appreciated." She fanned at her neck. "It's warm walking in the sun!"

Chewing on her lower lip, Emma glanced over her friend's shoulder. "Where is Gideon, anyway?"

"Gideon?" Hannah set down her purse on the floor next to the counter. "I think he went with your *daed* and another man behind the barn."

Emma groaned. "Oh, help, I know what that's about, for sure and certain!" She didn't wait for either Hannah or her sister to ask before she answered the unspoken question. "Gardening for next year. I just know it. *Daed*'s so worried about us not having fresh vegetables now that Anna isn't here. She did the gardening, remember?" With a frustrated sigh, Emma sank down onto the sofa, the baby still cradled in her arms. "I reckon he'll be expecting me to manage the garden, then!"

Gardening was the last thing on Emma's list of favorite things to do. Between the dry, dusty feeling of dirt on her hands and the warm sun heating up her back, there was very little about gardening that she found appealing. She much preferred working indoors, keeping an orderly house and working on her quilts.

"It wouldn't hurt you to garden a bit," Irene offered gently. "I feel so close to God when I'm working outdoors. How will you ever feed your own family, Emma?"

"Family?" Her eyes grew large and she stared at Irene, an expression of disbelief on her face. "*Daed* is my family and we are getting on just fine, *danke!*"

"One of these days—"

Emma interrupted her sister, refusing to let Irene finish the sentence. Undoubtedly it would lead to the same topic: marriage and motherhood. "*Nee*, Irene. You know that I'm quite content with my independence." She ignored a look from Hannah, who was clearly amused. Irene, however, frowned. She was always dismayed at Emma's avoidance of courting, never mind her determination to remain single forever!

To avoid the topic, Emma glanced down at the sleeping infant in her arms. "I'll leave mothering and nurturing to those who do it so much better than I ever could. Like you!" She said the last part with kindness, knowing full well that her sister had always wanted a large family, even if she was currently experiencing days of weariness and feelings of being overworked.

The table was set for the noon meal when the men returned to the kitchen. Emma noticed that Gideon made a great effort to avoid making eye contact with her. For a moment she watched him with curiosity, realizing that he was still upset with her about what she had come to call "the Ralph Martin and Hannah situation." With a slight roll of her eyes, she shifted the baby in her arms and pretended to not be offended by his silence. Instead, she watched as he played with the two older boys while Irene put the food on the table.

His patience with his nephews impressed her, especially given that he was an old *buwe* with little or no experience with *kinner*. His face lit up when the young boys clambered around him, asking him to toss them into the air. This he did with great delight, despite Henry's dismay that one of his grandsons might get injured.

When the two boys finally settled down at the urging of their *maem*, they begged Gideon to share stories about their *daed* when he was their age. Gideon was only too willing to oblige, much to his *bruder*, John's, dismay.

"Not the story about the loose cow, please," John mumbled to Gideon, which only caused young Henry and John Junior to beg to hear the story about how their *daed* had let a cow escape the dairy rather than milk it at chore time.

Listening to Gideon tell the story, Emma found herself smiling. *What a right* gut daed *he would have made*, she thought.

With lunch on the table, Irene called everyone to be seated. Henry assumed his position at the head of the table, and after he cleared his throat ever so slightly, everyone bowed their heads to say the silent blessing over the prepared food. When Henry shifted his weight, the subtle sign that prayer was over, a new round of activity resumed. Plates of bread and bowls of steaming vegetables were passed around the table, the adults helping to serve the younger children so that food was not spilled upon the fresh tablecloth.

Henry opened up the conversation. "Gideon offered to plow the old garden patch, Emma," he said as he reached for the boiled potatoes. "Fresh vegetables next year will keep us all healthy. I'm not too keen on those store-bought foods, you know. Those *Englische* use chemicals that are certainly killing us!"

Exasperated, Emma rolled her eyes.

Not one to be discouraged, he pointed his fork at Emma. "It's true! And all those sweets with refined sugar!" Clicking his tongue in disgust, he shook his head and turned his attention to Irene. "You best be using only that organic sugar."

"I am, *Daed.*"

Emma caught Irene's eye when her *daed* wasn't looking and mouthed the words *I told you so.* Both women suppressed their amusement and bent their heads down, choking back laughter by avoiding each other's gaze. Even Hannah joined in, familiar by now with Henry's concern for proper eating habits and good nutrition.

Indeed, Henry's concern was not a new one. His reputation among the *g'may* included more than just his being a godly man with a fierce sense of piety. He was also known to fret about just about anything and everything under the sun. As he continued to lecture Irene about what was permissible to feed his grandchildren, Emma caught a smile sneaking on Gideon's face. When he glanced up and saw that he had been discovered, the smile turned into a grin and she too found herself smiling back.

After tending to the needs of her *kinner*, Irene took a deep, satisfied breath and began to focus on enjoying her own food. "What news, *Daed*, of Francis Wagler? Has he come back to meet his new *maem*?"

"*Nee*," Henry replied, wiping at his mouth with the back of his hand. "Curious that. I have heard nary a peep about him. Emma, what says Anna?"

The eyes of the adults shifted to Emma, and for just a moment, she wanted to squirm. Instead, she merely shrugged her shoulders. "She shared a lovely letter that Francis had written to congratulate his *daed* and Anna. He apologized for not attending their wedding, but apparently his *aendi* in Ohio is ill."

With a disgusted wave of his hand, Henry dismissed Emma's comment. "That woman never was well thought of! Never letting that boy come back to Lancaster and making Samuel travel to Ohio to see him."

"*Daed,*" Irene said softly. "He is a young man now who can make up his own mind."

Despite the validity of Irene's comment, Henry shook his head in disgust. "Bah!"

Gideon spoke up next. "I never quite understood that arrangement, I confess," he stated, properly setting his fork down on the side of his plate.

Henry shook his head. "None of us did, Samuel most of all, I imagine."

For a moment a silence befell the table. To speak further of the situation would be inappropriate in front of the young *kinner.* However, Emma knew that everyone was thinking back to the year when Francis's *maem* had passed away and her older *schwester* had convinced Samuel to allow her to raise the young boy. What was to start out as just a few months had turned into several years. With Samuel left in Lititz to tend to his aging parents and work toward paying the enormous medical bills incurred from their illnesses, he had little option except to permit his only son to be raised in Ohio by his deceased *fraa*'s family. A most unusual situation, indeed.

Ever the peacemaker, Emma sighed and tried to shift the conversation back to a more positive tone. "*Vell,* the letter that Francis sent to Anna was rather positive, and he did apologize for not having been out here to visit yet, and promised a future trip to Lancaster. Surely he means well. I've never heard anything but kind words about Francis from Samuel and Samuel's family."

"Kind words gathered from the once-a-year visit Samuel must take to Ohio to see his own son?" Henry's disapproval was more than apparent. The silence from the other adults seated at the table spoke volumes. Emma seemed to be the only one ready to forgive Francis for his apparent neglect of his own father.

When the meal was finally over and the after-meal prayer was said, the men retired to the front porch, freeing up the space while the women gathered the dishes and cleaned. Hannah held the baby, giving both Emma and Irene a break while they worked side by side, just like old times, at the kitchen sink. The younger children sat on the floor, fitting together pieces of an alphabet puzzle in a long line across the kitchen floor.

Emma was just drying the last dish when she noticed someone walking across the front lawn toward the house. She squinted to get a better look. With a slight gasp she turned to Hannah. "Paul's here!"

"Paul?"

Emma shushed her sister with a quick glance and lowered her voice to respond so that their words would not carry through the open window. "Paul Esh."

"The bishop's son?"

Hannah shifted the baby in her arms and managed to reach a hand up to quickly smooth back her hair so that it lay properly under her prayer *kapp*. Raising an eyebrow, Irene quickly understood what was happening. She suppressed a smile and turned back to her task at hand of wiping down the counters.

"Good evening, ladies," Paul said as he walked into the kitchen. "I understand there is a finished quilt to be picked up...a quilt in need of binding, *ja?*"

Hannah smiled but said nothing, too shy to speak up.

"How good of you to remember, Paul!" Emma glanced at Hannah and made a quick face at her, encouraging her friend to say something.

"Remember? How could I forget!" He noticed Irene and hurried over to shake her hand in proper greeting. "How right *gut* to see you, Irene! Will you be staying for the weekend then? I'm sure that the church members would love to see you after communion."

Irene shook her head. "*Nee*, Paul. We will be returning home this evening. We need to be in our own district for communion tomorrow morning." She dried her hands on the front of her apron and joined Hannah on the sofa, reaching out to tuck the blanket back from the baby's face. A soft expression of love crossed her face, and she lifted her eyes to look at Hannah. "They are so precious when they sleep, ain't they?" she whispered.

Curious, Paul stepped forward and looked down at the bundle in Hannah's arms. Emma watched with delight as she saw his own emotion on his face. As the oldest son of the family, Paul did not have any nieces or nephews yet. His experience with *kinner* was limited to his own five siblings. From the way he looked at the *boppli*, it was clear what was on his mind.

"Will you be staying for a spell, Paul?" Emma asked.

He looked up as if startled from his thoughts. "*Nee*, Emma," he said, turning his attention away from Hannah with the baby and directing his focus onto her. "While I would so greatly love to stay to visit, I must return home, for we're to visit family this evening."

With a simple clicking of her tongue, Emma expressed her disappointment.

"However, I did want to stop by to pick up your quilt. We'll be in that area and it's the perfect chance to drop it off at the Hostetlers'."

As usual his thoughtfulness touched Emma, just one more reminder that Paul Esh would make a *wunderbaar gut* husband for someone. She knew, from the twinkle in his eye, that the someone in question, the one he had in mind to court, was none other than Hannah.

"Then I shall not delay," Emma said cheerfully. "I'm just so grateful that you are able to take it, Paul."

"My pleasure."

Emma glanced at her sister. "Irene, *mayhaps* you might help me collect it? I'll need help wrapping it."

She had only just finished the final stitches the previous evening. Earlier that morning she had made Irene study it in great detail to ensure that she had not overlooked any area or that any stitches were loose.

Now they climbed the stairs to the second floor, leaving Paul and Hannah alone. Emma could hear them talking softly and wondered what they might be discussing. She hoped it was Paul asking to take her to the singing the following evening, for Hannah was not an official member of the *g'may* yet and therefore could not attend the communion service in the morning. This would be Paul's only chance to ask Hannah to ride to the evening youth singing.

Carefully they folded the unbound quilt and set it upon Emma's bed. If Irene suspected that Emma took more time than she needed to wrap the quilt in a clean white sheet to protect it from dust along the journey, she said nothing. Yet Emma felt the heat of her older sister's eyes upon her as she worked. She tried to ignore Irene's inquisitive stare and began to hum a hymn as she went about her task.

When they finally returned to the kitchen, Emma was disappointed to see that Paul had retreated outside and was no longer keeping Hannah company. Carrying the wrapped quilt in her arms, Emma headed outside to where the men were gathered on the porch.

"Ah, there you are!" Paul said happily and reached to take the quilt from her. "Is this the most prized quilt that I have the distinct honor of taking to the Hostetler's for binding?"

She flushed at his words.

"Now that I have it, I will make haste so that I can catch up with my family," Paul said, unaware or merely oblivious to Emma's discomfort. "I shall see you all at communion tomorrow, *ja?*"

"Not all," Emma quickly offered. "Hannah will not be there."

For a moment Paul looked downcast and disappointed as if he had not previously realized that. "Such a shame that she will not enjoy worship and fellowship with us," he said, a genuine inflection of sorrow in his voice. After a moment's pause, just enough to pay proper respect to the mention of Hannah's misfortune, Paul brightened and lowered his voice as he said, "But, of course, I shall look forward to seeing you instead."

Her mouth fell open and she stared at him as he started to carry the packaged quilt to the buggy. She had expected more of a solemn response, not a quick recovery at her reminder that Hannah would be absent from worship. But

Paul seemed quite content as he walked a few steps then paused, glancing over his shoulder at Emma. "*Mayhaps* you might assist me in putting the quilt in the buggy. I would prefer that you lay it the proper way so that it does not wrinkle or get mussed."

Ignoring the amused look on Gideon's face, she followed Paul, more out of curiosity than a need to actually assist him. Once she joined him at the buggy, she was surprised that he made no motion to leave. Instead he stood there by the buggy for a moment, fiddling with his hat and shuffling his feet.

"Paul?" she asked. "Is there something else?"

He glanced over her shoulder, making certain that no one was close enough to overhear.

"I have brought something for you," he whispered, his eyes still roaming behind her to ensure that they were alone. "The other day, when we were in the carriage on our way to my *aendi*'s, you asked for a Bible verse for the collection you and Hannah are making, and I have brought it."

She wondered at his attempt at secrecy over something so trivial. "How kind of you!" was all that she could think of saying.

There was another moment of hesitation and he leaned forward, lowering his voice once again. "You may not want to put it in the book, Emma. I think you will understand why after you read it."

She did not have the chance to respond before he had slipped a small folded piece of paper into her hand.

"I shall see you at the communion service on Sunday then, Emma," he added, his voice soft as he took a step backward and adjusted the straw hat on his head. He swiftly untied his horse from the hitching post and climbed into the buggy.

At no time did he look at her again. In fact, it seemed as though he were avoiding her on purpose.

How odd, she pondered, a confused frown on her face. Only when his buggy disappeared down the road in the direction of Bird-in-Hand did she look down at the paper. With a quick glance over her shoulder to make certain no one was observing her, she quickly unfolded it and let her eyes drift over the neatly written words:

> *Husbands, love your wives, as Christ loved the church and gave himself up for her, that he might sanctify her, having cleansed her by the washing of water with the word, so that he might present the church to himself in splendor, without spot or wrinkle or any such thing, that she might be holy and without blemish. In the same way husbands should love their wives as their own bodies. He who loves his wife loves himself. For no one ever hated his own flesh, but nourishes and cherishes it, just as Christ does the church.*

It took her a moment to reread the verses, and then, with a squeal of delight, she hurried back into the house, calling out for Hannah. Irene looked up, stunned by Emma's show of exuberance.

"My word, Emma! What's that about?"

Ignoring her sister, Emma ran to Hannah and thrust the paper in her hands. "Read this! Read what Paul has given me for your collection!"

With trembling hands, Hannah took the paper and let her eyes slowly digest each word. She chewed on her lower lip, frowning at one point as she read it. "Oh, dear ... "

Emma was surprised by Hannah's calm reaction. "What do you mean, 'oh, dear'?"

"I'm not sure that I understand …"

Snatching the letter from Hannah's hands, Emma started to read it aloud, pausing when she read "husbands should love their wives as their own bodies."

"Don't you see? That's a secret message to you!"

"It is?"

Emma rolled her eyes and sighed. "Well, of course it is! And here. Look at this part." She pointed to the words "for no one ever hated his flesh, but nourishes and cherishes it."

"If a husband should love his wife as he loves his own flesh, he's clearly telling you that he cherishes you!"

"He is?"

Shaking her head, Emma handed the paper back to Hannah. "I'm afraid you must be too stunned to realize what this means, Hannah! He is clearly smitten by you!"

Irene pursed her lips and frowned. "Emma…"

Silencing her sister with an absent-minded wave of her hand, Emma focused on Hannah instead. "It's only a matter of time," she said, hugging her friend. "And to think that you'll be Paul's Hannah! Isn't that just *wunderbaar*?"

Hannah laughed and clutched the paper to her chest, holding it against her heart. Her face shone with joy and Emma laughed in delight. Neither woman paid any attention to Irene or noticed Gideon's disapproving look as he stood in the doorway, frowning at Emma's latest misguided attempt at matchmaking.

❧ Chapter Seven ❧

A GENTLE BREEZE BLEW through the open window, cooling the back of her neck as Emma sat on the hard wooden bench, preparing herself for what was going to be an undoubtedly long day. It was Sunday worship, and the *g'may* was gathered at the imposing leather shop of Jacob Yoder. While the large room was usually full of supplies and inventory used in the Yoders' business, it was clear that the Yoder family had spent the previous week cleaning out the room in order to accommodate this special Sunday gathering.

While the Weavers' *haus* was certainly too small to have ever hosted a worship service, Emma had helped neighbors who had. She knew what was involved in preparing for that special day when all of the members of the *g'may* would descend upon the *haus* to sit in the rooms, now cleared of all moveable furniture and cleaned from the top of the walls to the corners of the floors. Days were spent washing windows and waxing the floors so that everything was as pristine and clean as possible. No one ever wanted a member of the *g'may* to walk away having noticed a cobweb or dirt in the room.

Most *g'mays* consisted of anywhere from twenty to thirty families—rather large families as six to eight children were

93

the norm, even more if the family were farmers. When the church districts eventually grew too large, as they usually did, they would split, creating two new districts. That had already happened twice in Emma's lifetime, and she suspected that it would happen again in the not-too-distant future, for they were already bursting at the seams as more of the younger members had grown, married, and were expanding their own families.

Today, however, unlike other worship meetings, this one was limited only to members of the church, for today was communion. Unbaptized members of the district, including the smaller *kinner*, were not permitted to attend service on that day and stayed home with older siblings who had not taken the kneeling vow yet. It was a day of reflection and worship that lasted well into the afternoon, unlike regular church services that would end with the noon meal and a short time of visiting.

As usual, upon arrival the women had folded their black wraps and removed their black bonnets, setting them in the entrance room, before gathering in a circle to greet one another. As she stood next to Anna, Emma's white cape and apron contrasted sharply with the black, heart-shaped prayer *kapp* that she wore upon her head. Today for communion all of the women wore black dresses, a symbol of the seriousness of the religious rite that they were about to undertake. However, only the unmarried baptized women wore white organza capes and aprons with the black prayer *kapps*.

For at least ten minutes she stood by Anna Wagler so that they could quietly talk while they waited for newcomers to enter, stow their outer garments, then walk through the awaiting circle of women to shake their outstretched hands and plant a quick kiss upon their lips. Just before nine o'clock the door to the back staircase opened and the bishop and ministers entered the room. They too greeted each woman with a firm handshake and nod of the head. Emma took a deep breath, bracing herself for the long service ahead of her.

After the bishops took their seats, the older women, based upon their age and marital status, walked single file to their side of the room. As usual, Mary Yoder led the line of women, as she was the oldest woman in the *g'may*, with Widow Blank and Katie Miller following her. When it was time for the unmarried women to take their seats, Emma assumed her place ahead of her friend Rachel Lapp, who was six months younger than her and, like Emma, unmarried.

Once seated, Emma watched as the men entered the room, the older ones sitting directly behind the bishop and ministers. The married men filed in next, again in order of age, before the younger, unmarried men assumed their own seats. Like many other things about the Amish, large gatherings were usually separated by gender and age—a hierarchy of sorts. Emma didn't mind, for she enjoyed the company of the women on those occasions.

As if on silent command, the men suddenly reached up to remove their black hats and placed them under their seats, with the exception of the young men seated against the back wall. They stood and hung their hats from the hooks on the wall behind them. It was a fluid movement, almost in unison, a movement that signaled the beginning of the service.

The silence lasted only a few seconds as one of the men, the designated *foresinger*, began to lead the rest of the members in song. It was Ben Lapp, Rachel's older brother, who assumed the important role this morning. He sang the first word of the appointed hymn, his voice following a chantlike tune, his eyes staring at the black, chunky hymn book, the

Ausbund, that he held with both hands. Full of songs written by the founders of the Anabaptists in the mid-1500s, this hymnal had been used for hundreds of years. Many of the writers of these songs had been imprisoned for their beliefs, or even martyred, tortured, and burned at the stake. Emma always felt a strong tugging at her heart when she held the book in her own hands.

When Ben finished chanting the first word of the hymn, the rest of the congregation joined him, singing the next word in the hymn using the same chant. Each word was drawn out, sung to a specific tune. As the voices rose in unison, singing each word of the hymn in a similar manner, a sense of peace fell upon the people seated on the hard wooden benches in the loft of the Yoder's shop.

During this first hymn Emma began to feel the Spirit of God washing her with His grace. As she sang the hymns, her mind traveled back in time to her ancestors, who had suffered and even died to ensure that she could worship freely on that very Sunday. Her heart opened, and she lost herself in the presence of God, who seemed to surround the gathering, His arms embracing all who were present as they lifted their voices up in songful praise of His glory.

When the congregation began singing the second verse, the bishop and ministers stood and exited the room. Emma knew that they were going to speak in private about the proceedings of the worship service. It was never planned in advance. Secretly she often wished that just once she could be a part of that discussion in the back room. How did they decide who would speak? Why did they choose the specific topics for the sermons? Today, however, she knew that the sermons, which would last for hours, would be similar to the ones at the spring communion: a retelling of the Bible's stories to remind the people to remain faithful to God.

Almost twenty minutes later the bishop and ministers filed back into the large room. By then the congregation had begun singing a second hymn. As soon as the leaders of the church were seated, the singing came to an abrupt halt at the end of the stanza, the congregation knowing that it was now time for the communion sermon.

The first minister stood up and began to preach. His voice took on a singsong quality, rising and falling in an unnatural manner. Emma listened to the words. The first minister, John Glick, began retelling the story of the creation of the heavens and earth. He continued with the history of Adam and Eve and continued until he retold the story of Noah.

Emma had always loved the story of Noah and how he listened to God, who instructed him to build the ark and save His creatures. She could only imagine how Noah's neighbors reacted to the strange structure that he worked on day in and day out, mocking him and harassing him. But, like any God-fearing man, Noah ignored them and followed God's instruction. The message was clear: God did not tolerate disobedience amongst His flock.

Unlike regular worship services when the congregation gathered together to eat from two long tables that were set up after the service was over, today's noon meal was eaten in shifts so that the ministers could continue with their preaching. Emma fought the urge to squirm on the hard bench, and as the hours passed, she had to concentrate on the words being spoken in order to avoid drifting to sleep.

With the unusually warm weather for fall, Emma was glad that there were fewer people at the worship service. Fewer people helped keep the room from getting overly warm. Still, as she waited for her turn to be called to the back room for the noon meal, her eyelids grew droopy and she had to pinch her own arm to keep herself from nodding off.

It was well into the afternoon when the communion took place. The bishop held the loaf of bread before the members of the *g'may*. He spoke about how the grains had been grown, starting as individual seeds before, through the process of harvest and baking, they had joined together to form into the very nourishment that was needed for survival. He compared this to God's Word, as much a nourishment for the soul as bread was for the body. One of the ministers took the bread from the bishop and broke it in half, passing one half to the men and the other to the women. After a person had broken off a small piece of bread, he passed it to another until each member of the *g'may* had partaken of this holy rite.

When it was time for the passing of the wine, the bishop spent a moment with a similar comparison, discussing the power of each individual grape after they joined together as one, much like their church community who lived, prayed, and worshipped together. He told the story of Jesus and how the wine represented His blood. Two cups of wine were passed in a similar manner as the bread had been. When it was Emma's turn, she took the smallest sip before quickly passing it to the young woman seated beside her. She had never been partial to the taste of wine, regardless of its place in the communion ceremony.

The final part of the service was the foot washing. Emma shifted on the hard bench, knowing that once again it would take quite some time before it was her turn to kneel before another woman and gently wash her feet in the bucket of water that was placed in the center of the room. It wasn't her favorite part of the service, since it was a truly humbling experience to be on one's knees and cleaning another's feet. However, she was looking forward to it as it signaled the end of the communion service and the approaching moment when she would finally be able to visit with some of her friends before heading back home.

After the service Emma stood with Rachel and two other young women, catching up on what was happening in one another's lives. They were eager to hear about the quilt she had made for the Mennonite auction and also to inquire why Hannah had not been at the service.

"She hasn't yet transferred her membership to our district," Emma explained.

"Then we won't see her later since there is no singing tonight," Rachel said sorrowfully.

This news surprised Emma. "No singing?" *Well,* she thought, *that certainly explained why Paul had not mentioned picking up Hannah that evening.* "Whyever not?"

"Don't you remember, Emma? The bishop said that communion Sunday should not have such gatherings at night. We should spend our time reflecting, instead."

Despite her disappointment, Emma kept her opinions to herself. "I had forgotten," she admitted.

At that moment she felt a hand on her arm. When she turned to see who was trying to get her attention, she was surprised to see her father standing there. He looked tired and pale. "Emma," her *daed* said. "I'm feeling poorly. It's too warm in here."

Concern crossed her face and she immediately touched his arm. "I'll take you home, *Daed*!"

"*Nee, nee.* It's all right. Gideon offered to take me home so that you can stay a while longer. I know how much you enjoy visiting with the women, and it's good for you to socialize."

She frowned. Gideon was a good friend to her *daed*, indeed. Still, there were times when she just wished that he would let her take care of her own father without any interference. "How can I enjoy myself if you are not well?"

Henry laid his hand on her arm and forced a soft smile. "I just need to lie down, and it's better if Gideon is there to help me. Besides, Paul was kind enough to offer to bring you home when you are ready. I trust that is fine with you?"

Barely did she have a chance to respond before Gideon had appeared by her *daed*'s side. He nodded in greeting at Emma. "You visit with your friends," he said, leaning forward slightly so that only she could hear him. "You don't get out enough. And I'm ready to leave anyway." If she wanted to comment that it really wasn't any of his concern whether she went out with friends or not, she held that thought in her mind rather than letting it slip from her tongue.

"I'll be home shortly," she reassured her *daed*, but he didn't hear her for Gideon was already escorting him down the narrow staircase to the exit on the first floor.

For the next half hour Emma helped the other women clean the dishes and pans. She enjoyed talking with her friends, young women that she had known for most of her life. They had gone to school together and worshipped together. But, unlike Emma, most of them were either married with *bopplis* or worked either full-time on their parents' farms or outside the house, tending to market or cleaning houses. It didn't leave a lot of time for socializing, except on Sundays.

The men were busy folding the benches and stacking them into the church wagon, a plain gray wooden box on wheels specifically used to store the benches and crates of *Ausbund* hymnals. Sometime during the following week two draft horses or Belgian mules would be harnessed to the wagon, and it would be delivered to the property of the next family scheduled to host the church service in two weeks. With everyone helping, it never took long to dismantle the worship room.

She felt a tap on her arm and glanced over her shoulder, not surprised to see Paul standing there.

"I'll be leaving shortly," he said, his voice a little louder than needed for she could hear him perfectly well. To her embarrassment, several people overheard him and raised an eyebrow. "I promised your *daed* I would take you home."

"That's so kind of you," Emma began. "But I think I prefer to walk today. It's so nice out and I'd love to have the exercise."

Her answer caught him off guard and he leaned forward, lowering his voice. "You wouldn't have me break a promise to your *daed*, would you? You know how he worries so."

Unfortunately Emma knew that Paul was right. If she walked home, her *daed* would wonder why Paul had broken his promise. No amount of reassurance that it was she, not Paul, who had insisted upon walking, would appease him. It was better to accept the ride rather than deal with the unnecessary ramblings and complaints over Paul's unfulfilled promise that she would undoubtedly be subjected to from her *daed*.

While she collected her wrap and bonnet, Paul hurried outside to prepare the horse and buggy. Emma took advantage of the time to bid farewell to her friends and to thank Katie Yoder for having hosted the worship service. Then, with a deep breath, she walked outside to find Paul waiting to help her get into the buggy.

For the first few moments they rode in silence. Emma stared out the window, watching the cows grazing in a nearby pasture. The leaves of the trees in the distance were just beginning to show signs of changing colors. Hints of red and yellow and orange lightly brushed the edges of green, creating a pretty picture that Emma tried to commit to memory.

"A lovely autumn we are having," he said, as if reading her mind. His words, however, sounding forced and stilted.

"Such a shame that Hannah couldn't be at the communion service," she replied, eager to pursue the topic of her friend with Paul. "Has she approached your *daed* about joining our church district?"

The casual shrug of his shoulders caught Emma off guard. Certainly he would know whether or not his intended *fraa* had requested to become a member of their *g'may*!

"I'm surprised you didn't inquire," she said softly.

He laughed. "That's not my concern, I reckon. It's between her and the church elders when she is ready to make that change."

With a frown wrinkling her forehead, Emma shifted her weight in the seat so that she faced Paul. Studying his profile, she wondered if he was teasing her. When she saw that he was staring straight ahead, his eyes scanning the road, she realized that he was not. A dark sense of dread began to fill her chest and she felt her heart beating rapidly.

"But Hannah and..."

Quickly he stopped her from continuing, his voice sounded a bit agitated. "It's not Hannah I wish to talk about, Emma."

"But she is a good friend of mine."

Sensing her irritation, Paul was quick to apologize. "I mean no disrespect. Of course, any friend of yours is a friend of mine."

The word *friend* caught her off guard. She couldn't tell whether he was being coy on purpose or not. "She enjoyed your verse," she offered, carefully watching his reaction.

"My verse? Why…" He paused and seemed at a loss for words. His eyes glanced at her, and then with the slightest of movements, he slowed down the horse so that the buggy stopped along the side of the quiet road. "I intended those verses just for you, Emma. I never meant for them to be seen by anyone else."

Her heart caught in her throat and she felt herself tensing up. This wasn't the conversation that she had expected. Not from Paul Esh, the man she had so clearly believed was interested in Hannah. "I don't think I quite understand, Paul."

"It was meant for you, Emma," he repeated.

She caught her breath and inadvertently jumped farther away from Paul. "Now I am quite confused! Hannah…"

He frowned. "This has nothing to do with Hannah, Emma. She's a lovely girl and I know how fond you are of her."

"As are you!" she quickly retorted.

At this, he laughed. "Oh, Emma! Surely you must know that my eyes are for one woman and one woman only. Why, if you'd let me talk, what I'm trying to say is that I wish to properly court you, Emma Weaver."

"Oh, help!"

"There is no finer, more godly woman in our *g'may*. Together we would have a wonderful future."

She shifted her weight so that she was staring directly at

him. Her mouth was hanging open and her eyes were wide. She couldn't believe what she was hearing and had to replay his words in her mind. Court her? Wonderful future? The shock of his words left her all but speechless. "Paul! This is Emma you are talking to, not Hannah! She is my friend!"

At the mention of Emma's friend, Paul made a face, confused at the sudden shift in the conversation. It was clear that the discussion had moved away from his ardor for Emma and to her friendship with Hannah. "I...I don't understand."

"Nor do I! All this time I thought you were interested in Hannah!"

At this statement, he gave a moment's reflection. "Hannah?" It took him another moment to realize what Emma had insinuated, and then, with a new look of understanding, he gave a soft laugh. "Oh, Emma, how sweet you are to think so fondly of your friend. But she has no background to speak of and her devotion to God is still immature at best. She is most pleasant, I will agree with you there. But to be the daughter-in-law of the bishop? I think not."

His words did not seem real to Emma. Was Paul Esh actually saying such things to her? "You gave her so much attention!" she countered. "You gave her the impression..."

He cut her off. "*Nee*, Emma, I gave no impression." He seemed momentarily disturbed by her accusation. "I merely was kind to a friend of yours. Any man would do the same thing. Hannah's friendship means so much to you. How could I not mirror that favor?"

"But the Bible verse that you wrote...?"

He smiled at her, his eyes softening as he spoke. "Surely you knew that Bible verse was for none other than you, Emma. Did I not hand it to you directly and say you might not want to publish it? And how could such a verse, a verse that glorifies the love between a husband and his wife, comparing it to the love of Jesus for His followers, not be intended strictly for the woman I wish to court!"

"Paul!"

Still smiling, he took a deep breath and reached to take her hand in his. At his touch, she tried to shrink away but his grip on her was too tight. He stared into her eyes, a dreamy look upon his face. "My dear Emma, I'm sure that you will need some time to think about this. Any sensible woman would. But I would like to announce our banns after the October baptism ceremony."

"Banns?"

It was all too much. Her mind was reeling and she could scarcely believe that this was happening. For a moment she felt as though she were floating on a cloud, watching the scene unfold in the buggy as a passive observer from above. How could she have gotten this so wrong? How could she have misunderstood that Paul's attentions were not intended for Hannah but for herself?

When he began to lean forward, she realized that he intended to kiss her. Putting her hand out, she pressed it against his shoulder and pushed him away. Thankfully he pulled back and blinked his eyes, a look of confusion upon his face as he tried to figure out what exactly was the meaning of this unexpected response from his intended.

Emma glared at him, embarrassed at the position he had put her in. Never in her life had she felt so violated as in this moment when Paul Esh, of all people, presumed that she would not only want to court and marry him but had even tried to steal a kiss. The humiliation of his actions was intensified by the fact that he had never once stopped to think that she might have an opinion on the matter that differed from his.

And she did.

"I am terribly sorry, Paul, but I do not wish to court you." She spoke the words sharply, trying her best to calm her beating heart. "Any interest that I had in you was as the presumed suitor to my friend."

The realization began to sink into Paul that Emma was not just surprised by his offer but shocked. The look of joy quickly faded from his face, replaced with stunned indignation.

"I think you should take me home now, Paul." She moved farther away from him on the seat, crossing her arms over her chest and staring out the window. The horse couldn't trot fast enough down the road toward her home, and she silently prayed that this whole conversation had merely been a dream, or rather a nightmare. Unfortunately when Paul finally stopped the buggy in front of her house, she realized that, indeed, it had occurred. And from the way that Paul didn't even say good-bye or wait to see that she was safe on the porch, she suspected that her astonishment was clearly matched by his resentment. And she knew that by misreading the situation her failed attempt at matchmaking had gravely offended him.

❧ *Chapter Eight* ❧

As EMMA WALKED down the road toward the Wagler home, she wrung her hands and fought the urge to cry. Despite the fact that the sun shone in the sky and birds sang happily as they flew overhead, Emma saw nothing but darkness and gloom around her. There was no beauty in the fields that she walked by, some of browning corn stalks and others of hay waiting for a final cutting. Everything was peaceful and serene around her, but that was certainly not how she felt on the inside. Unaware of her surroundings, she barely even acknowledged the buggy that passed her, even when the driver lifted his hand to wave in greeting.

No. Emma was definitely not herself. A shadow of despair had befallen her. She felt like a confused, tortured soul. It was a feeling she had never experienced before, and it left her with a heavy pit in her stomach. Always eager to provide guidance to others when it came to matters of the heart, she now realized that she was at a loss when she, Emma, was the subject of these matters.

She had spent a sleepless night, tossing and turning in her bed, unable to find peace and tranquility as she replayed time and again the scene with Paul in the buggy: his declared admiration for her, his apparent disdain for Hannah with the implication that she was not good enough for him, the anger she had felt with the realization that he had already included her in his future plans, and her outright refusal of his offer. The confused expression on his face haunted her. Paul, without saying any words, had made it quite clear that her reaction was not expected and how disappointed he had been in the rejection. And that must have meant only one thing: he had been under the impression that his affection for her was reciprocated. How had she let this happen?

Over and over again she examined all of the reasons she thought Paul was interested in Hannah rather than her, trying to determine at which point she had misconstrued his affection: their conversations, Paul's admiration of the quilt, his anxious offer to take it for binding, the Bible verse. As she began to look at the memory of these interactions with a fresh perspective, she realized how terribly wrong she had been all along. Indeed, she had misread everything about Paul Esh's intentions to court Hannah. In hindsight, now that she had clearer vision, Emma realized that she had missed the truth, even though it had been right there in front of her to observe.

When she arose in the morning, she didn't know whether she had slept at all. Her eyes felt almost as heavy as her heart. During the morning hours Emma went through the motions of doing her Monday laundry. Accidentally she hung up two pairs of her *daed*'s trousers without actually having washed them. Embarrassed, she quickly pulled them off the line and hurried back inside the *haus* to return to the laundry room. She hoped no one had seen her blunder because tongues would certainly wag, the grapevine claiming she was being prideful, hanging dirty laundry to appear harder at work than she truly was.

In the early afternoon she finally decided to pay a visit to Anna. In the past Anna had always been the one to provide her with advice and guidance in times of trouble. She had been like a surrogate sister, close friend, and *maem* all in one. It only made sense that Emma would go to her, to share her burden and confess her sins. The shame of what had transpired was far too great for Emma to bear upon her own shoulders. She needed Anna's wisdom and nonjudgmental opinion to help her get through this.

Shortly after dinner, their noon meal, her *daed* had gone to help the Yoders as best he could with their shop, moving inventory and boxes back into the upstairs room that had been used for worship the previous day. When he left, Emma quickly finished cleaning the kitchen then hurried out the back door, something she had wanted to do since early morning.

As she approached the house, she could see Anna outside, standing by the laundry line and folding clothes that had been drying in the sun. Next to her bare feet a wicker basket sat filled with white sheets, each folded carefully and neatly in a way that only Anna could do.

Going barefoot nearly everywhere was often interpreted by the *Englischer* as a lack of personal hygiene on the part of the Amish. But to the Amish wearing shoes only when absolutely necessary, usually not around the house or even in public during the warm summer months, was simply a way of life, a display of their modesty, simplicity, and humility toward their Creator and the community.

The green dress that Anna held in her arms was almost finished, so with one final fold, she set it atop the basket and waved at Emma, the delight on her face more than apparent at the surprise visit.

"Why, Emma! I'm so happy to see you!" Anna beamed as she clutched Emma's hand. Her cheeks were rosy and her eyes glowed. It was clear that Anna was experiencing a tremendous amount of joy in her new life as Samuel's *fraa*; as if she was finally fulfilling her destiny. Still, there was something extra exciting in her expression today. "I have such great news! A letter arrived." She laughed and clutched her hands together before her chest. "It must have been delivered on Saturday, and I never checked the box until this morning! Oh, how I wish I had looked on Saturday. Why, Samuel is just beside himself! He would have loved to have shared that *gut* news yesterday with the men after worship!" Another delighted laugh. "To think, after so long, Francis has finally committed to return to Lancaster!"

Despite the happiness in her friend's face, Emma could hardly contain her own tears. She lowered her eyes, avoiding contact with Anna's in the hopes of hiding her own shame. "I have heard, *ja*," she admitted. Indeed, her father had told her just that morning about the news of Francis's upcoming return after so many years away from Lancaster.

"Already?" Anna had a quizzical look upon her face. "How on earth did the news travel so quickly?"

Emma tried to smile. "Your husband stopped by earlier this morning," she said. "He wanted to share the good news with *Daed*."

Indeed, both Henry and Emma had been surprised when Samuel appeared on their doorstep. When he came in, Emma offered him a cup a coffee, and as the two men sat at the kitchen table, she overheard the announcement.

It was clear that Samuel was exuberant. In the past there

had been several times when Francis had written that he wanted to visit. Those letters had always brought joy to Samuel, and he would share the news with his family and friends. But something always came up at the last minute that resulted in the trip being canceled. This time, however, Francis wrote that he had already scheduled the driver and he intended to stay for a good long while.

The two men laughed joyfully, pleased that Samuel's son was coming home at long last.

"And mark my words," Samuel said to Henry, a twinkle in his eye as he scratched at his graying beard. "If I know my boy, he says two weeks, but he will be here earlier!" With a wink in Emma's direction, he added, "Francis was always known for his love of surprises!"

Despite the jubilation of the prodigal son's eminent return, Emma had found it hard to do more than smile in response. Even now she found it difficult to feign the joy that Anna so clearly displayed, for her own heart was still aching from the previous day's buggy ride home with Paul and its potential consequences.

Recognizing the despondent look in the younger woman's eyes, Anna put her finger under Emma's chin and tilted her head upward. The watery mist in Emma's eyes was too apparent from that angle, and the expression on Anna's face changed from joy to concern. "What is this, Emma? Tears? You have never been one to cry. What is happening, now?"

"Oh, Anna!" Emma replied, fighting the urge to sob. "I didn't come here because of Francis, although that is such *wunderbaar* news and I'm sure that you are ever so pleased!" A tear filled her eye and she reached into the pocket of her dress to withdraw a white handkerchief. "I came because everything has turned upside down. I am so ashamed and so bewildered. I don't know what to do."

Putting her arm around Emma's shoulders, Anna gave her a gentle squeeze of comfort before she began to guide her toward the house. "Come, come, now, Emma. Let's go inside the *haus* where we can sit and have a talk. It's been a while since you and I sat together, ain't so? And with so much change afoot, I'm sure that everything must seem much worse than it truly is, *schwester*."

They were seated on the sofa, Emma wringing the handkerchief in her hands as she began to search for the words to explain. "I don't even know where to start. Something most unpleasant happened yesterday, and I fear that I may have harmed my friend."

Anna reacted with a concerned look on her face. Clearly this was not what Anna had expected to be the source of Emma's troubles. "Hannah? Whatever has possibly occurred?"

Emma reached up to dab at the tear that was lingering in the corner of her eye. She looked at Anna and chewed on her lower lip. "It was never my intention to inflict pain upon her, or anyone for that matter. My intentions were just the opposite."

"*Ja vell*, misunderstandings do happen, and quite often, my dear Emma. I can't imagine anything so awful as to make you this distraught!" She let her arm drop from Emma's shoulders and folded her hands, resting them primly in her lap. "Now, why don't you tell me exactly what transpired and from the beginning? *Mayhaps* that would help us both make sense of the situation."

Emma gave a heavy sigh. How could she explain? She didn't even know where to start. "I don't even know how it happened, but Paul Esh..." She stopped talking, trying to find the right words, but she was at a loss for words. Instead a blush of humiliation covered her cheeks.

The slight pause in Emma's words gave Anna the chance to interrupt, a knowing smile coming upon her face. "Ah, so Paul Esh has come courting you at last, is that it?"

Stunned, Emma stared at Anna. "How…how did you know?"

Anna reached out and patted Emma's hand, a gesture of comfort and support that was usually shared between mother and daughter. "*Vell*, I certainly had my suspicions over the past year with his frequent visits and Sunday suppers at the house. Of course, just the other week I saw him gazing upon you when you were visiting with Irene. To another woman's eyes, his intentions were most clear, Emma."

"Not to me, they weren't!"

A laugh escaped Anna's lips. "It usually isn't, that is true!"

"*Vell*, that's not all." Emma swallowed, trying to find the courage to admit the rest. "I thought he was intending to pursue Hannah. Now, regrettably, I fear that she has set her expectations upon that very thought."

Anna raised an eyebrow and stared at Emma. "Why would she have done such a thing? Has Paul made promises to her?"

"*Nee, nee*," she exclaimed. "It's not like that." Shutting her eyes, Emma slumped back into the sofa. *Oh, the misery*, she thought. Why hadn't she listened to Gideon when he had warned her so many weeks ago? "This is all my fault, Anna. It was my hand in suggesting that he was interested in her."

"Oh, Emma…"

The disappointment in Anna's voice hurt Emma almost as much as the knowledge that she had unintentionally harmed her friend. Sitting forward, she pounded her fist against her knee and scowled, realizing that she was disappointed in herself. She went on: "I was so certain that he was interested, with his compliments about the quilt and the Bible verse that he gave to us for her project. I had left them both alone on several occasions and had witnessed their pleasant interaction upon my return. And I even had a hand in her turning down that Ralph Martin..."

"The nice farmer who leases Gideon's land?" Anna frowned. "Why would you have done such a thing, Emma? He's a lovely, godly man!"

Lifting her hands to her eyes, Emma rubbed them, frustrated with her own feelings of inadequacy. "So I have come to hear over and over again," she cried. "I will never try to matchmake again, Anna."

"That is a wise decision, Emma. What is it the Bible says? 'For we hear that some among you are leading an undisciplined life, doing no work at all, but acting like busybodies.' And you, of all people, know that courtship is a matter better left to the two individuals who are courting. It has been our way, the Amish way, for endless generations, and that is how it is meant to be. The privacy of such decisions saves the people who make them from such embarrassment, should things not quite work out, don't you reckon?"

Despite the gentle nature of Anna's reprimand, at those words, Emma started to sob, the tears finally spilling from her eyes. "I did act exactly like a busybody, didn't I? I'm so ashamed of myself!" Emma pulled at the handkerchief. "How will I ever face Hannah again?"

"Dear Emma, the Lord has always taught us that we must admit our sins directly and face those we have affected just as we face Him: with honesty and true remorse. The best way is to be straightforward and to the point, don't you agree? Knowing your friend, Hannah will recognize that your intentions were nothing more than the utmost of admirable. Whatever you did, you did it for her in the spirit of true friendship; Hannah will be the first one to recognize it. Forgiveness will be right behind your confession, of that I'm sure."

"We are to attend an applesauce canning this Friday at Hetty's," Emma sniffled. "I reckon I should try to confess to her before then. It would probably ruin her day to be told on Friday, and I don't think I can keep this inside me much longer! It's eating me alive, Anna. What do you think?"

"I dare not try to imagine how you feel, Emma" she replied sympathetically. "It should be a lesson to you, though. Only God can control such things, not you."

"I know," Emma cried. "Oh, how I know that now!"

"So when will you tell her?" Anna asked, trying to refocus Emma on the problem at hand.

"Wednesday," she stated after giving it a moment's thought. "She had said that she would come visiting on Wednesday, since she is working at market today and tomorrow. I suppose that Wednesday will have to do."

Anna nodded her head. "I should think that would be a fine time, and it would certainly give her a day or two to digest the news before going to the applesauce canning." There was a new gentleness to her voice, and the look in her eyes let Emma know that she was forgiven, as far as Anna was concerned. "And don't fret too much. Hannah is young, Emma. She will find her heart mended rather quickly, I dare say." There was a wistful look in Anna's eyes. "She is not the first young woman to have her hopes disappointed, I'm sure."

Sniffling, Emma nodded her head and offered a timid smile. She knew that Anna was correct. There was nothing left to do but to go directly to Hannah and confess what she had learned by way of Paul Esh's sharing his interest in herself rather than in Hannah. Hiding the truth would only lay a burden of self-inflicted guilt upon her own head and, Emma feared, create a growing strain upon their friendship. And that fear, that her meddling might have ruined what had looked to be such a great, lifelong friendship, was the one that caused Emma the most pain.

✤ Chapter Nine ✤

I T WAS WITH grave apprehension and a lump in her throat that Emma waited for Hannah's arrival at her home on Wednesday. While she was eager to explain what had transpired and to apologize for what she now saw as her intrusion and meddling into Hannah's life, she had mixed feelings about meeting with her friend. After all, she hadn't seen Hannah since Paul's most awkward proposal on Sunday after the communion service. The past three days had seemed to drag, time frozen as she waited for the moment when she would have to confess what happened and ask for forgiveness.

She knew that Hannah had been busy working at the local market in town for a neighbor woman who had fallen down a stair, twisting her ankle. It had been a good sign that one of Gladys's neighbors had asked Hannah. It certainly meant that the community accepted her. However, since Emma needed to have the discussion in person, rather than by letter or even by calling Gladys's house on a neighbor's telephone, she had no choice but to wait until Hannah could visit, a delay that had left Emma alone with her own feelings of shame.

Now that the day was upon her, the day that she would

finally have the opportunity to face Hannah and confess her dreadful sin, as she had finally come to look upon her deed, Emma found that she was emotionally torn. The thought of hurting her friend's feelings caused Emma great pain. If only she did not have to tell Hannah, she thought repeatedly.

Yet Emma also found herself hoping that the confession would free her soul from the self-inflicted punishment of constantly berating herself. Over and over she had chastised herself for butting in on a situation that was none of her business. The horrible feelings that went along with this realization were punishment enough and almost more than Emma could bear.

She spent the morning pacing in the kitchen while trying to find both the courage and the right words she needed for sharing the news with Hannah. In her mind nothing sounded even remotely gentle and kind enough to communicate the impending letdown to her friend.

At one point Henry walked into the kitchen and stood, just for a moment, at the door, watching her with a mixture of curiosity and concern on his face.

"Wie gehts, Dochder?"

"Daed!" His presence surprised her and she jumped, her hand rising to her chest as if to still her beating heart.

There was a thoughtful gaze in his eyes as he stared at his daughter. At that moment it dawned on Emma that, *mayhaps*, her *daed* also suspected Paul was sweet on her. If that were the case, it explained why her *daed* had insisted on Gideon bringing him home from church, thus leaving the perfect opportunity for Paul to have some time alone with Emma. Of course, her *daed* would never think to ask if she was courting Paul. Such relationships were usually kept secret to avoid the embarrassment of situations similar to what Emma was currently facing. For him to know what actually transpired would only be one more complication to deal with, Emma thought.

Still she easily could see from his expression that he suspected something serious was on her mind. Whether he was expecting, or merely just hoping, that she was trying to figure out a way to tell him that she was to wed Paul Esh, Emma wasn't certain. All she knew was that she would never breathe a word of the proposal to anyone besides Anna.

"Something troubling you, then?"

The look on his face expressed yet another emotion that Emma had not considered prior to this moment: apprehension. It dawned on her that, if she were to marry, whether it was to Paul Esh or anyone else for that matter, she would move away from the small house where she had been born and raised. The house that had seen her mature into a grown woman. The house that had witnessed all that had been said and done throughout her growing years. But it was also and *mayhaps* as importantly, the house where the bond between father and daughter had been forged, especially of late, since Emma had replaced Anna as his caretaker and the mistress of the house. If she were to marry, that would leave her *daed* alone in the house, a thought that she could not bear to think about. Certainly he too had made that connection, and while most likely grappling with his need to accept that Emma might marry one day, even though she often protested otherwise, he had never thought it would be one day soon.

"*Nee, nee,*" she said, doing her best to reassure him. "Just deep in thought."

He didn't look quite convinced.

"Honest, *Daed,*" she said with a forced smile. "Everything

is right as rain!" She prayed that God would forgive the little white fib. It would be better for her *daed* to never know that Paul had proposed to her. *Let him suspect but never know*, she told herself. The last thing she needed was for her *daed* to catch wind of what had actually happened. After his warning just a short month prior about playing matchmaker, he would be most disappointed and opinionated about her role in this terrible misunderstanding. "I thought you were off to help Daniel Zook at his store today!"

"*Ja*, I am," he confirmed, finally choosing to believe her.

Despite Henry's weak hands and poor eyesight, limiting the extent of his involvement with his friends and neighbors, he still found ways to help in the community. Daniel Zook was an old friend of Henry's who ran a small leather goods store. From time to time Daniel needed to leave town on business and often asked Henry to mind his store and collect payments. If there was one thing Henry Weaver could do better than anyone else in the *g'may*, it was greeting and dealing with customers.

"But he doesn't need me until nine thirty." He glanced at the clock that hung on the wall over the kitchen window. It was ten minutes after nine. "I've come inside to let you know that I'm leaving now."

She responded with a simple nod of her head.

He glanced at her one last time. "Your shoulders sure do seem heavy with burden, Emma. If there is something you wish to tell me, I could spare a few minutes."

"Nothing that I can't handle, *Daed*," she replied with another forced smile. His good opinion of her meant more than anything in the world. To confide in him meant risking that. She contemplated asking for his advice, but after talking to Anna, she decided that her meddling had done enough damage, and to share the intimate details of what had passed between her and Paul would only continue the possible harm, not just to her standing in the community but also to Paul's. Her *daed* would be embarrassed to know that she had refused him, that was for sure and certain.

With a quick glance at the counter, she diverted his attention with a quick, "And you almost forgot the cooler with your dinner that I packed! We can't have that, can we now? You'd be forced to eat someone else's food and it would be full of nonorganic things, for sure and certain."

The teasing tone of her words went unnoticed by her *daed*. "Bless you, Emma," he replied. "So thoughtful of you to have packed it for me."

And with that, his concern evaporated as he took the cooler, planted a soft kiss upon her forehead, and left Emma to herself, to continue her fretting in peace.

Promptly at ten o'clock Hannah arrived with a smile on her face and a warm embrace for her friend. The greeting only caused Emma a tightening in her chest, and she felt herself fighting back tears just as Hannah pulled away.

"What is wrong, Emma? Is everything all right at home? Is it your *daed*?"

"*Nee, nee*," Emma quickly responded. "He's fine. Tired more frequently, *ja*, but fine."

Hannah set down her purse on the counter and turned to face Emma. "Then what is it? Tell me, dear Emma."

Clearing her throat, Emma dove forward by replying, "I fear I have some bad news, Hannah. Come, let's sit." Emma forced herself to guide Hannah to the sitting area where they could face each other from the comfort of the sofa. "I fear that my news has to do with someone else: Paul Esh."

A look of grave concern crossed Hannah's face, the color

draining from her cheeks. "Oh, dear. Has something happened? Is he ill?"

"He is not ill," Emma was quick to counter, her heart torn at Hannah's quickness to worry about the well-being of the young man, the very young man who had nary a care for her in return. "However, something *has* happened." She paused, searching for the proper words. Despite her days of trying to prepare the words to break the news to her friend, Emma realized that actually speaking to her was harder than she had anticipated. With a deep breath she reached out and took Hannah's hands into hers. For a few seconds she stared at her friend, forcing herself to meet her eyes, even though she would have much preferred to look away. "I...I have to confess to you something that has been weighing heavy on my heart. Unfortunately I haven't had the chance to see you until now..."

"Don't delay any longer, Emma," Hannah said, her voice edged with panic. "Tell me, please."

The time had come to disclose what she so dreaded unveiling. With a deep breath Emma bowed her head as she spoke. "I fear that I have been gravely mistaken in my opinion about Paul Esh. While he has occupied much of our time, interest, and discourse, I have come to learn that he was not interested in courting you."

"Oh." The slight gasp that escaped Hannah's lips spoke of her surprise at Emma's announcement. "Might I ask how you came to this realization?"

It was the question that Emma had been dreading. She had hoped that Hannah would not ask it. Perhaps she did not have to answer it after all. To confide the truth would hurt her friend even more as well as break the confidence that she had shared with Paul. His proposal, while unexpected on Emma's part, was not something to be shared. She had weighed her options over the past few days and knew that, if asked, she would have to find a way to convey the truth without causing further injury to Paul or distrust toward her.

"He confided in me, Hannah," she began slowly. "He informed me that his interest was not in you but ..." She paused and swallowed, averting her eyes. "His interest was somewhere else." Another pause. "With someone else."

Clearly this news stunned Hannah. The color drained from her face and she gasped. "Someone else? Oh!" Gone was the previous joy she had exuded when she had walked into the house. The expression of pain on her face ripped at Emma's conscience.

"I'm afraid so."

"Who?" Hannah ventured to ask, her voice trembling slightly.

Emma took a deep breath and lifted her chin, staring her friend in the eyes. "His interest, it seems, is in me."

With a very soft voice Hannah simply stated, "I don't understand" and tried to withdraw her hands from Emma's. She was met with resistance.

"I didn't understand either!" Emma responded quickly, holding on to Hannah's hands as tight as she could. "I never once suspected it, and it took me quite by surprise. I can assure you that I do not reciprocate those feelings, nor will I ever." Realizing how that last part sounded, she quickly added, "My interest in Paul Esh was only on your behalf."

"I...I see."

Emma wished she could read Hannah's mind. What was she thinking? Did she think that Emma had deliberately and willfully stolen her intended beau? Such a consideration tore at Emma's heart. To be thought of in such a light upset her greatly, for she always strove to be considered an upright and honorable person. Someone who encouraged a friend to pursue a young man and then tried to steal his affections was neither of these things.

"Oh, Hannah!" she cried, the emotion in her voice unmistakable and sincere. "I am so terribly sorry. My meddling has proven to be my downfall, although it was only with the best intentions, I assure you. How can you ever forgive me?"

It took a moment for Hannah to respond. She stood up and walked across the floor, her back to Emma as she stood by the kitchen table. With hunched shoulders, she appeared deflated, as if the wind had been knocked from her. Reaching down, she ran a finger along the back of a chair. Her mind was elsewhere as she digested this news that Emma had shared with her; as for Emma, she waited patiently for Hannah to speak.

"I suppose that was a rather ambitious dream," she whispered. "I mean, who am I to marry someone like Paul Esh?"

"That's not true!" Emma cried. "What is ambition anyway? To think that you are less than another and must work hard to prove yourself? You did not have an overly ambitious dream, Hannah! You can achieve great things!"

Hannah turned around, and despite the sorrow in her eyes, she smiled. It was a sad smile for she finally understood. "*Nee*, it is true," she replied calmly. "Someone of Paul's standing in the community would not court a simple plain country girl like me."

If Emma wanted to argue, she knew that she couldn't. Paul had almost admitted as much to her when he had sought Emma's hand. His comments had haunted her as much as the misunderstanding that had resulted from her interference in Hannah's personal affairs. So instead of contradicting her friend, Emma merely said, "Paul Esh is a fool if he doesn't see how *wunderbaar* you are, Hannah! And if he puts himself above others, he has only God to answer to on that! He will be missing out on a right *gut fraa*!"

"*Mayhaps*," Hannah reluctantly admitted. It was obvious, however, that she did not believe that. With her confidence destroyed and her heart broken, there were few words that would be able to comfort her at the present moment; that much was clear to Emma.

"Hannah," she said softly. "I thought I could help you acclimate into the community, and I was so hopeful that I was correct about a match between you and Paul. I misread his feelings. I should never have gotten involved. I fear that I have failed you as a friend as well as a sister in Christ. I can only, once again, ask for your forgiveness for having tried to play a hand in this confused mess." She looked up and pleaded with her eyes. "Please, Hannah, will you be able to forgive me?"

"My dear Emma, how could I not forgive you?" Hannah smiled through her tears. "While I am most disappointed in your news, I know that you would never intentionally lead me astray."

Jumping to her feet, Emma ran to her friend and they embraced. Tears fell from Hannah's eyes, but she laughed as she cried. Emma joined her, letting fall the tears that she had been holding back since Sunday. For a few long moments they cried on each other's shoulders, offering words of comfort and an occasional, tearful laugh at the situation.

Wiping at her face, Hannah was the first to break the embrace. She pulled back and took a deep breath, as if seeking an inner strength that she did not feel. "I shall have to be brave and face this news with the strength of the Lord behind me and know that some day He shall guide me to my proper husband, if that is indeed His will."

Emma placed her hands on Hannah's shoulders and stared at her, determined to show her own confidence in what she was about to say. "You will find your husband, Hannah. God will lead you to him; you can be sure and certain of that. You believe me, *ja*?"

Hannah nodded and sniffled at the same time.

"And I promise," Emma added solemnly, reaching up to dry the tear that clung to the corner of her eye, "I will not meddle anymore."

Both young women laughed at that statement and once again embraced in an affectionate, sisterly hug.

Despite the emotions of the meeting, Emma felt an enormous weight lift from her shoulders. She said a silent prayer, thanking God for granting her a second chance to prove what a right *gut* friend she was. Now she would rely on Him to help her refrain from meddling when her opinions and guidance were neither required nor needed.

❧ Chapter Ten ❧

THE SKY WAS overcast, gray clouds hovering on the
horizon and creating a gloomy feeling about the day.
There was a chill in the air, carrying a hint of the
impending change of seasons. Clearly the long hot days of
summer were over, even if some days still were warm and
sunny. Today, however, was not one of those. While the official start of autumn was still a few days away, Emma and
Hannah both wore thick black sweaters over their dresses
along with thin black knee socks with their shoes, an uncomfortable feeling after so many months of going everywhere
barefoot. With yesterday's drama behind them, they were on
their way to attend their weekly visit with the widows.

Their visits with Mary Yoder and Katie Miller were very
similar to the previous week: short visits with small talk and
simple treats of cookies and tea that Emma had packed in
a basket for the women. Both of the older women shared
whatever letters they had received earlier in the week from
friends and family, both near and afar. After twenty minutes or so Emma would excuse herself to wash and dry the
dishes, taking care to put everything back exactly the way
she had found it so as not to burden either Mary or Katie
with having extra chores after their visitors left.

It was at their third stop, Sarah Esh's house, that they encountered the first of two surprises for the day.

Sarah was a frail woman who used a walker to get around her small house. But she always greeted her visitors with a wide smile and a cheery invitation to come in and visit, sharing the rocking chairs in her sitting room. With great apprehension Emma knocked at the door, with a quick glance at Hannah to give her support to get through the visit. Both of them wondered if Paul would show up today to visit her. Neither one had talked further about what had happened with Paul, but they were nervous at the thought of running into him for the first time since he had proposed to Emma.

"*Wilkum!*"

Emma smiled as the door was opened and Sarah's face peered out, a big bright smile lighting up her face. "*Gut mariye*, Sarah! We've come to sit a spell, if that's all right with you."

"Come in, come in," she insisted, showing a sign of surprise as if this was not a weekly routine and she had not seen them in months, then stepping back from the door so that Emma and Hannah could enter. "How right *gut* of you to come visit!"

"Now, Sarah," Emma chided gently. "I wouldn't miss our weekly visit for anything!" Her words caused Sarah's smile to broaden even wider. "I brought along some sugar cookies that I made just this morning!" She lifted her arm, indicating the basket that she held. "And fresh meadow tea, too."

Without waiting for an invitation, Emma quickly began to move toward the kitchen. She knew where everything was kept and quickly had a tray prepared with paper napkins, cups, glass jar of tea, and the covered plate of cookies.

"Shall we go sit, then?" She moved over toward the sitting area, waiting for Sarah to sit in her burgundy-colored recliner. "This will probably be the last tea of the season, I reckon," she sighed, bending down for Sarah to serve herself.

"Concentrate!" Sarah announced forcefully as she accepted a glass from the tray that Emma held before her. The single word startled Emma, and for just a moment she wasn't certain what Sarah had meant. "You must make concentrate tea syrup in order to have some in the winter months."

Laughing, Emma set the tray on the oval coffee table and sat down in her assigned rocking chair. The glass of cool tea in her hands, she stared into it for a moment as if pondering over Sarah's words. "I thought you meant I needed to concentrate better!" Both Sarah and Hannah joined her in laughing at Emma's comment. Once everyone was situated and enjoying their refreshments, Emma finally responded to Sarah's suggestion. "Anna and I made that tea syrup one year. I thought that it doesn't keep as well and spoils my enjoyment of the tea."

Sarah shook her head and clucked her tongue several times, before lifting her cup to her lips to taste the tea. "Well done, Emma," she said approvingly. "Just the right blend of sugar and mint."

"*Danke*," Emma said. "Anna taught me *vell*."

A moment of silence fell over the three. Emma watched as Sarah reached for a cookie, taking a healthy bite as small crumbs scattered down the front of her navy blue dress. She was about to say something when Sarah carelessly wiped them onto the floor.

Clearing her throat, Hannah set down her cup and broke the silence. "I found a powdered formula at the Sharp

Shopper!" She smiled eagerly at Emma. *"Mayhaps* we could try that for the colder months?"

"Powdered? Oh, help!" Slapping her hand against her leg, Emma sank back into the rocking chair and shook her head in wonder. "Whatever would *Daed* have to say about *that*?"

Both Sarah and Hannah laughed, knowing full well that Henry Weaver would find something to say about such an unnatural version of a truly delicious, if not medicinal, potent drink. Emma was pleased with Hannah's response. Contrary to her fears, Hannah had seemed to respond to the dreadful news of the previous day with a strong continence. She was proud of her dear friend for being so strong in the face of such a devastating loss.

After tasting the tea, Sarah set the glass on the small side table next to her chair. "You come to visit me every week and bring me news," she said, a mischievous smile on her face. "Today I have news for both of you!"

Emma looked amused and raised an eyebrow, glancing at Hannah, who also appeared delighted in this unusually sassy side of Sarah Esh. "News? Oh my!" She winked at Hannah. "Do tell us! I can hardly wait!"

The older woman's eyes sparkled and she leaned forward, her elbows on her knees as she lowered her voice, sharing her secret. "I don't reckon you have both heard about my nephew Paul, *ja*?"

At the mention of Paul, the very man who had caused such angst for the two of them, Emma stiffened and glanced at Hannah. Her cheeks suddenly looked pale but she maintained her composure as if bracing herself for the worst news. Emma certainly hoped that he hadn't told anyone about what had transpired between them. Even if he omitted her name and confided in his family, such news would be devastating to Hannah.

"*Nee*, Sarah," Emma responded, choosing her words carefully and speaking slowly. "I can't say that I have heard any news of Paul of late."

Hannah merely shook her head.

Receiving the response that she wanted, Sarah looked delighted as she finally shared her gossip. "He went off to Ohio, he did! Just Monday last. Wanted to visit with a bishop out there, learn more about their *g'may* and different practices." She smiled, unable to hide her pride in her nephew. "You mark my words. That young man will be chosen by the lot one day. Not a finer, more godly man has ever graced our church district."

With a sigh of relief and ignoring the blatant pride in Sarah's words, Emma pressed forward. "Monday after communion service? Was that an expected trip then?"

"*Nee*, not at all. His *daed* said that Paul felt the calling from God to take such a spontaneous trip. Imagine that!" Another smile. "God touched him, that boy."

Hardly likely, Emma thought, still bitter at what she considered a clear deception on the part of Sarah's ever-so-godly nephew. While Emma would never share the intimate details of that conversation with anyone, she did suspect that her rebuff had caught him off guard, and he had run to Ohio to hide his shame. If her entire opinion of Paul Esh had changed dramatically after that dreadful buggy ride home, her respect for him had now vanished at this unexpected announcement.

"And I wouldn't be too surprised if he returns with a bann to be announced too!" Sarah giggled in delight.

Choking on her tea, Emma set down her glass on the

table and reached for a paper napkin to wipe at her mouth. Her eyes flickered to meet Hannah's, and she wasn't surprised to see that her friend was blinking rapidly as if fighting tears. Gone was that facade of strength she had been portraying. And, as startled as Hannah was, Emma was equally as shocked. Had he not just proposed to her five days prior?

"Banns?" Emma managed to ask with a shaky voice.

Sarah nodded her head emphatically. "That's what I said."

"Oh, I heard you," Emma retorted. "I just didn't believe what I heard."

Sarah laughed at Emma's reaction.

"That would be most sudden, wouldn't it?" Emma asked.

What she really wanted to ask was how on earth Paul Esh could propose to her on one day, leave town the next, and then have rumors spreading that he would return from Ohio with a *fraa*! It was unthinkable. While Emma knew that she could never voice her opinion on the matter, she also knew that tongues would wag along the Amish grapevine. The speculation on such a situation had the potential to ruin any chance of Paul Esh ever being nominated to serve the church.

Waving her wrinkled hand at Emma, Sarah dismissed the question and shook her head. "You young people put too much emphasis on this courtship business. In my day..." she began, a wistful look in her eyes as she fell back into her memory, a favorite place for many of the widows that Emma visited, it seemed. "Courtship was more direct. Select the partner on values and morals. God provides the rest over the years. Is it not better to marry a righteous and God-fearing man than to seek romance? What you call 'romance' and 'love' only comes with time, girls. Not during a few buggy rides. Mark my words on that." She pursed her lips together.

"Is it any wonder that so many of you young folk are getting married later and later in life, and some not at all. Too particular you are, I'll say!"

Hannah quickly stood up and excused herself, explaining that she needed to use the restroom. Emma's eyes trailed after her, hoping and praying that the pain of her heartbreak was not more than her friend could bear.

But that was not to be the only surprise of the day.

In silence Hannah and Emma walked to their final destination: the home of Hetty and Old Widow Blank. Sarah's announcement had seemed to take the wind out of their sails, and neither one knew what to say to the other.

"Why, Emma Weaver! How *gut* of you to come!" The door opened before she even had a chance to knock. Hetty grinned and reached for Emma's arm, pulling her into the kitchen. "What a surprise we have for you! I just know that you'll be as excited as we are!" She turned to her aging mother. "*Maem*! Won't Emma be just thrilled with our surprise?"

The elderly woman leaned forward and cupped her ear. "Eh?"

Hetty repeated herself, louder this time. "Our surprise! Won't Emma be excited?" But it was clear that her mother still could not hear her and she responded with a disgruntled shrug of her shoulders and looked away.

"Let me guess," Emma said sweetly as she set her basket on the table and began to unload the goodies that she had brought with her for the two women. "Another letter from your dear niece, Jane?"

It was part of their routine. Every Thursday when she visited, Emma was subjected to listening to Hetty read and sometimes reread letters from Jane. And every week Emma smiled politely, commenting on one or two lines from the missive, knowing that to talk about Jane gave Hetty such great joy, despite the fact that Emma found most of Jane's letters one thing and one thing only: dull.

"A letter!" Hetty giggled and clapped her hands in delight, more childlike in her response than Emma found pleasing. "A letter, *Maem*. Emma asked if we received a letter!" Clearly Hetty was delighted with whatever her surprise was, a surprise that Emma was beginning to dislike before she even knew what it was. "*Nee, nee*, Emma. It's better than a letter!"

"Well do tell, Hetty," Emma coaxed, starting to feel irritated, as she was still unhappily digesting Sarah Esh's news. "Surprises are meant to be shared at some point, otherwise there is no point in having them, is there?"

Grabbing Emma's arm, Hetty led her through the kitchen and into the small sitting room that was down a narrow hallway. "Come see for yourself what surprise we have for you. And, oh, I just know you will be delighted, delighted, delighted!" She clucked her tongue happily.

No sooner had they walked through the doorway and into the sitting room than Emma's eyes fell upon a young woman. She sat straight and proper in the ladder back chair with her legs crossed at the ankle and tucked under her skirt. She was darker skinned, clearly from having worked outside in the fields or gardens. Yet she was fresh and pretty, with bright brown eyes that sparkled and plump lips that smiled ever so slightly. There was something familiar about the woman, but Emma knew that she had never seen her before this day.

"I don't believe we have met," Emma said politely, stepping forward with an outstretched hand to greet the pretty young woman. "I'm Emma Weaver."

The woman smiled, again just a hint of an upturning of her lips. "We have met, but it has been many years," the woman said, her voice soft and gentle with just the faint touch of a different accent.

And at that moment Emma knew.

"Jane?"

Hetty giggled and clapped her hands. "I knew you'd recognize her! I knew you'd know Jane, even after all of these years!" She turned to call out to her mother. "Didn't I tell you, *Maem*?" She didn't wait for an answer, for her *maem* didn't even appear to be listening, but turned back to Emma. "I told her! I said that if anyone would recognize our dear Jane, it would be our Emma! Oh, for sure and certain!"

If she felt humiliated and dismayed at having heard that Paul Esh's declarations of admiration for her had already been brushed away by taking an unplanned trip to Ohio in search of a substitute *fraa*, Emma's heart jumped further in her throat at the realization that the beloved Jane, the one with a perpetual aura of goodness, grace, and perfection, the one that Hetty constantly talked about, was finally sitting before her, grown up and proper, with an air of godliness about her that Emma found overly powerful. This was Jane? Twelve years ago she had left a mere child, and now she returned as a woman who clearly had just as much confidence as she did beauty.

Masking her surprise, Emma was quick to take ahold of Jane's hands and give them a warm squeeze. "This is such a *gut* surprise, indeed!" she managed to say, doing her best to sound genuinely pleased. It wasn't easy and she worried that her voice sounded strained. "Your *aendi* has been so kind as to share your letters with us each week. Why, I feel as though we are the best of friends already!"

Jane smiled in response but did not speak.

"From the last letter, there wasn't any mention that you

were planning a trip to Lititz!" Emma forced her own smile onto her face, a bit puzzled by the reserved nature of the woman before her. While they were the exact same age, Jane seemed years older and much more formal in her demeanor. Emma wondered whether or not that was a trait of the *g'may* in Ohio where Jane had been raised. "Had you planned this visit for long, then?"

"A van was coming from Ohio and I wanted to surprise my *aendi* and *grossmammi*," she explained. It was a simple explanation that did not directly answer Emma's question.

Emma glanced at Hetty, observing the joyous delight on the older woman's face. Indeed, she couldn't remember a time when Hetty looked so happy. "Well, I do think you have achieved just that!"

After introducing Jane to Hannah, Hetty encouraged the three young women to sit down and visit. For a few awkward moments, they sat in the small sitting room, uncertain of what to say. Hetty took the liberty of telling the story of Jane's arrival, how she had simply appeared at the door, and oh, wasn't this reunion delightful? Then, in a burst of nervous energy, Hetty began to fuss over Jane, worrying that she was hungry. When Jane did not immediately reply, Hetty quickly excused herself, stating that she needed to fetch a tray of freshly baked cookies and lemonade from the kitchen.

Eager to leave the room, for she needed a moment to collect her thoughts from this second surprise, Emma had offered to assist her in the kitchen, but Hetty flatly refused any help. It was clear that Hetty was in her glory and wanted nothing more than to take care of Jane and their two visitors. It was also clear that today would not be a short visit.

Hetty had no sooner left the room when an awkward

silence fell over the three young women. The only noise came from the clock hanging on the wall, the gentle ticking sounding loud as it echoed in the room. Emma quickly realized that any conversation would depend on her taking the initiative. Hannah was too shy and Jane, apparently, was overly quiet.

"It has been so long since you left Lancaster for Ohio," Emma began, searching for something to say…anything! "I reckon you don't remember much, but, of what you do, does it seem much different?"

"Different and the same," Jane responded vaguely, a hint of a polite smile on her lips. "But delightful, nonetheless."

Emma fought the urge to frown, not understanding the response that Jane had provided. Just as before, when she responded to questions, she provided no real answers. In fact, her responses made it impossible to converse, something that did not sit well with Emma.

Determined to probe further, Emma asked, "And when, exactly, did you arrive?"

"Just yesterday evening," Jane responded.

Hetty reentered the room, the tray in her hands as she padded across the floor to set it down on the table by the sofa. "You'll never believe this, Emma." Hetty gave a delighted laugh, pausing to push her glasses back from the tip of her nose. "Guess who she drove all the way from Ohio to Lititz with?"

Another surprise? Emma thought that she surely could not stand another one. "Why, I'm sure I couldn't do any such thing!" she managed to say. "Do share!"

Jane smiled and looked down at the floor while Hetty handed a glass of lemonade to Emma. "Would you believe if I told you that she rode with Francis Wagler!" she said with

137

another amused laugh. "Can you imagine? How unusual and wonderful! Both Francis and Jane returning to Lititz and in the same van!"

At this news, Emma lifted an eyebrow. Francis wasn't due for a visit for another week, according to what Samuel had told her *daed* on Monday. "That *is* rather unusual!" With a curious look upon her face, she turned to Jane. "I hadn't realized that you knew Francis!"

Again, there was no immediate response from Jane.

Hetty, however, quickly jumped in. "Oh, I'm sure not," she said excitedly. "Francis was in a different *g'may*, after all. Farther away. Why, during all my visits out to Ohio to see my dear Jane, I never once bumped into him." She turned to her *maem*. "Isn't that right, *Maem*? We never once saw Francis Wagler in Ohio." A pause. "Francis! Ohio!" she repeated loudly before returning her attention back to her three young guests. "And there she sits! Jane has come to visit us at last!"

"What a joyous homecoming! Surprises abound for us all!" Emma lifted her voice, forcing it to sound more cheerful than she really felt. Once again Hetty giggled in delight, and even Hannah smiled at the older woman's happiness. Emma went on: "And you rode all that way with Francis? Why, do tell! What sort of person is Francis Wagler? We are all most curious!"

As if curious about Emma's question, Jane tilted her head. "He's a fine, godly man, I presume. I found no reason to think otherwise."

"Is he agreeable then?"

"Why, no more so than anyone else, I reckon."

Emma frowned. How many hours in the van must they have spent together, and all that Jane could say was that he was no more agreeable than anyone else? "Did you have an interesting conversation, then?"

A simple shrug of her slender shoulders accompanied yet another vague reply. "As interesting as one could expect from spending six hours in the company of another person while traveling in the same vehicle."

Emma suppressed a sigh. She felt as though she were attempting to milk a dry cow, trying to get answers out of Jane. Yet no matter what question she asked of the young woman, her response provided absolutely no useful information. Immediately Emma knew that she did not care for this young woman who appeared far too proper and much too vague to satisfy her need for information.

Emma spent the rest of the visit smiling and adding an occasional "Oh my!" in response to Hetty's continual stream of discourse, most of it flattering Jane in one way or the other. Ever so discreetly her eye monitored the clock on the wall, counting down the minutes until she could risk excusing herself to return home without a chance of offending Hetty, her *maem*, or Jane. Furthermore, the realization that she would have to spend much of the next day with all three of the women at the applesauce canning caused a queasy feeling in her stomach. How on earth would she be able to survive such a day subjected to Hetty's chatty tongue and Jane's evasive and practically silent demeanor?

❧ Chapter Eleven ☙

THE FOLLOWING AFTERNOON Emma returned home later than anticipated from the applesauce canning at the Blanks. It had been almost one o'clock when she left, and she took advantage of the mobility that having the buggy provided to stop at the natural food store, which was only a mile out of her way. She needed to replenish some of the staples in her pantry, and the stop would save her a trip on the following day. More importantly, with such a hectic and emotional week behind her, she was looking forward to a quiet Saturday at home. She needed the time to relax, reflect, and recuperate.

As expected, the applesauce canning was a long, drawn-out affair. While there were several young women there, including her friend Rachel, and many of the older women from the neighborhood who should have distracted her and kept her entertained, it became evident that this was not to be. The conversation, which usually would have delighted Emma, focused on two things and two things only: Francis Wagler's return to Lititz and Jane's surprise visit from Holmes County. Neither topic interested Emma and, with Jane's continued ability to respond to questions without actually responding, Emma quickly lost the inclination to even pretend an interest in the discussions.

After peeling and coring dozens of apples, and being forced to listen to Hetty's endless prattle about Jane—almost as if Jane were not sitting there to engage in the conversation herself, something she apparently rarely did—Emma was more than ready to leave when the last jar of applesauce was sealed in the water bath canner and the small kitchen was cleaned. Hetty had wanted her to stay and sit for a while, perhaps have some coffee and a piece of cake that she had prepared the previous day for her guests. Emma, however, had no intentions of staying even one minute longer. With feigned regret, she made her apologies for not being able to linger.

"I really must leave," she said. "*Daed* will surely be expecting me soon."

Hetty frowned. "It won't be the same without you, Emma."

At that, Emma merely smiled. "That's most kind, but you do have Jane here to delight you with lovely conversation and stories about Ohio!"

Nobody noticed the sarcasm in her voice.

Hetty merely nodded her head in agreement. "This is true! Oh, bless Jane's heart for making such a long journey!"

With a big sigh of relief, Emma hurried outside to put the harness on her horse and hitch it to the buggy. The horse could not trot fast enough to carry her away from the Blanks' home.

By the time that she finished shopping at the food store, it was almost two o'clock. She had run into a few of her friends at the store and paused to catch up on the latest news. To her dismay, they too only wanted to talk about the unexpected arrival of both Francis and Jane. Fighting the urge to roll her eyes, Emma had barely been able to keep a smile on her face as she listened to the excited gushing of her friends. She couldn't excuse herself fast enough.

Ten minutes later when she directed the horse into the driveway, she was surprised to see that there was another buggy parked there. Her first thought was Gideon must have stopped by to visit with her *daed*, as he often did on Friday afternoons after leaving his business early. Only, upon closer inspection, she noticed that it wasn't Gideon's buggy. She could easily identify his buggy with the small rectangular orange reflector bars on the back so perfectly aligned, as if he had measured the distance between them with a ruler. No. This buggy had fewer reflectors and she did not recognize the haphazard pattern.

With no other visitors expected, she found her curiosity piqued. Who could possibly have come visiting, she wondered.

She was quick to unhitch the brown mare from the buggy, carefully leading her into the stall. Reluctantly, after hanging up the harness and bridle, she curried the horse, knowing that her *daed* would be displeased if she left the sweaty horse unattended after such a workout. Still, she knew that she hurried through the task and whispered a soft apology to the horse as she shut the stall door behind herself and quickly put away the grooming supplies.

Back in the driveway she reached into the opened buggy door and grabbed the box of groceries. With a swiftness to her step, she hurried to the house, eager to find out who had stopped to visit her *daed*. When she left him, he had been busy at the kitchen table, his shoulders hunched over as he scribbled furiously on a white notepad. His focus had been on making a list of tasks that needed to be done around the house and barn prior to the onslaught of winter. With the ever-reliable Farmer's Almanac predicting an unseasonably cold winter this year, Henry wanted to be prepared for days, if not weeks, of confinement inside the house. He hadn't mentioned a visitor so she was certain that he was as surprised as she by whoever had appeared on their doorstep while she was gone.

Shifting the box of food on her hip, Emma managed to kick open the door so that she could slip through and enter the house. To her astonishment, seated around the kitchen table were two men with her father, one of whom was Samuel Wagler. The other, a tall man with broad shoulders, without doubt was his son, Francis.

When she walked through the door, all three men raised their heads and looked in her direction. But it was Francis who stood up quickly and crossed the room. He was handsome. That was the first thing that she noticed about him. Certainly he did not favor Samuel, who, while not unattractive, had broader features than Francis. The second thing she noticed was the charismatic way he carried himself. Unlike many Amish men, Francis was clearly most comfortable meeting and interacting with new people, even women.

"You must be Emma!" he said cheerfully as he reached to take the box from her arms. Without being asked, he set it upon the counter, all the while still talking. "It's right nice to meet you. I've heard so much about you from Anna! Why, I feel that we are practically siblings!"

His forthcoming manner of addressing her startled Emma, yet there was something charming about his sparkling blue eyes and his quick, lopsided grin that made her instantly like him. His skin was tanned and spoke of having worked mostly out of doors during the past seasons. His clothes were very similar in style to the Amish men of Lancaster County with the exception that his blond, curly hair was cut differently, more modern, and from the looks of it, styled at a barber rather than cut at home, which Emma immediately thought was rather worldly. A quick glance at the hats that rested upon the counter pointed out another difference: his had a much broader brim than what would be accepted in the Weavers' *g'may*.

"Wilkum, Francis," Emma said, warming up to him immediately.

It was hard not to, for there was a nearly contagious energy about him. She found herself drawn to it, a fact that troubled her immediately for she had never felt such an instant favor toward anyone, neither female or male. He was as handsome as he was charming, and Emma immediately wondered at Jane's evasive responses from the previous day. Surely there could not be enough praise said about the man that stood before her!

"Just yesterday I had the pleasure of visiting with your travel companion from Ohio and I learned then of your early arrival. And only just now I've returned from an applesauce canning at that same house where it was all that Hetty could talk about," she said, trying to not sound snide or to reflect the boredom she had felt all day. "That and the return of her niece, of course."

Francis snapped his fingers, a grin still upon his face. "And here I thought that we would surprise you today! I hoped that my arrival would be kept a secret for a day or two." Despite his expressed disappointment, the teasing look upon his face made it clear that he didn't mind.

His boyish glee caused her to laugh. "I'm not certain how it works in Holmes County," she said lightly. "But in Lititz secrets are just about as hidden as laundry hanging outside to dry on wash day! The Amish grapevine carries rich fruit, it seems!"

At this statement, everyone laughed, and the mood was set for an enjoyable visit. However, as she sat down at the far end of the kitchen table, Emma caught the knowing look exchanged between Samuel and her *daed*. She fought the urge to cast a harsh look in their direction, knowing exactly what both men were thinking and perhaps hoping, although she knew that neither would say a word.

Ignoring them, she returned her attention to Francis. He seemed oblivious to the reaction of the other two men. Casually Emma couldn't help but remark, "How fortuitous that you managed to ride along with Hetty's niece. It must have helped to pass the time, being able to converse with someone. And your *daed* must have been quite glad to see you so soon. After all, I thought you were scheduled to arrive next week."

Francis retreated back to the chair where he had previously sat, pausing to lean over and pat Samuel's knee. "It's one of my favorite pastimes," he said. "Surprising others. While one cannot indulge in such pleasures with just anyone, I knew that coming home early would be warmly regarded by my *daed*!"

At the use of the word *home*, Samuel lit up and grinned, placing his large hand over his son's. "Very true, my son. Very true."

"Your *daed* did mention how you love surprises! Why, if I recall properly, he predicted you would come sooner than the appointed date!"

Francis looked at Samuel, a warm and tender expression on his face. It was clear that, despite the separation of time and distance, the young man was fond of his *daed*. "Did you now?"

For the next half hour the discourse of the gathering focused on Francis. He delighted them by sharing stories about his life in Holmes County, living with his *muem*'s *schwester* and family. He had nary a negative word to speak about anyone, and all of his stories were told as if they were the grandest adventures in the world. His zest for life was contagious, and he had a captive audience whenever he spoke.

Emma quickly learned that he was a carpenter with his *onkel* and cousins. However, just as farm work was becoming scarce in Lancaster, there was also an overabundance of carpenters in Holmes County, making it difficult for Francis to find employment. While many young men were moving to smaller settlements out west in states such as Indiana and Missouri, it was Francis's intention to explore the possibility of relocating back to Lancaster. He wanted to start his own carpentry business, an announcement that surprised Emma and Henry, but one that was met with a hearty cheer of delight by Samuel. Clearly anything that kept his beloved son in Lititz was more than acceptable to Samuel.

"There are a lot of carpenters here too," Henry pointed out.

"But lots of development, from what I can see," Francis countered with confidence. "Good carpenters are always needed."

She thought that a queer statement in response to what her *daed* had said. After all, if the abundance of carpenters was what drove Francis from Ohio, it seemed like an awkward argument to argue the reverse as support for moving to overcrowded Lititz. Still, the joy on Samuel's face could not be denied, and she was not about to say something that could dampen the mood in the room.

"*Mayhaps* Gideon could use some help," Emma offered, glancing at her *daed*. "At least until you become established."

Samuel seemed impressed with her statement. "A good thought, that!"

Henry slapped his hand on the edge of the table in agreement. "I shall talk to him the very next time I see him! Brilliant, Emma! Always thinking, you are!"

With a slight shake of his head, Francis inquired further about what she had said. "And who is this Gideon?"

It was Henry who answered. "Gideon King. My daughter Irene's brother-in-law. He builds storage buildings for the *Englische*. A good sort of fellow."

"And a rather established young man," Samuel added.

"Well, not so young…" Emma blurted out then blushed when her *daed* scowled at her. Once again Emma had spoken before she thought. Silently she reprimanded herself, knowing that her *daed* would certainly correct her later.

"While at your age, we must all seem ancient," Samuel said lightly, not having taken offense to her comment, "at our age, Emma, everyone seems young!"

Samuel's comment caused a brief stir of laughter, and even Emma had to smile. So it was decided that an introduction would be made between Francis and Gideon, although Emma immediately noticed a change in the exuberance that Francis had displayed earlier. While the men continued their discussion, once again focusing on Francis's family in Ohio, Emma watched the young man, noticing that he had the ability to make himself amiable in all conversation that was agreeable to himself. However, when a topic arose that seemed to displease him, a dark shadow of a wall seemed to cloud his eyes.

The clock had barely chimed three times when Samuel

rose to leave. "I best get going," he said. "Regrettably I've other errands to run."

Francis stood as well. "I'd be happy to accompany you, *Daed.*" Then, with a slight pause, his eyes drifted to the window as if he had just thought of something. "Although I know that I should stop by to visit with the Blanks. Hetty was always so close to *Maem* when they were younger and most supportive after she passed."

"That she was," Samuel agreed.

All of this was news to Emma. She did not recall any such memories for, shortly after Francis's *maem* had died, her own mother passed away. While the Waglers were known among the Weavers' *g'may*, they worshipped in a different district, and Francis had gone to a different school. Henry and Samuel had been able to commiserate their loss together, but they had decidedly kept their *kinner* apart. It wasn't until Samuel had moved just that year into their *g'may* that Emma had become acquainted with him.

Her thoughts were interrupted when Francis sighed. "I'd hate for her to feel slighted if I didn't visit with her right away."

Placing his large hand upon his son's shoulder, Samuel beamed at the goodness that exuded from Francis with that one statement. "I'd be happy to drop you off," he offered. "It's not out of the way and I can pick you up on my return."

Trying to lighten the mood, Emma shifted the conversation back to one that was more enjoyable for parting guests, for she'd hate to have the Waglers leave on such a solemn note. "Such a shame you weren't there just an hour or so ago! You'd have delighted the group of women that were there. You were, after all, one of the main subjects of discussion," she said. "Although Jane said very little. She's not very talkative, I noticed." This last bit was added on purpose, and she paid extra attention to his reaction which, as expected, was devoid of any emotion.

He nodded his head. "I'm sure such a subject was weary on her nerves," he said.

Despite the flatness of his words, there was something about his tone that caused Emma to think twice. He was rigid and forced, the casual nature from their previous conversations suddenly vanished. "I'm sure you became familiar, having learned much about each other during that long ride from Ohio," she ventured to add, carefully monitoring his reaction. "Or had you previously known each other?"

"What?" He seemed startled by Emma's question. "Oh, not really. She lived in another *g'may.*"

"I'm sure you found her most agreeable," Henry added as he stood to see his guests to the door. "From all that Hetty tells us about her, she is the most godly of young women!"

"So it seemed, indeed," Francis said with a smile.

Emma stood at the kitchen counter, her eyes on the three men as they walked out to the driveway together. Slowly she unpacked the box of food that she had bought earlier that day but abandoned when she arrived home. She was curious about this new young man who had returned home at long last. While his natural mannerism was magnetic, to say the least, there was something else about him that remained to be discovered: a mysteriousness that caught Emma's curiosity.

With a new sense of purpose Emma decided that Francis Wagler was going to be a most welcomed and interesting addition to the community, even if Hetty's niece, Jane, most certainly was not!

❧ *Chapter Twelve* ❧

B Y THE TIME the following Saturday rolled around, Emma felt as though she was ready to collapse from exhaustion, and justifiably so.

Earlier in the week John King had stopped by their house to inform Henry and Emma that Irene had fallen ill. While Henry immediately began fretting, worried that she must have eaten something that was spoiled or not organic, Emma was quick to volunteer to go to her *schwester*'s aid. For the beginning part of the week, she stayed at the King's house so that she could tend to the *kinner* while Irene recovered. Taking care of Irene, five very active *kinner*, and a house full of people was something that Emma was not used to doing. Still, she did it without one complaint and was pleased to see that Irene was quick to mend.

By the time Emma returned home on Wednesday afternoon, she was looking forward to going to bed early that night and having a peaceful morning. She needed the sleep, and there was quite a lot of work to catch up on at her *haus*, that was for sure and certain: laundry needed to be washed, floors needed to be scrubbed, food needed to be stored for the winter, and meals needed to be prepared. However, within one hour of her return, her *daed* walked through the door from his afternoon stroll with news that changed her plans.

He was quick to welcome her back, commenting that the three days she had been gone felt like three weeks.

"And Irene? She is better now?"

Emma rolled her eyes. "Of course! I wouldn't have left otherwise!"

"She is using *Englische* food!" He said it as if that was the worst thing a person could do. "I've told her time and time again to eat only homemade food or food grown by our people. But I heard she was at that Sharp Shopper!"

At this, Emma frowned. "I highly doubt that, *Daed*. It's too far from their farm."

"I know what I heard," he said. "Poisoning those *kinner*, I tell you."

She laughed at the stern look on his face. "I can assure you that she is *not* poisoning the *kinner* and she was *not* shopping at Sharp Shopper!" Then, with a teasing gleam in her eyes, she added, "*Mayhaps* Giant Foods but definitely not Sharp Shopper."

And then he told her the news: during Emma's absence, Jenny Glick stopped by to inquire if Emma might go to market on her behalf that Thursday and Friday. Hiding her displeasure when she learned that her *daed* had committed her to standing in for Jenny, Emma reluctantly went to bed even earlier than she had planned. After all, Jenny's market was in Maryland and required that she arise at four o'clock in the morning in order to catch the commuter van.

To her further dismay, when Saturday final arrived, respite was not in order for Emma, as the ever diligent Henry Weaver had arranged a working bee at their house. Wielding his previously prepared list of "Must-dos" to prepare for the winter, he had convinced the Waglers, Blanks, and Gideon to come help check those tasks off of his list.

"I do wish you had waited another week," she lamented to her *daed* as she finished washing the breakfast dishes. She knew that she had dark circles under her eyes and her bones felt weary. The tranquility of tending her own home and spending quiet days quilting were much more appealing to her than the constant labor of mothering five children, tending a sick sibling, and then rising so early to travel so far to wait on *Englische* tourists, all for a meager eighty dollars a day at that!

"What is it that the Scripture says? 'Do all things without murmurings and disputings.'"

Emma scowled at him. "I am well aware of what Paul says in Philippians. And I am not disputing anything." She lifted her chin and pressed her lips together, defending herself with a touch of defiance in her voice. "I was merely stating my personal opinion."

Henry chuckled. "You do have a way of doing just that frequently, I dare say."

In response she tossed a dishcloth at him, which he caught and broke into laughter. Despite her fatigue, she couldn't resist joining him.

Gideon was the first to arrive, as always prompt, if not early, when scheduled to visit or help. He sat at the table while Emma prepared him a cup of coffee. If she noticed that he watched her with a curious expression on his face, she chose not to say anything. However, as the minutes passed, she became increasingly aware that his eyes repeatedly traveled to her person, and on more than one occasion, he deliberately drew her into the discussion. She was not vain about her looks, far from it. Nonetheless, Gideon's frequent glimpses in her direction made her more self-conscious about her drawn face and the dark circles under her eyes. And she was not comfortable with that.

Thirty minutes later the Waglers arrived. As Francis entered the room, his clothes more suited for visiting than working, Emma noticed a new energy and light come into the group. He had apparently already made the acquaintance of Gideon, for they greeted each other without introduction. Emma soon learned that Samuel had taken Francis to Gideon's place of work for an employment application, and as a result, Francis had started working there just a few days after that meeting.

With great curiosity Emma watched the interaction between the two men, noting that Gideon suddenly became more quiet and reserved as Francis took over the direction of the conversation, lighting up the room with joyful stories and jokes. When the rest of the group laughed, Gideon seemed to begrudgingly spare a forced smile and nothing more.

By the time Jane, Hetty, and her *maem* arrived, the men were already outside, working to plow over the garden from last spring in order to spread some cow manure over it. To Emma's dismay, she also learned that her *daed* insisted upon expanding it, for he wanted to plant rows of corn and other vegetables for canning. Inwardly she groaned at the realization that it would be up to her, and her alone, to tend to that garden, which meant more work and less quilting.

Inside the house Anna and Emma cleaned out the pantry, doing an inventory of what food would need to be purchased in order to stock up for the cold winter months. While she had plenty of canned peaches, chow-chow, relish, and, thanks to the canning at the Blanks the previous week, an ample supply of applesauce, it was clear that she was low on other essentials: beets, meat, and tomatoes. Luckily Henry had purchased ground meat from a local Amish butcher so that the women could work on preparing meat and meatballs for canning. Already the stove in the workroom had a black enameled pressure canner heating up the water that was required to seal the canning jars.

"I'm so sorry we're late," Hetty gushed when they breezed in through the door. She hung her wrap on the hook by the door and helped her *maem* do the same. "We had an unexpected visitor that delayed us," she continued, a delighted look on her face. "And you will never believe who it was and what we were told!"

Emma peeked around the corner of the pantry where she was reorganizing the shelves after having wiped them down before returning the inventory to their proper places. She noticed that Jane wore a freshly washed and pressed apron, not typical for a working bee.

When neither Anna nor Emma inquired as to this grand news that Hetty was clearly so eager to share, Hetty proceeded to share it anyway. "Sarah Esh stopped by," she began, washing her hands at the sink so that she could begin helping with the meat canning process that Anna was already working on. "She came with the most amazing news!" Hurrying over to where Anna was working, Hetty immediately began to help, knowing exactly what needed to be done without either waiting for or requiring instructions.

With the freshly washed mason jars now lined up on the table and the box of ground meat on the floor, she scooped up raw meat, squishing it between her hands to make small meatballs which she pushed into the jars. "You know she stops by, or at least has been since Paul's travels to Ohio."

Hetty looked up and seemed to ponder something. "Isn't that something? Francis and Jane arrived from Ohio at the same time as Paul left! It's almost as if we swapped our youth!" She seemed delighted with her rather judicious observation.

"The news, *aendi*," Jane urged, but quietly, trying to refocus Hetty on what information she had started sharing before getting sidetracked.

"*Ach ja, ja*! The news!" Quickly Hetty dipped her hand into the salt box and sprinkled some into the jar of meat before wiping the lip with a ratty-looking cloth. "Why, she had only just received a phone call that very morning!" She quickly tightened a lid on the jar and handed it to Jane to put into the pressure cooker to seal it. "The bishop has a phone shanty next to his house for emergencies, you know."

Everyone nodded, for this was a well-known fact, and it had been for quite some years. Emma fought the urge to roll her eyes and felt Anna nudge her with her elbow, a reminder to behave.

"So, she received this phone call from Paul! He is out in Ohio, remember?"

"How could we forget?" Emma said sweetly, hoping that she had masked her bored sarcasm.

Another giggle of delight. "It seems he is returning! And, can you believe it, with a brand new *fraa*!"

A silence fell over the room and Emma almost knocked over the clean jars that she was arranging for Hetty to fill with ground meat.

"They were married on Thursday! Lydia was quite upset that Paul did not wait for his family to return and partake of the services," she added solemnly.

Even Anna expressed her surprise at this news. "I can only imagine! My word!"

"He's only been in Ohio less than two weeks!" Emma exclaimed, unable to hold her tongue any longer.

"Sarah said that the woman, Alice Hertzler, is an old family friend. Apparently Paul and this woman had been writing to each other for months!" No one noticed Emma's gasp of disbelief. "They'll be returning this week."

Emma was still reeling from the shock of Hetty's announcement. Paul had been writing to this Alice woman all along? Being denied by Emma had caused him to flee to Ohio and return with a bride? The turnabout stunned her.

"I'm sure Sarah and the bishop were disappointed, indeed," Anna added. "No wedding here?"

Hetty shoved meat into the jar, her fingers pressing it down before reaching for the salt. "Apparently he said that it would have been a hardship on her family to travel here." She pushed the jar toward Emma. "I think it's a nice surprise."

Anna shook her head and clucked her tongue. "Samuel would be just devastated if Francis pulled a surprise like that."

Emma finally managed to respond. "I would expect something like this from Francis who seems to delight in surprising people," she reminded Anna. "But Paul? It's most out of character!"

Jane finally spoke up. "But practical, wouldn't you agree? Rather than trouble his *daed* during wedding season with having to travel to Ohio, which would have severely limited the weddings in his own *g'may*, this Paul seems to have removed that burden and expense, sacrificing having his own family there for the benefit of the local couples about to wed during the upcoming season."

Her words seemed odd to Emma. What did Jane know about the *g'may* and who was rumored to be courting whom?

"Why, I only suspect two couples in our *g'may* of marrying this season," she said out loud, thinking of Rachel and Elmer as well as another younger woman who was rather vocal about her large garden of celery, a clear and very public indication of an upcoming wedding in November.

"One never knows," Jane said softly.

The one thing Emma did know was that she would have to alert Hannah to this news as soon as she could. While Emma was beside herself at Paul's two-timing behavior, she could only imagine the emotional wounding that Hannah would feel to learn that not only had he never been interested in her, but also that Hetty's words from the previous week at the applesauce canning had proven prophetic. If Hannah had been upset at the suggestion that this might happen, she would be devastated at the news that a wedding had actually occurred!

By the time the dinner hour arrived, the table was set as well as an additional folding table set up at one end to accommodate all of the guests. Emma assumed her spot next to her *daed*, and to her delight, Francis sat next to her. After the silent blessing, he immediately began the conversation, sharing his exploits over the past week with the others at the table. Several times he directed his conversation toward her, and Emma felt the color rise to her cheeks at his attention.

With the garden plowed over and the manure spread, the guests had a leisurely dinner. Following the after-prayer, they retired to the living room to continue visiting while Anna and Emma quickly cleaned the dishes.

For the first few minutes they worked in silence, listening to the conversation and laughter that came from the far side of the room where the sun shone through the glass windows onto the sofa, recliner, and folding chairs that had been set up for company. Anna occasionally glanced over her shoulder, smiling to herself as she observed her husband and stepson deep in conversation with the other guests.

When she had a moment, however, Anna quietly cleared her throat and leaned over toward Emma. In a soft voice Anna inquired how she was feeling. Emma was uncertain whether she meant the situation with confessing to Hannah earlier the previous week or the news about Paul's sudden marriage.

"I'd be telling an untruth if I didn't say that I have lost quite a bit of respect for Paul," Emma admitted, lowering her voice so that no one overheard her. "That seems either rash or deceptive on his part, and either way, I am not impressed."

Anna seemed to digest this, taking her time to respond. She was drying the last plate when she finally turned to Emma. "It's not up to us to judge," she replied thoughtfully. "The Bible tells us that we reap what we sow. I do believe you have experienced that yourself most recently."

Emma understood that statement to reference her dilemma with Hannah. Heat rushed to her cheeks and she lowered her eyes in deference to Anna's reminder.

"However, since Paul was not interested in your friend and you were not interested in Paul, I see no harm in what he has done. In fact," she added cheerfully, "I look forward to meeting this Alice."

Emma only wished that she could mirror Anna's kind sentiments.

By the time they finished cleaning the kitchen and joined the rest of the gathering, it was clear that the focus of conversation had finally shifted away from Francis. Only now it was focused on Jane. She sat demurely on a folding chair, having apparently insisted that her *aendi* and *grossmammi* take their seats on the more comfortable sofa.

Emma moved her own folding chair to the outer skirt of the circle as there was barely enough room to be a part of it. She listened as question after question was asked of the young woman, most of them being directed at her from Francis. For a few minutes it appeared as if no one else was in the room, just the two of them, and Emma felt the heat rise to her cheeks. When she glanced around, she noticed that Gideon, Samuel, and her *daed* were hanging on to every word that Jane said in response to Francis's thoughtful questions about her life in Ohio, her *g'may*, and her family. She also noticed that, unlike the previous week, Jane's answers flowed much more easily than when she had responded to Emma's own questions.

The final straw, however, was when Gideon began to squirm in his seat. Something was bothering him; that much was clear. He fidgeted and took deep breaths, clearly agitated over something. Finally he jumped up from his seat and retreated into the kitchen. When he returned momentarily, he held a glass of water in his hand, which he proceeded to hand to Jane.

The gesture was a peculiar one and Emma found herself perplexed. Was it possible, she wondered as she watched Gideon's staring at the young woman, that he had taken a romantic interest in her? Her suspicions were only further aroused when it was time for the guests to begin leaving: Gideon insisted upon taking Jane and the Blanks home, claiming that, despite their house being in the opposite direction, there was no imposition at all on his time.

"It would be my pleasure," he said with a slight dipping of his head.

Hetty seemed especially pleased. *"Danke,* Gideon," she gushed. *"Danke!* That would be ever so *gut,* especially for my *maem.* It's such a long distance for her to walk and, *vell,* we are not as fortunate to have the income or property to keep a horse and buggy." She leaned over and tapped her *maem*'s shoulder. "Isn't that most kind, *Maem?* Gideon offered us a ride home." When it was clear that her *maem* hadn't heard properly, Hetty repeated the key words again, this time louder. "Gideon. Ride. Home."

When the gathering disbanded, Emma stood at the kitchen counter, her hands aimlessly drying a plate while she watched out the window. It struck her as odd that she felt a growing ache in her stomach as she saw Gideon help Jane and Hetty into the backseat of the buggy before offering his assistance to Hetty's *maem,* who sat next to him on the front seat. As the buggy pulled away, she stared after it for a long while, her mind far away until her *daed* teased her that the plate was certainly dry by now.

Startled back to reality, Emma gave a weak smile and quickly put the plate away in the open cabinet next to the sink. She couldn't quite put her finger on what bothered her so much about the possibility that Gideon's offer to take the three ladies home was not just neighborly kindness but due to interest in a certain young woman from Ohio. It was something that gave her pause to reflect and wonder while she finished drying the dishes.

❧ Chapter Thirteen ❧

EMMA COULD HARDLY believe what Gideon had just said to her. How had he come to this conclusion? He barely knew the man! She was sitting on the sofa, staring at him with her mouth agape, stunned by his words. It wasn't often that she was held speechless, but Gideon had managed to do just that. It took her a long moment to compose herself before she was able to speak.

"Gideon, what do you mean that you don't like Francis?"

The thought was disconcerting. To not like Francis Wagler? From the few interactions that she had with the man, he had been pleasant and cheerful, and his presence lit up any gathering. With great pleasure Emma had witnessed his attentiveness toward his new *maem*, Anna. Wherever he went, people seemed to flocked to him like moths to a lantern. Even today, after worship service, Francis was surrounded by a group of young men and quickly had them laughing, the center of attention and clearly admired by all.

Gideon frowned, leaning forward and rubbing at his forehead. "I didn't exactly say that, Emma," he said, his voice sounding stressed. "Once again, if I dare say, you are putting words into my mouth!"

Was she? She wasn't too sure of this.

After the worship service Gideon had offered to bring her home since Henry had previously made plans to visit and play Scrabble with the Glicks. The grueling week ending with those dreadful long days left Emma exhausted, and she begged to be excused from any social obligations. Even during the sermons Emma fell asleep twice, and when it came time for the kneeling prayer at the end of the service, she could barely keep her eyes open. The last thing she wanted was to accompany her *daed* in his social visits. Thankfully Gideon noticed her fatigue and insisted upon taking her home, for which she was secretly grateful. Considering how tired she was, the walk home seemed daunting. Even if it were only a mere mile, she knew it would feel like ten!

To her surprise, after Gideon stopped the horse in front of her house, he got out of the buggy as well. She watched as he pulled out the horse's halter from under his seat and quickly put it over the horse's head, covering the bridle with it and securing the reins. He hooked a lead rope to the under-side of the halter, clipping it to a small round metal piece, and tied the horse to the hitching post. Then, without even asking permission, he accompanied her inside the house as if he intended to visit.

For a split second his boldness took her aback. It was most unusual for a man to visit with a woman alone in a house. Such a situation was reserved for courting couples, and even then, being seen to enter a vacant *haus* could cause many tongues to wag. In fact, a young woman chanced having questions raised about her reputation if she were caught alone in a house with a young person of the other gender. Certainly the bishop would want to question the couple as to their intentions.

However, since this was Gideon, and he was a member

of the extended family, even if only by marriage, she pushed the thought out of her mind and decided that an hour of company was not necessarily a bad thing, especially because he was a dear friend.

At first the visit seemed awkward. She became conscious of the fact that she had never really been alone with Gideon in the house for an extended period of time. During his frequent visits over the years, Anna or her *daed* was usually home. Of course, there were times *Daed* might leave to take his daily walk or to tend to a task outside of the house, but that was usually at the tail end of Gideon's visit and therefore would not be construed the same way as Gideon visiting Emma when she was home alone. Emma had never really given a second thought to such short periods of time spent alone in Gideon's company. His frequent presence in the house seemed very natural, even expected. Today, however, was different. It certainly spoke volumes about his comfort level with the Weavers to have accompanied her into the *haus*.

The initial conversation focused on her. She didn't mind that at all and actually appreciated his concern, especially when he asked her about her week helping Irene. Certainly he must have learned from his *bruder* that Irene had fallen ill. Emma had told him about Irene and the *kinner*, sharing stories about Little Henry and John Junior, who seemed to be the most mischievous boys that either one of them had even known.

"Reminds me of a young girl who shared a similar gleam in her pretty blue eyes," Gideon teased lightly.

Emma ignored his comment and proceeded to tell him about having gone to market for Jenny Glick.

"Such long days," Emma sighed, shaking her head wearily.

165

"And the long commute in that packed van! I am so glad that my quilting brings enough income to avoid having to work at the market every week."

Gideon nodded in agreement. "I reckon days at market are no different than working a dairy farm. Rise before the sun, retire with the moon."

"I do prefer to work at home," Emma admitted. "It's nice to be near *daed* and to enjoy the comforts of home and community."

"You do that rather well," was his reply. She wasn't sure whether Gideon meant that as a true compliment or a comment in badinage. She certainly was not one to shirk obligations or labor. But the fact was that she preferred working indoors to outdoors, solitude to exposure. She had always found the stares and the questions from the *Englische* tourists and visitors at the market rather odd and uncomfortable.

The pleasant tone of the conversation, however, suddenly shifted when Emma inquired about how Francis was working out as a carpenter at his storage building business. His response caused Emma to question him.

As Gideon sat in Henry's recliner, he stared at her with another of his side looks, one that clearly conveyed his never-ending disapproval. "What I said," he began again, speaking slowly and carefully, "was that I have gained the suspicion that he cares more for his own pleasure than for a hard day's labor. How you can possibly construe from that statement that I don't 'like' Francis is beyond me."

She almost smiled at how Gideon mimicked her when he spoke the word *like*.

"And for such a young man, he seems far too independent and worldly, in my opinion."

"You seem rather determined to find flaws in his character," she pointed out.

"*Mayhaps*," Gideon owned. Candor was one of his traits that she both admired and disliked. Gideon was never one to pretend to be someone he was not. However, that same trait caused him to speak his mind, sharing his thoughts and opinions even when they were not popular or sought. "But it is quite easy to do in this particular case," he added.

Emma leaned forward and pointed her index finger at him. "Ah ha!" she said, unable to hide her pleasure at having tricked Gideon. "There! You are judging him. One does not often judge someone who is in good favor! Therefore, you admit you do not like him!"

Gideon laughed. "You are in my good favor, yet I find myself judging you rather often."

"Bah!"

"It's true," Gideon confessed, a sparkle in his eye and light tone to his words.

While there was truth to his statement, Emma took it good-naturedly. "Indeed, you do it as frequently as possible, it seems!"

He laughed. "You certainly seem to give me just cause!" A comfortable silence befell them, the gentle teasing having created a warm feeling in the room. It lingered for just a few long seconds before Gideon spoke again. "You speak of my judging Francis. What say you of Hetty's niece?"

The rapid shift away from Francis caught her off guard. "Jane? What of her?"

He eyed her carefully. "It is most apparent that you are not very fond of Jane."

"Me?" Emma placed her hand upon her chest. Try as she had to hide her dislike of Jane, it was clear that Gideon was not going to be deceived. Still, unlike Gideon, she tried to maintain her innocence against his accusation. "Oh, heaven! Whatever would give you that impression?"

"My dear Emma," he said, shaking his head with that all-too-familiar amused smile on his face. "The deep sighs, the glazed look, and your unusual silence during any conversation involving her speak volumes. You forget how well I know you!"

"And I, you!" Emma shot back. It unexpectedly irritated her how much Gideon presumed about her, all the while not considering or admitting his own attentiveness to the young woman. "For as much as I may not be partial to Jane and, indeed, count the days for her return to Ohio, I sense that you, on the other hand, dread that day!" The words slipped out before she could stop them and she immediately caught her breath, staring at Gideon with wide eyes, not quite believing that she had just uttered those words.

He sat in the chair, left thumb under his chin and his index finger rubbing back and forth above his upper lip, a familiar gesture he often adopted when pondering someone's words. The longer he waited to respond, the more Emma braced herself for a reprimand. Surely it was coming, she reasoned, for she had spoken far out of turn about something that, once again, was not her business.

Oh, she knew that she was correct in what she had said, for she had noticed on more than one occasion that Gideon seemed to favor the pretty young woman from Ohio. Hadn't he hurried to get her water, concerned for her comfort when she was responding to the barrage of questions from the group? Hadn't he insisted upon going out of his way to take her home? And how many times had she caught Gideon staring at Jane during service? It wasn't hard to count them, for much to Emma's discomfort, Jane had sat between her and Rachel.

Clearly Gideon was smitten with Jane. Only it wasn't until this moment that Emma realized how much his attention to Jane truly bothered her. She had always presumed Gideon would remain an old *buwe*. He was well into his thirties, and during the time that she had known him, he had not shown an inclination toward marriage. There was actually a time, not very long ago, when she wondered whether he would ever marry or if he was just as comfortable remaining an unmarried man, an old *buwe*. She knew several men in the *g'may* who preferred to leave these matters up to God and readily accepted the fact that a *fraa* and some *kinner* were not what He had in mind for them. They may have tried to court someone, but after a rejection or two they took it for granted that such things were not in His plans.

Of course, if Gideon *were* to take a wife, Emma knew that his frequent visits to their house would cease. He'd be obligated to spend more time with the family of his *fraa*. *And once there were* boppli... Emma shuddered at the thought. Why, if Gideon fancied Jane and married her, Emma would most likely see him only at family gatherings that included his *bruder* John and Irene. Even worse, her *daed* would be devastated at the loss, that was for sure and certain.

During the time that these thoughts raced through her mind, Gideon remained quiet. He too was reflecting upon her words, and she couldn't read his reaction. Certainly, she thought, another of his lectures would follow, and she braced herself for the inevitable.

It took what seemed like a very long time to finally come, and when he eventually spoke, she realized that she had been holding her breath.

"I think I understand the situation much better now," Gideon said, a thoughtful tone in his voice. He leveled his gaze at her and, without any expression on his face, stated his thoughts. "You are prejudiced against Jane."

While the brevity of his lecture surprised her, his words caught her completely off guard. Such an accusation was on the verge of insulting, for it made her look as if she thought herself superior to another human being. "Pre-ju-diced?" The word, each syllable of which she made a point to emphasize, seemed to echo in her ears. "Why, I highly doubt that I am prejudiced against anyone!"

He gave her a skeptical look, raising an eyebrow, but remained silent.

"If it were true, and it is not, I can assure you," she stammered, trying to find the words to defend herself. "Then I imagine I am prejudiced against Jane just as you are prejudiced in her favor! Likewise, you are prejudiced against Francis while I am partial to him."

"I think there is more to this than your simple summation," he replied softly. "While I have questions about Francis's work ethic, that is for certain, your disdain for Jane is deeper. Perhaps it stems from something that you are not used to: losing regard within the community, for she seems to steal much of the attention that would otherwise be directed toward you. In addition, you favor Francis for the exact opposite reason."

Jumping to her feet, Emma put her hands on her hips, glaring at him. "Now you are accusing me of pride! You insult me!"

"*Nee*," Gideon said, rising to stand before her. Since he was taller than she, he stared down into her face, his eyes shifting back and forth in short little bursts as he studied.

"*Nee,*" he repeated. "I do not insult you for I speak the truth. However, Emma, you have given me something to ponder, something I had not expected to consider before now."

Frustrated, she crossed her arms over her chest and continued scowling. Whatever was he talking about? "You speak in riddles!"

Despite the tension in the air between them, Gideon wore a calm, if not almost peaceful expression on his face. It contradicted how Emma felt, for the visit had been most pleasant until this moment. "Time will tell, I reckon," he said thoughtfully.

At this, Emma took a deep breath. She wanted him to leave the house. Her head was beginning to hurt, a painful throbbing at her temples indicating that her fatigue was giving way to a possible migraine. It was time for Gideon to go. "I'm afraid I feel a headache coming on," she said and glanced at the clock. "I'd like to lie down for a while, before *Daed* returns."

Always the gentleman, Gideon nodded his head and quickly retrieved his hat from where he had hung it on the hook by the door. He delayed his exit by a few, drawn-out seconds as he fingered the brim of his black felt hat. He looked up and stared at her one last time. "I do hope that you feel better, Emma Weaver," he said. "And I think we shall continue this conversation at a later time. There is much more to be said on the matter, I assure you."

Without another word he placed the hat upon his head and hurried through the door, a faint smile on his face, leaving Emma perplexed. She could hear his boots on the porch as he walked across it and descended the steps. A few minutes later, the sound of his horse's hooves and the metallic hum of his buggy wheels filled the air. She listened until she could no longer hear them before she uncrossed her arms and retreated to the sanctuary of her room, hoping that a long nap would help her forget Gideon's words and replace the bouts of ill humor she felt as of late with her typical cheerfulness and joy.

Somehow, however, she knew that it would take a lot more than a short nap for that to happen.

❧ Chapter Fourteen ❧

ON TUESDAY AFTERNOON the Weavers received an invitation to attend a welcome dinner planned for Paul and his new wife on Thursday afternoon. It was written on lavender stationery and delivered by Paul's younger *bruder*, who stayed only long enough to receive the Weavers' response. Apparently the newly married couple was scheduled to arrive in Lititz on Wednesday, and the Esh family wanted a proper gathering the following day in order to introduce Alice, Paul's wife, to the community.

Henry Weaver was quick to respond in favor of joining the celebration and even went so far as to turn to his *dochder*, inquiring whether she might have time to make some schnitzel pies for the guests.

While Emma didn't feel like facing Paul, she knew that refusing to attend would cause more questions and raised eyebrows than was worth the trouble, especially if her *daed* suspected that Paul had asked to court her. With a forced smile on her face, Emma replied that she would happily make schnitzel pies to bring along for Paul, his bride, and their many guests. Her response was met with enthusiasm by the *bruder* and a look of approval from her *daed*.

By the time Thursday came around, Emma was mentally

173

prepared to put on a brave face and greet Paul's *fraa*. The five previous days had given her enough time to get accustomed to the news. Despite her inability to make any sense of his rash decision to engage in a whirlwind courtship with what amounted to no more than a complete stranger, letters or no letters, Emma remained determined to wear a smile as her armor and to use laughter as her shield. A positive attitude, she reasoned, would improve any situation.

What Emma had not, however, expected was to take such an immediate dislike for the woman who had so conveniently filled the role that Paul had originally planned for her!

Alice Esh was a larger woman, not necessarily overweight but definitely big boned. Her hair was already graying, which gave her the appearance of being older than Paul, despite the fact that they were rumored to be the same age. While her face was certainly pleasant enough, it was easy to see that she would have to avoid gaining any weight for it to remain so. Unlike Hannah, she immediately made known her preference for the plain, cuplike Ohio prayer *kapp* and vowed that she would not change to the heart-shaped style worn in Lancaster. Her voice carried in the room so that when she made this statement, several older women clucked their tongues and raised their eyebrows.

Without doubt, the Amish grapevine would have a comment or two about such a remark by Alice Esh!

Upon meeting her, Emma smiled and welcomed the newcomer to Lititz only to be informed by Alice that the town was so akin to the Dutch Valley that she felt the similarities outweighed the differences. And from that point forward Emma never got in another word. Alice was not necessarily a well-spoken woman, but speaking was one thing she apparently did well and for a long time. Once captured by Alice Esh, Emma had a hard time escaping her attention and discourse.

Paul stood among the men, rarely lifting his eyes to seek out his new bride. Emma noticed that fact right away and wondered whether or not Alice was as talkative with her husband as she was with the women in the room. Without doubt, Emma began to wonder at the attraction between Paul and Alice, for she was as different from her as night was to day. She also pondered the irony that Hannah would have been a far better match for Paul than this loud, boisterous, and overly conversant woman from Ohio! She was curious as to how such a match had possibly occurred. But her curiosity was soon to be satisfied.

"It was my *onkel* who introduced us," Alice said in her raucous voice to the small gathering of young women who circled her. "He's a bishop, you know, in one of the largest *g'mays* in the Dutch Valley." The way she drew out the word *largest* hinted at pride, and Emma fought the urge to make a comment. Not that it would have mattered, she realized, for Alice Esh went on talking, apparently more interested in hearing herself speak than in engaging in an actual conversation with her unfortunate captive audience.

Emma quickly lost interest in the conversation, but she knew she could not leave the circle of young women around the guest of honor without appearing rude or, even worse, like a disgruntled jilted woman. After all, she had no idea who else, besides her *daed* and Anna, might have suspected Paul's interest in her.

Instead, while Alice prattled on about her *onkel*, Bishop Kaufman, Emma pondered this new bit of information. Was it possible that Paul had sought out Alice Hetzler to not only repair his self-esteem but to also build up his standing within the community? With his *daed* heading up their *g'may* and Alice the niece of another bishop, was this a marriage of true emotion or merely convenience and social suitability? She highly doubted the former, which therefore gave her cause to suspect the latter.

It wasn't until after the meal when the singing commenced that Emma managed to break free from what she had begun to think of as Alice's audience. The older women were washing the dishes and Emma slipped outside to cool off. With over two hundred people in the *haus*, it had grown increasingly warm, and Emma needed a moment of quiet to think.

She hadn't expected to encounter Francis standing on the porch. Clearly he had the same idea. He grinned when he saw her and invited her to join him. He was leaning against the railing, his eyes scanning the farm fields that surrounded the Esh's *haus*. While the bishop did not farm, per se, his wife and three *dochders* ran a small garden center from spring to autumn, while his sons planted hay which often yielded three or even sometimes four cuttings per season. The older boys helped grow plants and flowers in their greenhouse, and the Esh women sold them at the garden center. It was enough to keep the family living modestly without taking up too much of the bishop's time so that he could minister to his flock.

"Have you enjoyed yourself so far today, Emma?" Francis asked.

"I always enjoy meeting new people and engaging in good fellowship," she responded, trying to be as diplomatic as possible without telling a lie.

He must have seen through her for he laughed. "Good

fellowship, it seems to me, would require the participation of multiple people in a conversation and not just the ramblings of one."

Emma was startled by his frankness and almost thought to say something. However, since she actually agreed with him and interpreted his candor to mean that there was a budding intimacy between them, one shared by friends, she kept her thoughts to herself. "I'm sure it's overwhelming, given that you most likely don't remember many of the people here."

He gave a little grunt in agreement, nodding his head. "True, indeed! At least you have your friends nearby," he added. "Hannah, Rachel, Jane…"

"Jane?" Emma couldn't help but interrupt him. "Why, I barely know Jane, I suppose. I'm not certain I would consider her a friend." Then, to soften her words, she quickly added, "Yet, anyway."

"There's always time," Francis observed.

"*Ja vell.*" Emma shrugged. "But she is to return to Ohio in…what…another week or two? What is the point, really?"

"She seems pleasant enough," he offered. "Although I do find her complexion a bit weathered for my taste." He laughed when he said this and Emma smiled at his comment, which clearly hinted that Jane came from a farming background. While there was nothing vulgar about a young woman working on a farm, for many Amish women did it, there definitely was a different level of sophistication among children who grew up on farms as opposed to those who lived and worked among the *Englische*.

"I hadn't noticed," Emma said, surprised at the urge to defend Jane. "She still seems refined and proper. Her manners are…" She hesitated and looked for the appropriate word. "Respectable."

Francis shrugged his shoulders. "*Mayhaps* I cannot separate her manners from her complexion." He laughed again and Emma wasn't certain whether or not he was teasing her.

"And how are you getting on working with Gideon King?" she asked, eager to change the subject. Her opinion of Francis was changing rather rapidly, for she had not appreciated his comments about Jane's appearance. She hoped to divert his attention to a new topic to counter the negative feeling she began to feel from his rather unkind observation.

"Carpentry work is carpentry work," he said with a shrug of his shoulders and bored look upon his face. "And storage sheds are easy enough, I reckon. Not much creativity in it. In fact, it's rather dull." He leaned forward and brushed at something on her shoulder. When she looked down, she saw a piece of lint upon her dress. While his gesture smacked of familiarity, she appreciated the thoughtfulness behind it. "And how have you been, Emma Weaver? We didn't have time to talk after last Sunday's service, and I noticed you were absent from the youth singing that evening."

Forgotten was his comment about Jane's complexion. "I had such a long week," she admitted. "Between helping my *schwester* Irene and her *kinner*, then tending to market, I needed to rest Sunday evening."

"Your friend Hannah was there," he mentioned.

Emma brightened at that news. It was a right *gut* sign that Hannah was fitting into the community and especially the youth group if she attended a singing without Emma. While they had not seen much of each other this week, Hannah had whispered to her earlier that very day that she had some exciting news to tell her. Based on what Francis had just informed her, she wondered if it had to do with someone asking to take her home after the singing.

"As it were, without you there, I felt obliged to offer both her and Jane a ride home." This additional information caused her heart to swell at the insinuation that he would have rather offered her a ride home. But her stomach sank as she realized that Hannah's exciting news did not involve a new beau on the horizon. At least not from the previous week's singing, she assumed.

When the door opened and several young men emerged from the house, Emma was quick to excuse herself and return inside before her presence was missed. Once inside she searched the room, eager to find Hannah. To her surprise, Hannah was talking with Gideon and Samuel in the back of the kitchen, so as not to disturb those singing in the larger gathering room. Eager to find out Hannah's news, Emma wasted no time to hurry over there.

"There she is!" Samuel called out jovially when Emma approached. "I had some of your schnitzel pie. Delicious as always."

She bowed her head at his compliment. "No more so than any other, I presume."

Gideon's amused look at her attempt at humility did not go unnoticed, and her thoughts flickered back to the previous weekend when they had shared words. She chose to ignore him.

Turning her attention to Hannah, she gently laid her hand upon her friend's arm. "I thought that I would see if you wanted to visit afterward at our house," she asked. "When the gathering breaks up."

To Emma's surprise, Hannah glanced at Gideon then looked back at Emma. "I...I..." The way that she stammered over her response indicated that she wanted to accept Emma's offer, but something, perhaps another commitment, was hindering her from being able to do so. Clearly whatever it was made her uncomfortable.

Gideon saved Hannah from having to answer. "I've already volunteered to take Hannah home afterward. Gladys left already, and there is a threat of rain."

The proper recourse would have been to invite both of them to visit. However, Emma was still smarting from Gideon's perceived injury to her ego the previous Sunday. With her chin tilted stoically in the air, Emma feigned disappointment. "What a shame," she replied. "Perhaps over the weekend then? *Mayhaps* this off-Sunday?"

Hannah cast another furtive glance at Gideon.

"Am I missing something?" Emma asked, half in jest, half in annoyance. She felt like there was a secret among the group, one that she was not privy to, and that did not sit well with her.

"I meant to speak to you about this, but I haven't had the chance," Gideon said, addressing Emma directly. "If the weather holds up, we've planned a picnic at the Yoder's pond this Sunday to get to know Alice Esh in a less formal setting."

Emma could only imagine who was included in this "we" that had taken care to plan such an excursion without including her in the planning process. "I see," she managed to say.

The stiffness of her reply seemed to amuse Gideon. He leaned forward and lowered his voice. "Don't fret. You *are* invited, Emma," he said in her ear, his breath warming her neck and causing her to blush; whether it was his close proximity to her or the fact that her reaction had been so transparent, she wasn't certain.

Frowning, she leaned away from him and gave him a disapproving look, one that caused him to chuckle to himself as he returned to an upright position.

It took another fifteen minutes for Emma to finally have Hannah's undivided attention. The older people had begun to leave while the younger, unmarried adults lingered around Paul and Alice, singing. It was the perfect opportunity for Emma and Hannah to catch up without fear of being interrupted.

"What was this news?" Emma ventured to ask.

Hannah's face lit up and she smiled shyly at Emma. "You'll never guess whom I ran into at market this week?"

So that was where Hannah had been! Emma tilted her head and held her breath, waiting to hear this big revelation that caused her friend to glow from head to toe. "I'm sure that I can hardly imagine!"

"Elizabeth Martin!"

Not being familiar with the name, it took Emma a few seconds to realize that Hannah was referring to Ralph Martin's sister. "Oh!"

Hannah nodded. "And they've invited me to visit!"

"They?"

Hannah averted her eyes. "She was not alone."

Of course she wasn't. Strasburg was far enough away from the market where Hannah was working that it would not make sense for her to travel such a distance by herself. Certainly Ralph would have accompanied her, eager to run his own errands rather than make a separate trip at a later date.

True to the promise that she had made to herself about

meddling in other people's affairs, Emma did not respond, not wanting to sway Hannah one way or the other. After all, she reasoned, it was up to Hannah to decide whether she wanted to encourage that courtship or possibly pursue what was looking like a potential interest in her from Gideon. She didn't quite understand why, but the thought of Gideon actually wishing to court Jane or Hannah did not sit well with Emma. It was as though she had always presumed that they were both going to remain single forever, bickering and arguing well into their old age.

Mayhaps, she told herself, there is, indeed, someone for everyone. After all, who was she to question God's plans?

❦ Chapter Fifteen ❦

DESPITE IT BEING October, typically a chilly and rainy time of the year, the weather could not have been more pleasant. The sun seemed to shine large in the sky, a peculiar sky which was a most unusual blue with nary a cloud to distract from the color. A true Indian summer as unseen for quite a few years had befallen Lancaster County. The regular group that gathered at the Weaver house for Sunday supper had, indeed, decided to pack their food into baskets and enjoy their fellowship by the Yoder's pond down the road instead of sharing the late afternoon meal inside of the home.

The grassy banks smelled like autumn, and the backdrop of color-changing leaves on the trees made it a perfect afternoon. While the adults seemed to languish in the sun, enjoying what might well be their last leisurely day spent outside until the following spring, Emma, however, was more quiet than usual. Her mood had soured since she had attended the Thursday gathering to welcome Alifce Esh to the community.

On Friday Hetty and Jane had descended upon Emma, completely unannounced and with Alice in tow. If she had not warmed up to Alice at the gathering earlier, she felt even less inclined to change her opinion now. Immediately upon her arrival Alice began staring at everything as if scrutinizing the way Emma kept house. Despite the house obviously being kept in pristine condition, Alice seemed to tilt her nose in the air, a look of disdain upon her face.

To add to her irritation, Francis had stopped by toward the end of the three women's visit. His stay, however, was immediately cut short. He claimed to have seen the horse and buggy hitched to the post when he was passing by and decided to stop, for he recognized it as belonging to Paul Esh. Emma, however, cast a sideways glance at him, curious as to how he could have seen it from the road. Furthermore, she wondered why he was riding down her road at three in the afternoon, for she was fairly certain that Gideon's carpenters worked until later in the day.

Regardless, his stop seemed most fortuitous, if not short-lived.

Hetty had promised to take Alice into town since they had the use of the Esh horse and buggy. However, Jane begged to be excused, claiming that a headache had befallen her. Two solutions were immediately offered. The first was suggested by Hetty, who insisted that she'd walk home with Jane and volunteered Emma to ride into town with Alice. The color must have drained from her face for Francis quickly offered the second solution: to escort the ailing Jane home so that Hetty's afternoon plans with Alice would not suffer.

Emma wasn't certain which solution was the better of two evils.

Despite his attention and mild flirtations, Emma hadn't been able to shake off the feeling that something was wrong. She was flattered by his attention, that much she could not deny. And just for a short while she thought she might have found someone who could capture her interest. But something had changed, something she couldn't put her finger upon. Whatever it was, she had quickly realized that Francis was not the man for her.

Still, coming to this realization did not positively impact her mood. There were other things amiss in the community. Winds of change were blowing through their small *g'may*, and she wasn't certain she liked what she was feeling.

On Saturday afternoon Hannah had stopped by, a shy glow upon her face—a glow that, without words, told Emma her friend had good and important news for her. With her *daed* sitting in the recliner, Hannah sat on the sofa visiting with Emma while she sketched out her next big project: a queen-size quilt for an *Englische* woman who was friends with the Glick family.

When the clock began to chime, announcing that it was four o'clock, her *daed* excused himself for his casual afternoon walk, finally providing the much-desired privacy that the two women wanted so that Hannah could share her secret with Emma. Indeed, Emma sensed that her friend could barely contain herself, but the presence of her father had made it impossible for Hannah to confide in her.

"I went to visit with the Martins last evening," she admitted, avoiding Emma's eyes for fear of seeing disappointment staring back at her. "I made certain that it was a short visit; I didn't want to seem overly intrusive."

"Of course," Emma responded, not certain what else to say in response to this news.

"I was ever so nervous, Emma!" Hannah confided, her voice sounding stronger. "I was so afraid that they would treat me differently, especially Ralph."

"Did they?"

Hannah shook her head. "*Nee*, not at all! In fact, before I left, Ralph took me into the barn where he keeps the pigs. Apparently, he had just received his new contract delivery last week." When Emma made a face, Hannah could not repress a giggle. "It didn't smell half as bad as you'd think. And so adorable and precious!"

"They are small now, so I believe you. But when they grow bigger, you'll be the one to believe me."

Taking a deep breath, Hannah sighed as if greatly satisfied. "I felt much better upon leaving," she said. "I sensed no disdain on the part of Elizabeth, and Ralph remained as pleasant as always. There were no hard feelings there, and that, if nothing else, frees my mind from worry."

It took all of her resolve to not speak out, to question Hannah's words. Emma wanted to inquire what worry had besotted her mind to begin with? Just because a man proposes, does the woman always have to respond in the positive for fear of hurting his feelings or diminishing her status in the eyes of his family? From her own experience, Emma knew the answer was a firm "*nee!*" However, Hannah's lack of self-confidence in this particular matter was a source of much reflection for Emma into the late hours of the night.

And then Sunday arrived.

At the picnic she immediately fell into a rather foul mood. It began when she noticed the excessive attention Francis bestowed upon Jane, who, to her credit, demurely deflected it as was proper for a young Amish woman. Still, Emma found herself resenting the open and particular attention that Francis gave to Jane. And when his attention did shift toward her, inquiring as to her unusually quiet temperament, she merely shrugged her shoulders and looked away.

But it wasn't until she saw Gideon that her temper shifted from slight agitation to full-blown irritation.

When he arrived, Emma's mouth fell open, for he was not riding in his regular gray-topped boxlike buggy but in an open carriage, a carriage typically reserved for courting couples. To her further distress, seated beside him was none other than Hannah, who seemed rather pleased to have been picked up along the way. Emma refused to inquire as to how the ride had been obtained: by chance or by plan. Neither answer, she realized, would appease the annoyance she felt.

And then there was Alice. Her demeanor was beyond forward, and Emma found herself doing all that she could to avoid being in her immediate presence. There was a vulgarity about the woman. She spoke her mind, laughed far too loud, and barely paid a lick of attention to her husband. For a newly wedded couple, the lack of communication and, for that matter, any signs of affection between the two were most surprising to Emma.

While she found the woman socially distasteful, it was increasingly clear that the feeling appeared to be mutual. Emma suspected that Alice was unaware of the fact that if Paul had his way with his original proposal, it would be Emma who bore his last name and not Alice. Still, Alice did all she could to blatantly disregard Emma by not including her in any conversations and interrupting any comments she tried to make. It was all too clear that Alice had not taken to her. While Emma found that she didn't particularly care that Alice was not partial to her friendship, she did, however, wonder why.

Additionally Alice practically announced that she was enamored with Jane, determined to help the young woman come out of her shell of propriety in order to attract a beau, so that she would not have to return to Ohio. When Alice glanced over at Gideon, Emma felt her heart pound, a sudden feeling of irritation developing in the pit of her stomach.

"It's so pleasant here," Alice announced as she linked her arm with Jane's. "Don't you agree? I love the landscape, so much flatter and spread out than in Ohio. Why, driving here today I saw a valley with a dozen or so farms! Simply breathtaking!"

"It is lovely," Jane agreed noncommittally.

"And the people, for the most part, are pleasant enough," Alice added. "If not a bit provincial, I suppose."

Emma rolled her eyes at that last statement.

"Isn't it interesting, Jane, that one of my favorite people here is another woman from Ohio?" Alice laughed at herself. "It makes sense, of course. We Ohio Amish simply better understand each other, *ja*?"

With Alice's hoity-toity mannerisms and rather verbose opinions, which she was all too willing to share, Jane's quiet reserve had not stood a chance of arguing against such a ridiculous proposition.

The only consolation for Emma was that, upon arriving at the gathering, she immediately noticed that, despite Alice's proclamation to the opposite at her welcome dinner a few days before, a *heart-shaped* prayer *kapp* now rested upon her head. Secretly it delighted Emma to imagine the conversations that must have taken place to convince Alice of the errors of her ways on that particular subject! Was it a compelling argument on Paul's part, or simply a spousal request against which she had no recourse?

Hetty sat upon the blanket, legs crossed under her and her dress tucked under her knees as she spread the food from the baskets for all to see. She fussed and prattled on, moving dishes and plates, assessing them, and then quickly rearranging them once again. The older woman's nervous energy did nothing to soften Emma's mood, especially when it dawned on Emma that, between Hetty and Alice, no one would ever be able to get a word in edgewise.

Disgusted with the negative feelings that seemed to dwell within her heart, Emma sat to the side, her eyes staring across the glistening pond. She tried her best to ignore the irritation that slowly arose within her chest. How so much could change in such a short period of time, she wondered. Everything had been so pleasant and predictable before Anna got married and moved away. Now it seemed that everything Emma thought turned out to be the complete opposite.

Her eyes fell upon Samuel, Anna, Hannah, and Francis, who were walking around the pond. Hannah had reluctantly joined them, encouraged by Francis. As the foursome rounded the far side, Emma saw that they were headed toward the large oak tree that had a wooden swing hanging from a branch. Emma smiled wryly, knowing which woman would be the one that, inevitably, sat upon it, a man standing behind her to gently push the swing so that she could enjoy the breeze as she swung through the air: Francis and Hannah. Would that not make a suitable pair! His charm could serve as cover for her shyness, and her reserve would atone for his overfamiliarity.

"Emma! Emma! Come join us! You shouldn't sit alone on such a beautiful day!"

She glanced over her shoulder at Hetty and forced a weak smile. "I'm just admiring the beauty of this glorious day God gave us. Soon it will be winter, ain't so? Won't be many more opportunities to enjoy the outdoors without heavy coats."

Her excuse was met with nods of approval and Emma said a quiet prayer of gratitude to God for allowing her the wisdom to speak kindness and not the turmoil of such negative thoughts as the very ones that were brewing inside of her.

"Such a lovely young woman," Emma heard Hetty say to Jane. "So reflective and godly!" Hetty must have turned toward her mother for she repeated herself loudly. "Why, if ever there was a godly young woman, I always say that Emma Weaver is she! Oh, indeed! Don't I, *Maem*?" A pause. "Godly! Emma!" she repeated loudly. There was no response from her *maem*. "Why, I can only think of our own dear Jane as being as godly and righteous as our Emma." Hetty patted her niece's hand. "I am so blessed to know and love them both."

"We are fortunate indeed," Gideon commented.

At his words, Emma glanced over her shoulder, catching his eyes on Jane. When she followed his gaze, she noticed that Jane was more than unusually silent at Hetty's double compliment.

There was, however, a voice that spoke out in disagreement. "There is a time and place for reflection," Alice said teasingly, yet in a haughty tone grating on Emma's nerves. "Personally, I find isolating oneself from a group to smack of pride." Her loud voice carried in the wind. "Are we not good enough? What say you, Paul?"

To Emma's relief, Paul did not respond to his wife's question.

Oh bother, she thought and stood up, rejoining the group

on the blanket so as to stop any further potentially controversial statements.

Pretending that she had not heard Alice's comments, she sat next to Hetty and reached out for a cup to pour herself some fresh lemonade. To both her relief and displeasure, Emma realized that, despite her sarcastic complaints just seconds before, Alice was already moving on to something else, directing her attention to Jane, as she inquired about the small Amish community where she had been raised. It was almost painful to watch the abortive exchange, because as Alice enjoyed hearing herself talk, despite her questions of Jane, she refused to let another person steal her stage. That left Jane in the lurch, for whenever she tried to get into the conversation, Alice would merely talk over her.

Bored, Emma sipped from her cup and let her eyes drift. The Waglers and Hannah were headed back toward the group, Francis walking beside Hannah, making her giggle at his comments. As Emma returned her attention to the long-winded Alice, she caught Gideon watching her. She tried to smile and was about to say something to him when she realized that, once again, Gideon's eyes were actually not quite upon her but on Jane.

Her heart sank, and for reasons unknown to her, she felt even more irritated. She was sorry that she had let Alice's comments goad her into returning to the group. She had been much happier by herself, regardless if this talkative, loud woman thought she was prideful or was just teasing. Her irritation only increased when the Waglers and Hannah returned, all smiles and sunshine from their little adventure.

Francis knelt down in the grass by the blanket and noticed the dark mood over the group. "Now, now," he started, plucking a piece of grass and tossing it at Emma. "What's this? A gloomy picnic party?" He laughed as Emma plucked the blade from her lap and played with it between her fingers. "Let's play a game, shall we? That should liven up the mood of the gathering."

"A game?" Hetty seemed delighted at the prospect. "Oh yes, let's play a game. What shall we play then, Francis?"

"The suitcase game!"

Hannah laughed. "I used to play that in school when I was learning English!"

Emma fought the urge to roll her eyes.

It was Gideon who inquired about the game next. "You must share the rules," he said. "I fear it's been quite a few years for some of us since we've played such a game, and some of our Ohio transplants might not be familiar with it." He smiled at Jane. Perhaps he only meant to draw her in as a politeness, but the gesture further soured Emma's mood, even if Jane seemed to ignore it.

"It's easy, really." Francis shifted his weight so that he was no longer kneeling but sitting on the ground. "We used to play it with the alphabet and take turns, listing items we would pack in a suitcase to go on a trip. As we take turns, you have to repeat whatever items were previously mentioned, in the same order, then add your own."

Jane smiled and Hetty laughed outright.

"Of course," Francis said slowly. "We don't have to pack a suitcase. We could change it up a bit. Perhaps we could alphabetize words about Emma instead."

At this change to the game, Emma frowned and looked up. "Me?"

"To cheer you up! You look so glum!"

Emma dared not protest more lest she draw unwanted attention to herself. Silently she hoped the idea would die a quick death. However, Hetty quickly seconded the notion and Hannah also thought that it was a grand idea. If Samuel, Anna, or Gideon thought the game unsuitable, they held their tongues. And Jane seemed to sink into a deeper silence, if that were possible.

Not to anyone's surprise, Alice had something to say about Francis's suggestion. "A game?" She raised an eyebrow and stared at Francis for a moment. "A schoolhouse game? I think I'll pass on that one. Come along, Paul. Let's go walk around the pond! I saw Francis pushing Hannah on that swing over there. That seems like something we should do!" Without waiting for his answer, she began walking.

Obediently Paul followed, pausing to take breath and stretch as he stood. "No parlor games for this old married man," he said. "Besides, I'm certainly not clever enough to think of anything that might amuse anyway, especially Emma." He said this last part under his breath, but Emma had clearly heard it.

As he hurried after Alice, Emma scowled and wondered which one of them would actually push the other on the swing.

"Shall we begin? Remember, we are to cheer up our Emma, so be as clever as you can!" Francis displayed a childish delight at the idea of this game, blatantly ignoring the glances exchanged between Samuel and Anna and the decided disinterest of Jane. "I'll start and say a word that I feel describes Emma, starting with the letter A. Hannah will continue, repeating my word then adding one that starts with the letter B. Hetty, you'll do the same, only your word will start with C."

"Just one word? Only one?" Hetty interrupted him, her voice cheerful and delighted at the thought of this game.

"Oh help!" She gave a soft laugh. "Describe our Emma? That should be easy, shouldn't it?" She looked around and smiled. "Why, I'm sure that I could think of dozens of interesting words to describe our dear Emma!"

Irked at being pushed into the center of attention, Emma turned to Hetty and said, "I'm sure you'll find it most difficult to speak just one word of interest at all!" As soon as the words slipped from her tongue, Emma caught her breath and bit her lower lip. She hadn't meant to say it out loud. And the sharpness of her tone clearly indicated that there was no hint of teasing behind her words.

Silence befell the group. But it seemed to take a moment for Hetty to realize the meaning behind what Emma had said.

"Oh!" The older woman frowned and lowered her eyes. "Oh my," Hetty said softly, her liveliness quickly evaporating. The color drained from her face as her eyes widened. "I see...I mean, I think I understand what Emma means." She glanced around at the downcast eyes that avoided hers. "I suppose I should be silent now so as not to further...well, there I go again, being disagreeable, I imagine..." She paused. "I...I'll...*mayhaps* I might go for a walk, I reckon." Without any further words, Hetty rose to her feet, a hand at her throat, and hurried away.

The silence that surrounded the group deepened.

Emma felt the heat under her skin. Refusing to look at anyone, she knew that her cheeks were turning crimson from embarrassment. Instead, she shut her eyes and pressed her lips together, wishing that, once again, she had thought before speaking. The nasty tone and horrid words that had slipped past her lips were uncharacteristic of Emma, that was for certain, but whether she could be forgiven was yet to be determined.

"I suppose it is a bit too silly of a game," Anna finally offered, a gentle way to break the silence as she forced an air of cheerfulness that no one felt. "*Mayhaps* it's just better if we have dessert before it's time to return home for evening chores, *ja*?"

Despite Anna's attempt, there was still a heavy tension over the group. Emma gave a quick glance around and noticed that no one was either nodding in approval or, for that matter, even looking at her. No one, that is, except Gideon. The displeasure on his face did not need words, and he gave a single shake of his head before he stood and followed in the direction of Hetty.

Disgusted with herself, Emma jumped to her feet and walked up the incline toward the road. The tears started falling before she made it there, and once away from the group she allowed herself to sob as she started the long walk home by herself. Each footstep brought her more pain as she berated herself. How could she have said something so cold, rude, and insulting? The look in Gideon's eyes, so full of disappointment, stayed with her long after she left the pond.

She didn't go immediately home, however. Instead, she let her feet take her down the back roads so that she could be alone and calm her nerves. The last thing she wanted was to return home and face her *daed*. If he thought that she had been crying, the questions would never end.

The sun had started its descent over the horizon and a definite chill was now in the air. Emma did not know whether the shivering that had overtaken her was coming from the outside or from the inside, on account of the icy words she had directed toward Hetty. Those words were, indeed, very uncalled for. Emma knew only too well how Hetty held her in such high esteem, often looking upon her as a niece or even a daughter of sorts, especially after Emma's *maem* had passed. For Hetty, Emma was the daughter she never had. She had even confided to Emma that if she had ever married and reared a daughter, she would have wanted her to be just like Emma. While Hetty, despite being over twice her age, did not have Emma's wits, her poise, and certainly nothing close to the same effect on others, she often tried to emulate Emma, considering her as a role model in all and everything that she did or said. Emma was well aware of the quasi veneration bestowed upon her by her surrogate *aendi*, and while not admitting it publicly, could not help feel a little vanity at such reverence. Not a very Christian feeling, she had told herself time and again; so she was quite ambivalent about it, sometimes accepting it, yet at other times, genuinely feeling undeserving of it.

Today, however, she had definitely committed an act of wrongdoing and displayed an unchristian behavior, belittling one of the people who loved and admired her the most.

While walking the back roads, the same roads that she had taken so many times before when making her rounds of visits to the elderly and less fortunate widows in her *g'may*, Emma pondered the changes that were taking place not only within the community, but also and especially—within her. Was she starting to lose faith? Was her set of beliefs and values crumbling? *What is happening to me?* she asked herself, a heavy wave of sadness invading her soul.

"Emma!"

As she was just about to walk past the mailbox and turn up the driveway, she was startled by the sound of someone calling her name. She had been so distracted by her thoughts that she hadn't heard the horse and buggy approaching her from behind. When she turned to see who it was, she felt her stomach flip-flop: Gideon.

He directed the horse to pull the buggy up to the driveway and then stopped, stepping on the brake and jumping down to the macadam. There was a sharp look in his eyes as he walked around the back of the buggy to face her.

"Where have you been?"

She lifted her chin defiantly. "Walking home."

"You left an hour ago!"

Had that much time truly passed? She glanced again at the sky and noticed how quickly daylight was slipping away.

"What do you want, Gideon?" she asked, steeling herself against his inevitable reprimand and ensuing lecture.

"How could you do that to Hetty?" he demanded. "How could you be so unfeeling toward a woman so dear to you? Badly done, Emma! Badly done indeed!"

"It…it was meant in jest, Gideon," she said, although the words sounded meek and contrived from the moment she spoke them.

"I can assure you," he said angrily. "In jest it was *not* taken! You have wounded a woman who has no greater flaw than constantly praising Emma Weaver, both in front of her and when she is not near. Why, Hetty considers herself part of your family! You are as dear to her as Jane!"

"I highly doubt that!"

"Whether you believe it or not, I frankly don't care." He stood with his legs apart and his arms hanging stiffly at his sides. His short tone indicated just how vexed he was with her and her terrible behavior. "What I do care about is the fact that you just demonstrated such an uncharacteristic lack of compassion, and as a result humbled her, not just in front of friends but in front of her family!"

She was stunned by the anger and hurt that he wore on his expression. While she had known that her words had disappointed him, she had no idea how much! She fought the urge to cry once again. "What would you have me do? I shall apologize when I see her next."

"What would I have you do?" he repeated her question, mockery in his voice. "Why, Emma Weaver, I have proven myself, time and time again, to have your best interests at heart and to be a true friend. My counsel, while most often ignored, has always been faithful. What would I have you do?" He took a deep breath and shook his head. "The only thing you can possibly do is to prove to me that I was justified in putting my faith in you!"

Without waiting for a response, he spun around on his heel and marched back to the buggy and climbed aboard. She watched as the horse began to trot, pulling the gray-topped buggy down the road and away from where she stood. As it disappeared around the bend, she felt a hollow in her chest, a hollow that was both empty and heavy at the same time. With her head hung down, she slowly walked up the driveway and headed to the house, too distraught over what had just transpired between Gideon and her to bother masking her feelings from her *daed*.

✤ *Chapter Sixteen* ✤

EMMA EMBARKED ON her regular visiting schedule on Thursday, only this time she went alone, for Hannah had committed to help at the market all week long, as several of the regular workers had been in dire need of time off. With the beginning of the wedding season upon the community, many of the young Amish women who normally worked at the market traveled to different church districts or even to other states to attend the weddings of extended family or friends.

Weddings were always joyous occasions, especially for Amish youth, as the celebrations often presented the opportunity to travel to new places. As a result, Hannah was scheduled to work every single day of that week. Additionally she hadn't been able to come visiting during the evenings either, a fact that had Emma both curious and relieved. She wondered whether Hannah was avoiding her or too busy doing something else, such as taking buggy rides with a certain young man. On the other hand, she wasn't exactly in the mood for company after what had happened on Sunday, so the solitude was a welcomed respite.

After the dreadful events during the picnic she had spent most of her days alone at home, refusing to leave for even the smallest errand. She even turned down a trip to town with Henry to get some supplies for the pantry. This strange development in her behavior sent Henry into a tailspin. He worried and fretted over Emma, threatening to call the doctor by Wednesday should her demeanor stay the same. Due to his concern, Emma forced herself to make her Thursday visits, but she did so with a heavy sense of dread for her final stop.

Gideon's words still seemed to ring in Emma's ears. The fact that he had not stopped, not even for a quick visit during the early part of the week, added to her self-torment. Try as she might, she just couldn't understand why she had said such a horrid thing, especially to a kind soul like Hetty Blank. And indeed, to think that she might have lost respect in the eyes of so many people upset her greatly. But it was the loss of Gideon's favor that bothered her the most, she reckoned.

And that particular realization had given her several sleepless nights.

On Thursday morning she took the roads for her weekly visits. Her first three stops seemed to go by too quickly. And, to further add to her burden, upon reaching the third house, she discovered that Alice was already at Sarah Esh's *haus*, visiting with the older woman.

Alice greeted her with a cold reserve that Emma could not help but find surprising, given their limited number of encounters. Granted, there had been that episode during the picnic at Yoder's pond, but Emma did not expect a woman who barely knew her to have already passed a judgment because of the unfortunate deed that had, undoubtedly, been reported to Paul and her. While Emma did not particularly care for the woman, she did her best to mask her feelings.

This apparently was not the case with Alice. Her contemptuous looks and superior airs angered Emma, but she did her best to remain even tempered so that no one could ever complain about her behavior again.

She did, however, wonder what caused this newcomer to her *g'may* to behave in such an overly condescending manner toward one specific individual. Since Alice and Paul had not witnessed her awful behavior toward Hetty, Emma could only presume that Paul must have made a negative comment about her to his *fraa* in order to cause discord between the two, perhaps his way of covering his tracks and ensuring that Alice never knew that he had proposed to Emma before asking for her hand.

Frankly such suspicion did not surprise Emma.

"Isn't this just lovely?" Sarah said when Emma sat down to join them. She smiled, beaming from ear to ear. "Two visitors in one day!"

Alice inhaled sharply. "Now, Sarah," she said as if the two were the closest of friends. "I know that Paul visits you on a weekly basis." She glanced at Emma, speaking in a sharp and measured tone. "I was only too happy to take his place today as he has business in Pequea." She emphasized the word *business*, filling it with self-inflated importance. "Besides, we are family now, ain't so? Visiting with you is my pleasure, you know!"

Emma couldn't help but recognize that Alice was trying to establish her seniority over her. She was a woman who commanded attention, whether deserved or not. She was boisterous and loud, traits that Emma did not find particularly attractive in a person, never mind a woman! Being new to Lititz, Alice had already made it abundantly clear that she was never going to sit silently in the background. Her unexpected visit to Sarah attested to that fact.

It also dawned on Emma that, based upon her words, Paul's *fraa* intended to visit on a regular basis, and in all likelihood, she would continue visiting on Thursdays, most likely to make her visits perfectly coincide with Emma's. It looked like an attempt to take credit for what Emma had been doing for several years, or possibly even push her out. The thought of having to spend time in Alice's company made Emma want to groan out loud, yet how could she extricate herself from a long-standing commitment without causing comment? Emma struggled hard to keep a smile upon her face.

As usual, Alice dominated the conversation, her loud voice booming in the small room. By the time she managed to make her excuses, Emma found that she had a pounding headache, whether from being subjected to Alice Esh for thirty minutes or from dreading her next and final visit, or *mayhaps* both, she did not know.

It was later than usual when she knocked at the front door of the Blanks' house. Despite the cool temperature, she felt small beads of sweat slowly tricking down her back. Her heart rapidly beat inside of her chest as she waited for what seemed like an eternity. Would they refuse her? Would she never get to apologize for the injustice she had done to Hetty Blank? Would her deed ever be forgiven?

A minute passed before she heard shuffling behind the door. She had almost given up, starting to turn away to retreat, in defeat, to return home to suffer some more. However, the door finally opened and Emma was surprised when Hetty's *maem* herself welcomed her and invited her inside. As soon as she crossed over the threshold and shut the door behind herself, Emma looked around at the small kitchen. It was too quiet in the house, and she couldn't help but wonder where Hetty and Jane were hiding.

Emma followed Hetty's *maem* into the sitting room and, just as she was about to sit, caught a glimpse of Jane through the doorway. She was pale and disheveled, hunched over and still in her nightclothes. Seeing Jane in such a state startled her, for, despite their short-lived acquaintance, Emma had never seen her as anything less than impeccable and pristine in appearance. The young woman disappeared down the hallway, and Emma could hear Hetty talking to her, her voice low and soothing. Emma's curiosity was piqued and she wondered what was going on with Jane.

"Excuse me for not greeting you. I was tending to Jane. She's terribly sick, you see," Hetty explained apologetically when she finally joined Emma in the sitting room. She assumed her regular seat, a look of grave apprehension upon her face which Emma worried was targeted toward her and not really toward Jane's illness.

"Oh, dear," Emma said in return, genuinely concerned. "I caught a glimpse of her just now. She didn't look well at all! Has a doctor been called, then?"

Hetty shook her head and her *maem* clucked her tongue, obviously having understood Emma's words. "*Nee*," Hetty replied sorrowfully. There were dark circles beneath her eyes. "Jane suffers in silence, it seems. She refuses to be seen by anyone."

"Why, that's preposterous!" Emma was shocked by Hetty's words. To be ill and refuse treatment? "Is she in pain?"

"She claims she has pain in her chest and is experiencing difficulty sleeping" was the simple reply from Hetty. "But no fever or chills. But the tears! She is blinded with the tears, a sorrow that I just cannot understand, I confess." Shaking her head, she clucked her tongue three times before adding, "I just don't know what to make of it." She paused and lifted a finger to wipe at her eye. Emma realized that Hetty was fighting tears herself. "I worry that it is because she does not wish to return to her home next week. *Maem* and I will both miss her so. I'm just surprised that she *might* be afflicted with so much emotion at her departure. That causes me extra grief as well, I reckon."

With a deep sigh, Emma sat back in her chair. She felt as if she wanted to disappear. She hoped that her own poor behavior toward Hetty had not contributed to Jane's illness. After all, Jane seemed a rather fragile creature and doted on her *aendi*. Guilt washed over her and Emma bent her head, ashamed once again at how she had spoken to the older woman at the picnic. Yet the situation provided a timely opening for Emma to do her best to comfort Hetty and *mayhaps* make her forget the awful words she had spoken to her this week past.

"I shall pray for all of you to feel better," Emma said. The statement was made with conviction and it was clear that she meant her words.

"*Danke*, Emma," Hetty replied, nodding her head in approval. "You are always so kind."

The word *always* stung, the irony not lost on Emma, despite the fact that Hetty had not meant it that way. She hung her head and looked away for a moment, a lump forming in her own throat. How gracious of Hetty to say something so kind, she realized, when she, herself, had been so cruel. "*Mayhaps* not always," Emma managed to say. "And for that, I am so sorry, Hetty. I don't know what got into my head and I must sincerely beg your forgiveness." It was a speech she had practiced over and over again, although now that she spoke the words, they did not sound ample enough in their depth to convey what she was really feeling.

To her relief, Hetty smiled and patted Emma's knee in reassurance. "No need to beg for anything," she said quietly. "Forgiveness was given before it was needed."

For a moment Emma wasn't certain what to make of Hetty's remark. Had she been in need of forgiveness before that day at the picnic when she made such a careless remark? Had her perpetual impatience with Hetty been so transparent? "I'm not quite certain how to react to that, I fear," she managed to say, fighting the emotion that welled in her throat. "You humble me."

"Then speak no more about it, dear Emma." And with that, nothing further was ever mentioned on the subject of the incident at Yoder's pond.

Emma, however, had been given food for thought from the most unlikely source. Long after she left the Blanks, she continued to evaluate her behavior. Upon returning home, she sat by the window before the new quilt that was spread in the quilting frame, but her finger merely held the thread, not moving through the fabric as her eyes stared out the window.

While Hetty had been quick to forgive her, Emma couldn't help but wonder how Gideon would react to such an apology. Would he relinquish his displeasure with her? After all, his harsh words had been so full of emotion and disappointment they still echoed in her ears and tugged at her heart. She didn't understand, exactly, why she was so unsettled, especially since everything had been made right with Hetty. She began to sew, but was so distracted that three times she had to undo her stitches, for she made them too far apart.

It was just before supper when her *daed* was taking his daily stroll down the road when Hannah surprised Emma with an unscheduled visit. She had been able to leave work early and had asked the driver to let her off at Emma's house.

"Oh, Emma!" she said gaily as she practically skipped through the kitchen toward the sitting area. "I have such *wunderbaar gut* news!"

The glow on Hannah's face made Emma temporarily forget her own reflections, which had been causing her such misery all afternoon. She spun around in her chair and somehow found laughter on her lips. It felt good to see her friend so happy, even if she, herself, felt so miserable. "Pray, tell me at once! I'm in great need of happy news!"

Practically falling into the chair next to Emma, Hannah clutched her hands to her chest and smiled. "You'll never guess who stopped into market today!"

Truly Emma could not, and she admitted as much.

"Why, let me give you some clues!" Hannah said gleefully.

Emma returned Hannah's smile. "All right then," she said, playing along. "Go ahead and let's see if I can guess!"

For a moment Hannah seemed to think about it, as if delightfully plotting her strategy to drag out the game. Her eyes glowed and the smile never left her face. "Let's see..." she began. "A young man!"

"That's your clue?" Emma felt her dark mood slowly lifting. "I don't think that narrows it down at all! Not fair. I want another hint."

"He's handsome," Hannah offered.

"Clearly! Otherwise you wouldn't be so giddy with joy!"

Emma laughed. "Although we shouldn't put such emphasis on looks now, should we?"

Another moment of pause as Hannah tried to come up with a more clever clue to properly suggest the subject of her delight. "He's been visiting me at market."

Now this was news, indeed. She searched her memory, trying to recall that Hannah had mentioned someone stopping to see her at the market. She couldn't remember any names. "You never told me someone was visiting you at market!"

"*Ja*, I did!" Hannah paused. "I think I did, anyway!" Laughing, she leaned forward as if sharing a big secret. "Just this day, he stopped in and inquired about ordering celery! He was most serious and stared me straight in the eye!"

Celery. A main dish at all Amish weddings and usually planted in the gardens for households that suspected a marriage in the autumn. However, plenty of Amish had neither the space nor the advanced warning to plant enough celery in their gardens. Plenty of farmers, particularly the Mennonites, grew fields of celery for this very purpose, selling it at market to the Amish families that would soon be in need of such. For a young man to suggest such a need directly to Hannah could very well indicate that he was intending to ask for her hand in marriage.

Emma was stunned: two proposals in less than one month? She had never heard of such a thing! And then it dawned on her. "Ralph Martin again?" Hadn't Hannah mentioned she saw Ralph and his *schwester* at market? Hadn't she recently been asked to visit them, and despite Emma's raised eyebrow, she had gone? Certainly she meant Ralph Martin.

"No, goose!" Hannah laughed again, delighted that she

had tricked her friend. "Why would I think of him? Have I not learned anything from you?"

"Francis Wagler?"

At this, Hannah looked startled. "Francis? Why on earth would you suppose him?"

"He did offer to take you home from the youth singing," Emma suggested. "He told me so himself. Saved you from walking home. And he seemed rather friendly to you at the picnic."

Waving her hand dismissively, Hannah shook her head. "*Nee*, not Francis. If he's fond of anyone, it's you!"

"Me?"

"Indeed! Didn't he suggest you as the subject of that game?" Hannah didn't notice that Emma stiffened at the mention of what she had come to think of as the "incident" at the picnic. Instead, Hannah giggled as she urged Emma to continue. "Now, guess again!"

"*Mayhaps* it would be easier if you just told me, then."

"I can't believe you can't guess," Hannah remarked, clearly disappointed for she obviously thought the answer was obvious. "Gideon King!"

The walls seemed to close in upon Emma. The reality struck her and she felt weak. Her throat closed and her heart pounded. Of course, she realized. Her mind reeled over the past few weeks, how Gideon had been attentive to Hannah. He had taken her home in his buggy after the Esh gathering. He had apparently planned the picnic by consulting Hannah first. Why, he had even brought her to that very picnic! The realization that Gideon might have been secretly courting Hannah struck her with such a force that she couldn't speak.

"Emma!" Hannah said, her tone light and cheerful. "You act surprised! Say something!"

"I'm...I'm not quite sure of what to say," she managed to whisper.

"Congratulate me, then!"

That was one thing Emma knew she could not do. "This...this seems rather sudden," she stammered, aware of the sinking feeling inside of her chest.

"No more so than Paul and Alice, I reckon" came the quick, defensive retort.

"But he hasn't asked you," Emma said, although it was more of a question than an actual statement.

Hannah stiffened at what Emma was implying as if offended. "*Nee*," she admitted. "He hasn't. Not yet." Her expression changed and she lifted her chin defiantly, an air of confidence about her that surprised even Emma as she added, "But he will."

Still stunned, Emma sat in her chair and simply stared at Hannah. The thought of Gideon King actually marrying anyone, especially her friend Hannah, was more than she could bear. If anything, she realized, she'd prefer to see Gideon marry Jane, for then, at least, she would not have to feel jealous of a friend.

Jane.

Emma's mouth fell open and she realized that, despite Hannah's confidence, she could very well be mistaken. Gideon had been just as attentive to Jane as he had to Hannah, staring at her at church and at the picnic and including her with his little joke about Francis's game. The old Emma might have said as much, but the new Emma, determined to speak with pleasantness in her heart, hesitated enough to carefully think through her response. The words raced through her head and she quickly assembled a more kind and thoughtful statement than what she was actually thinking.

"*Mayhaps*," she began gently, "you should keep this to yourself, Hannah, until he actually asks you. There might be danger in letting your feelings run ahead of yourself." Emma spoke slowly, pausing before she continued, for she hoped that her words would not offend. "I suspect that we have learned not to presume we know the outcome of a man's thoughts when it comes to love, especially after what happened with Paul, *ja?*"

She knew from Hannah's reaction that it was far too late for that. Clearly Hannah knew something that Emma did not. Paul was long forgotten, and Hannah's heart was turned to Gideon. There was nothing Emma could say to warn her that *mayhaps* Gideon King was not interested in her at all but had his sights set on another: Jane.

"Why, of course I wouldn't dream of telling another soul!" Hannah gushed.

"And...and you are quite certain of his affection?" She hoped that her voice did not betray the disbelief that she was feeling.

"Most undoubtedly!" Hannah giggled and clasped her hands in front of her, giddy with happiness. "Such a kind and thoughtful man," she said out loud, although it appeared as if she were talking mostly to herself. She seemed to be thinking of something that gave her secret delight. Returning her attention to Emma, she smiled. "I knew it for sure and certain when he went out of his way at the picnic."

The dreaded picnic. That again! Oh, how Emma wished that picnic had never taken place. "Out of his way?"

She nodded her head emphatically. "*Ja*, the picnic! He must have suspected how uncomfortable I would have been to arrive alone, and he insisted upon bringing me in his buggy. His courting buggy, no less!"

The image of Hannah's face, glowing with delight as Gideon had guided the horse and buggy into the parking area flashed before Emma's eyes. Had that not been the very first moment when Emma had realized that she too had feelings for Gideon? "I see," Emma managed to say.

"Do say something else, Emma!" Hannah seemed to plead with her. "Tell me that you are happy!"

"Your happiness is all that I have ever wanted," Emma said softly, hoping that her words masked her true feelings.

While the statement was true, Emma knew that she could never congratulate her friend on such a union. Fortunately her words seemed to satisfy Hannah's need for affirmation. She reached out and took Emma's hands, holding them tightly as she stared at her friend. "And I have you to thank for this!"

"Me?"

"You told me to believe in myself and to aspire to greatness. You even encouraged me to take note of his behavior!"

Inwardly Emma cringed, wishing that any encouragement had never come from her own lips. *Oh, that I had never known her,* she thought bitterly.

As Hannah prattled on about conversations she had with Gideon, Emma sank into further reflection, occasionally nodding her head and smiling as if she were, in fact, participating in the conversation. Instead, she was beside herself, her mind reeling at this unfortunate news. If only she had not been so focused on trying to arrange other people's lives, perhaps she would have paid more attention to her own. By encouraging Hannah, Emma now knew that she had lost the one person who, deep down inside, she may have always truly loved: Gideon King.

To make matters worse, the burden of this great loss rested entirely upon on her own shoulders.

When her *daed* finally returned home from his daily stroll, Emma could barely speak. With great apologies, she claimed a roaring headache and retreated to her room to lie down. She didn't get up again until the sunlight dawn slipped through her window. It had been a sleepless night, and she feared that it was not going to be the last one she would have for quite some time.

❧ *Chapter Seventeen* ❧

HERE WAS A general murmur spreading throughout the congregation. It started as a soft whisper before growing much louder, although everyone tried to be discrete in voicing their surprise. At first everyone seemed to look at one another, as if questioning the person seated next to them whether or not they had heard correctly. Then, still disbelieving their ears, they stared back at the bishop. It was as if they were waiting for him to correct the announcement that he had just made. Certainly he had been mistaken. When they realized that the bishop had, indeed, been correct in what he said, that they hadn't misheard him, their attention immediately shifted elsewhere.

Stunned, Emma sat upon the hard bench, trying hard not to look at the back of Anna's head. She clutched the *Ausbund* in her hands, thankful that she had something to hold on to. For a long moment she stared at it, trying to comprehend what had just been announced. Try as she might, she couldn't help but look up, fighting the urge to glance in Anna's direction. However, in looking elsewhere, she noticed that half of the church was, indeed, staring at Anna, the other half at Samuel. It was hard not to do so. Only when Hetty dabbed at her eyes with a handkerchief did people begin to look at her too. Undoubtedly her tears were a mixture of happiness for her niece's betrothal as well as sorrow that Jane would undoubtedly move away.

As was common at the end of the worship services during the month of October, and sometimes November too the bishop announced upcoming weddings. For many in the community, it was the first time that a secret relationship between a young man and young woman were made public. After all, courtship tended to be a private matter. The family, however, would most likely have been tipped off in advance, for planning purposes more so than for approval seeking.

Today, however, the reading of the banns had caught the community off guard. When the bishop stood before the members, clearing his throat, an energetic hush fell over the room. It was an exciting moment, the moment when wedding banns were announced. Who would it be, people were wondering. Some may have had suspicions, for some couples were more open about their courtships. Others, however, followed tradition and were very secretive.

The couple that was announced on this day had followed tradition, perhaps too much, for it was announced that Francis was to wed Jane in four weeks.

In response to this surprise proclamation, everyone seemed to look at the Waglers, wondering how much they knew about this relationship that had been kept secret from everyone. From the stoic expressions on their faces, they too must have only just learned about Francis courting Jane, perhaps as recent as just days before the banns were announced. Clearly Samuel was surprised by his son's choice, not just in his selection of a bride but also in his conduct in being so secretive.

Rachel reached out and touched Emma's hand, a covert

gesture that she wasn't certain how to interpret. Glancing at her, Emma questioned her friend with her eyes, but Rachel looked away, as if ashamed. Not understanding why Rachel would have such a reaction, Emma gently withdrew her hand and continued staring straight ahead, listening to the bishop finish his announcements.

Once the worship service was officially over, the volume of the chatter in the room increased. A small group of women gathered around Hetty, who seemed delighted by the attention. Emma was about to join the small group when Alice Esh barged into it, standing beside Hetty and taking over the conversation.

"I sense that the engagement of Francis and Jane comes as a surprise to most. Why, I saw him walking with her in town just a few days ago. How could anyone not recognize it?"

Hetty started to respond, but Alice didn't let her finish her sentence.

"Of course, when he first came he paid an awful lot of attention to another," Alice added, her eyes darting over their heads to where Emma stood, as if to make certain she was listening. "It's no wonder Jane was sick this week. Most likely heart sickness over worrying about her beau."

Shocked and dismayed, Emma backed away, then hurried into the kitchen. So was that why the announcement came as such a shock to the *g'may*? Was that why Rachel took her hand in sympathy—because everyone thought that Francis had been courting her? And now everyone must think she was heartbroken at the announcement of the secret engagement. Mortified, she refused to meet anyone's eyes. Instead, she quickly snatched up a dish rag and began to tackle the dishes, wishing that she could just be invisible. *Perhaps*, she thought, *if I just act natural, no one will think anything is wrong.*

In hindsight Emma should have suspected something was amiss. After all, neither Francis nor Jane was at the worship service. Only after the bishop announced their betrothal did she realize they were missing. Had she noticed it earlier, she might not have been so surprised by their engagement.

As was customary, the future groom and bride did not attend service on the day that their banns were announced. Instead, they spent the day in private reflection, just the two of them together, usually at the bride's house. Emma could imagine that they were, just now, sitting down for the noonday meal, one that Jane would have made with great care. Today was an important day for her: once the banns were announced, she would be known as Francis's Jane for the rest of her life.

"Can you believe it?"

The hand on her shoulder and harsh whisper in her ear startled Emma from her thoughts. She turned her head, not surprised to see Hannah beside her.

Dish towel in hand, Hannah stood close to her so that others could not overhear. "It's a bit shocking, isn't it?" She picked up a plate and began wiping.

"*Ja*, I should say so!" Emma whispered back. "First Paul, now Francis! Surprises seem plentiful this season!" She tried to keep her words and tone light.

Leaning against the kitchen counter, Hannah crossed her arms over her chest and studied Emma. There was a look of concern upon her face. "Are you all right with it, then?"

"With what?" She decided to play ignorant.

"Francis and Jane!"

Emma rinsed another plate and frowned. "With their

announcement? I have no problem with Francis marrying Jane. I do believe it's a bit sudden, but as I continue to learn, it's not my place to interfere."

Hannah's eyes widened as she pondered Emma's words. "But that's not truc!"

"That I shouldn't interfere?" Emma laughed out loud at that thought.

"Nee, nee!" Once again, Hannah leaned forward, a quick glance around to ensure that no one might be able to eavesdrop. "I just overheard Alice telling others that Francis and Jane were secretly engaged all along! It's the very reason they both came back to Lititz! To meet his father and announce their wedding! But *mayhaps* their announcement was delayed when Francis met you and saw how his father hoped for an attachment between the two of you." Hannah gave Emma a sly look, as if congratulating herself on her subtle reasoning. "I reckon he didn't want to disappoint his *daed*."

But Hannah's explanation left Emma stunned. How could Francis do such a thing to Jane? Truly it must be a terrible burden to always be playing for the smiles and approval of whatever audience he happened to entertain, never mind how inconsistent and even untrustworthy that might make him appear once the truth emerged.

"And how did Alice know about the engagement?" It was a question that, once spoken, did not require an answer. Certainly Francis would have approached the bishop in advance of the worship service. The bishop would have interviewed him, asking questions about the upcoming union between the two. That information, apparently, had been shared with Paul, who, in turn, informed his *fraa*. "Oh, my!" Emma whispered, her eyes scanning the gathering as she sought out Alice.

She was seated at the table already, for the elderly and married women ate before the younger, single ones. From Emma's vantage point, she could see that Alice was engaged in a lively conversation, although from the looks of it, it was mostly Alice talking and everyone else listening. Surely she was retelling the story, eager to let everyone know that she, Alice Esh, had known before everyone else. Her position in the small community was clearly established: the new *dochder* of the bishop was the first to know the secret happenings in the *g'may*.

Disgusted, Emma looked away.

"I suspect his *daed* isn't too happy," Hannah said softly.

"Why ever not?" Emma didn't understand what there was for anyone to be unhappy about. "Jane's a nice enough woman," she added, omitting her opinion that she was rather dull and more than vague when she spoke. A thought dawned on her that, *mayhaps*, the vague conversation had been due to the secret engagement. The less said, the less chance of divulging what was best left unsaid.

Hannah looked equally as surprised. "He was rather attentive to you, ain't so?"

"No more so than to you, I reckon," Emma said defensively.

A blush covered Hannah's cheeks. "You know where my interests lie," she murmured, a reminder that caused Emma to freeze.

Their conversation abruptly ended when one of the women thrust a coffee carafe at Hannah and indicated that she should go refill the men's coffee, a task Hannah readily accepted. Emma shut her eyes, taking a deep breath as she tried to regain her calm. She simply wasn't ready for facing the inevitable: surely Gideon and Hannah's banns would be announced at the next worship service. *At least*, she thought, *I have two weeks to prepare myself.*

"Emma!"

She glanced over her shoulder, surprised to see Anna approaching her, a look of determination on her face.

"Why aren't you seated?" Emma asked, gesturing with a nod of her head toward the women's table. "You should be having dessert, Anna. I saw that Martha brought her apple strudel..."

Anna waved her hand and cut off Emma. "I'm finished and didn't feel up to visiting much." Abruptly she grabbed a dish towel and began to help Emma with the cleanup.

Every dish, plate, and utensil needed to be washed for the second sitting. It was busy work that Emma was thankful for today. Once the after-prayer was said over the meal for the first serving, a flurry of women would clear any remaining dishes and wipe down the table cloths in order to set it for the second group of people who needed to have their noon meal. Emma, however, wasn't feeling very hungry and had already decided to slip out the door when that happened.

"How are you feeling?"

Emma's heart sank. *Oh, no*, she thought. *Not Anna too.* "I feel just fine," she replied slowly. "Why do you ask?"

"Why, the announcement about Francis, of course! Are you all right, then?"

"*Ja,*" she replied nonchalantly, deflecting Anna's concern. "Of course. I mean, it's a bit shocking, I reckon. Being so sudden and all, although I understand that they were acquainted in Ohio..."

"Shocking indeed!" Shaking her head and clucking her tongue, Anna agreed with Emma, her disappointment in the clandestine way with which Francis had conducted himself more than apparent. "His *daed* was beside himself last night. To think, the deception that Samuel felt! After all these years, he had been so excited that his son was coming home only to find out that it wasn't because of him wanting to be near his *daed* but to marry Jane!"

Emma didn't quite understand why this would be so upsetting. She repeated her sentiments about Jane. "She's a pleasant enough young woman. I should think Samuel would be happy."

"I reckon," Anna said dismissively. "He just feels deceived. Why did Francis hide this from us? And to pretend that he didn't even know her and behave so solicitous toward others? Why, Samuel and I, we had been so hopeful..." She too left her sentence unfinished and glanced away, a look of embarrassment upon her face.

Ah, Emma thought, realizing what Anna was insinuating. Her cousin's genuine concern for her feelings touched Emma. She reached out to touch Anna's arm and smiled. "I do not feel deceived, if that is what you mean," she said. "And I'm truly happy for the two of them. If I had felt any interest in Francis, it was short-lived and mostly as a friend, anyway."

With a sigh of relief Anna smiled. "Oh, Emma! We were so worried," she admitted. "His *daed* and I, that is. You do know that Francis's attention toward you did not go unnoticed by many, including us."

"I can assure you that his attention to any of the young women was never inappropriate," Emma quickly suggested. Then, as the severity of the situation began to sink in, she frowned. It was one thing to be secretive but another to be deceptive, she thought as she recalled the uncomfortable discussion she had with Francis on the Esh's porch during a recent gathering. "Although I do question the extent of his trickery. He even went so far as to comment negatively about Jane to me!"

Anna shook her head and averted her eyes, ashamed for her stepson's behavior and unable to speak.

Emma continued. "I can't imagine the pain that Jane must have felt, not only hiding their relationship but having him try so hard to hide it so publicly!" Another image came to her mind of the previous Sunday. Francis had been so attentive to her and come up with that silly game, focusing so much on Emma when his true interest lay elsewhere. All the while, Emma realized, Jane had sat there, watching as Francis ignored her, despite the fact that they had been secretly courting. "Although it is no wonder Jane did not wish to see me the other day when I went visiting."

Anna nodded her head, agreeing with what Emma implied. Indeed, while Francis was a friendly and outgoing young man, it was most uncomely for him to have paid so much attention to anyone, especially if he was courting another.

Emma shook the image from her mind. It was too close to the other image that had haunted her all week: the look on Gideon's face when she had spoken so rudely to Hetty. She cringed at the memory and tried to focus on Anna instead. "Anyway," she said, "truly I greet the news with joy for the newly engaged couple."

"Such a relief!" Anna whispered happily, reaching out to gently squeeze Emma's arm. "Samuel and I were both so worried. The last thing either of us wanted was to see you hurt."

Emma responded with a light laugh. "He may have taken advantage of our friendship," she admitted, "but he most certainly did not injure me."

Indeed, she knew that it would take more than Francis Wagler to hurt her, that was for sure and certain. Her eyes scanned the table of seated men and fell upon Gideon. Despite still being single, his age permitted him to sit with the other married men. He was deep in conversation with them, listening to a man seated next to him. Hannah was refilling their coffee cups, lingering beside Gideon for a moment longer than necessary.

If Emma had originally suspected that he had interest in Jane, she now knew otherwise. He was actively engaged in conversation, no hint of disappointment or heartbreak upon his face.

As Emma watched, Hannah touched his shoulder to indicate that he should pass his coffee cup to her. To Emma's dismay, he smiled at Hannah, his face bright and cheerful. He said a few words to her, words that made Hannah laugh softly, a demure gesture that suggested a certain degree of intimacy that caused Emma to catch her breath. His eyes flickered in her direction, and when he caught sight of her, he smiled briefly before returning his attention to Hannah as she handed him the refilled cup.

Emma looked away, forcing herself to refocus on washing the dishes that were piling up by the counter.

Ja, she thought as she handed a clean but wet plate to the woman next to her. Since the Yoder's pond incident, Emma had finally come to realize that *mayhaps*, as far as she was concerned, there was more to her relationship with Gideon than just friendship. Maybe it was his reaction to her harsh words toward Hetty that had finally opened her eyes and her heart. No, she did not want to lose Gideon. She hadn't allowed herself to fall in love with anyone before because she did not want these feelings to come between herself and her *daed. Mayhaps* not even between Gideon and her. Indeed, she was content with the status quo, where celibacy allowed her to keep tending for *Daed* while enjoying Gideon's almost daily visits. But now, faced with the prospect of losing him to Hannah, she felt a terrible knot forming in her throat. It was not the announcement of the wedding banns for Francis and Jane that would hurt her, indeed.

❧ Chapter Eighteen ❧

THE SUNDAY AFTERNOON sun was starting its descent
in the sky when she heard the all-too-familiar sound
of a horse and buggy pulling into their driveway.
Emma had been sitting down, reading a devotional book.
The Bible verse for that day was rather fitting:

> But the eyes of the Lord are on those who fear
>   him,
>   on those whose hope is in his unfailing love,
> to deliver them from death
>   and keep them alive in famine.
> We wait in hope for the Lord;
>   he is our help and our shield.
> In him our hearts rejoice,
>   for we trust in his holy name.
> May your unfailing love be with us, Lord,
>   even as we put our hope in you.

All afternoon her heart had felt heavy and she had wanted
to cry. Now as she read and reread this verse, she realized
that she needed to lean on God to deliver her from the pain
that she was feeling. Only through her faith in Him would
she find the strength to get through the upcoming wedding

season, especially if Gideon and Hannah were to be one of the couples to take their nuptials.

So she was even further surprised to see Gideon walk through the door. He removed his hat but did not hang it upon the hook. Instead, he nodded his head in greeting toward her and strode forward to shake Henry's hand.

"Didn't expect to see you here today," Emma said softly, her heart pounding as she spoke.

Henry smiled warmly. "You'll be staying for supper, then?"

"I'm not certain I'll be staying long," he replied, an odd tone to his voice, and looked at Henry. "But *danke* for the invitation."

Disappointed, Henry shook his head and frowned. "You running off somewhere, then?"

With a sideways glance at Emma, Gideon gave a cryptic response. "That's yet to be seen."

He spent a few minutes with Henry, discussing things that they hadn't been able to talk about after worship. Emma tried to listen but felt distracted. Her mind raced and she continued to repeat the last part of the devotional verse: "May your unfailing love be with us, Lord, even as we put our hope in you."

It was no more than ten minutes after he arrived when Gideon looked up and stared at her. There was a fearful look in his eyes as he cleared his throat. "Emma," he said. "Might I have a word with you?" He stood up and gestured toward the door. "Perhaps a short walk?"

If Henry seemed genuinely surprised by Gideon's question, for he had never made such a bold request before, Emma was not. Quietly she followed him toward the door and down the porch steps. They walked side by side down the driveway, Emma's heart racing at what she knew was coming. *This is it*, she thought. Her heart felt heavy. This was the moment she would have to give up on him. The moment her life would change. Certainly Gideon was going to tell her about his desire to wed Hannah. Now that the dust had settled within the community in regard to Francis and Jane, he clearly had wanted to tell her in private to pre-empt a repeat display of communal surprise at the next worship service.

"I suppose we were all taken aback," he said solemnly. He sighed and looked at her. *"Mayhaps* you most of all."

"Whatever do you mean?"

He glanced at her quickly as if trying to read her reaction. "Why, Francis and Jane's announcement, of course."

"I understood that," Emma said, trying not to show her nerves as she braced herself for becoming his confidante about his desire to wed Hannah. "It was the second part. Why would I be taken aback more so than anyone else?"

That seemed to catch Gideon off guard and he hemmed and hawed for a moment as if searching for the proper response. "It was quite apparent that you were not unaffected by his attention," he said softly.

At this, Emma stopped walking and looked at Gideon. Was he serious or speaking in jest? When she realized that he was not teasing her, she shook her head. Had he also thought that she was interested in Francis Wagler? The embarrassment of the situation caused the color to rise to her cheeks. "I take exception to that," she said. "If his attention was ever directed to me, I can assure you that it was not returned."

Gideon raised an eyebrow.

"Nee, Gideon," she reaffirmed, her voice unwavering. "While I admit that I may have found him entertaining and

refreshing, especially when he first arrived, I never shared any sort of emotional connection toward him beyond strictly that of friend." She hesitated, forming the words in her mind before she spoke. "I'm quite content, more than you can probably imagine, that Francis and Jane should have a happy marriage and long life together."

A look of relief crossed Gideon's face.

She hadn't expected that reaction from him and she suddenly realized where she had spoken in error. If a happy marriage for two strangers made her content, he was reassured that her happiness in his news that he intended to marry Hannah would most surely be met with even greater joy.

"I envy them," he said wistfully. "Their secret is no more."

His words wounded her, and knowing that he was thinking of his own secret about his feelings for Hannah, Emma looked away so that he could not see the pained look on her face. "Envy is a sin," she snapped, stealing a quick glance at him.

He smiled. "I envy them in a good way, Emma." The amused look in his eyes upset her even more. She felt that all-too-familiar lump growing in her throat as she braced herself for the inevitable. "Would you like to know why?"

"*Nee!*" she blurted, feeling the tears too close to the surface. She feared they would fall when he confided in her. Then, realizing how impossible the situation was, she quickly tried to compose herself and repeated the word softly. "*Nee,* I don't think I do.... Words once said cannot be taken back."

He looked surprised. There was a lengthy silence between them. He removed his hat and fiddled with it in his hands. "I see," he finally mumbled. "I...I will speak no more on the subject then." He started to turn around as if to walk back in the direction from which they had come.

Shutting her eyes, Emma quickly prayed for strength. She knew that she had been wrong to cut him off. She also knew that she couldn't hide from the truth forever. "I'm sorry, Gideon," she called after him. Then, hurrying to catch up with him, she reached out to grab his arm. "I should never have said that. Please, tell me what you will. As much as I might dread it, I suppose I must hear it eventually."

When he lifted his hand to his brow, his expression pained, she realized that her words frustrated him. Turning his back to her, he took a few paces down the road before he turned back and dropped his arm. "Oh, Emma! I gather the courage at last and you destroy it with your words!"

She lifted her chin, searching deep within herself for the resolve to hear him through. What did it matter if he told her today or in three days? If she learned about it now or at the next worship service? If Gideon King wanted to marry Hannah Souder, Emma would just have to accept it as God's will.

"My apologies, Gideon. I don't mean to be so difficult."

He laughed, a laugh that spoke of irony, not mirth. "Difficult? Why, difficult is exactly what you are!" He took a few steps back toward her and placed his hands upon her shoulders. The fierce expression on his face startled her. His eyes blazed as he stared at her. "Do I even stand a chance with you?"

She answered his question with silence, for she wasn't certain in which direction this conversation was going. A chance? A chance for what? And then, for a moment, one brief, dazzling moment, as she caught a change in his expression, she knew. Gone was the intenseness from just a few seconds before. In its place was an unexpected tender look in his eyes. As he searched her face and a hint of a smile played upon his lips, to her surprise, she found herself suddenly not without hope.

"I...I reckon I don't understand," she finally whispered, not trusting her voice to conceal what she was starting to feel.

He bent his knees, just slightly, so that they were eye to eye. "Have you no idea of the depths of my emotions for you, Emma Weaver?" he said. "Have you no compassion for how formidable you are as an object of my heart? Difficult, you say. Indeed, that is putting it lightly."

Her eyes widened as she realized what he was saying.

"I've been watching you, all this time, fighting my feelings. By what right do I have to even hope that my affections might be returned? Such a lively and vivacious woman, clearly sought after by other, younger men, I thought. First there was Paul, who I suspected was secretly courting you."

"Paul!"

Gideon nodded his head. "But your insistence on his courting Hannah convinced me otherwise."

She was speechless.

"And then Francis Wagler arrived home." He did not wear a compassionate expression on his face upon mentioning the young man's name. "I thought to give you a chance, and when I saw how attentive he was toward you and how you defended him so, I knew that my chance had never been there at all." He looked defeated. "And then at the picnic..."

Her eyes searched his face, her mouth opening, just slightly, as if she wanted to say something. She couldn't. There were no words that were sufficient to express what she was feeling.

"I...I saw his influence over you when you spoke to Hetty." His eyes looked anywhere but at her. "It was only when the banns were read, I thought that, just *mayhaps*, I was wrong. But from the look upon your face, I see that I was not."

Emma stammered over her next words. "I...I don't know what to say," she managed to say. "I can't say that...I certainly had no idea...This is not what I expected..."

He shook his head, a look of pain upon his face. "Nor I," he admitted. "I'm far too old, I reckon, and apparently too proud. I never should have engaged in such self-indulgent emotional ambition."

Realizing that the moment was slipping away, Emma placed her hand upon his. "*Nee*, Gideon," she said softly, her heart skipping a beat. "It is I who has so many flaws. But I have been trying, oh so hard, to improve. And it has only been with your guidance that I have been able to amend my ways, although I am far from achieving a fraction of the humility and godliness that you have."

"You speak of flaws?" He laughed nervously. "I've spoken sharply to you so many times, scolding you as if you were a child, lecturing you as if you were a student! Why, I've pointed out every error or mistake that I thought you made!" He smiled, his eyes meeting hers at last. "And you! Why, you have borne it better than anyone!"

She hesitated, her eyes wide and bright as she dared to shift her hand, just slightly, so that it was pressed against his.

He glanced down at her hand, tucked so neatly in his, as if to make certain that he wasn't imagining this moment. The perplexed look on his face made her smile and take a small step closer to him.

And it dawned on him what that meant.

"I...I'm not good at this," he confessed awkwardly. "I mean, in all my years, which are plentiful for certain," he said, ignoring the small laugh that escaped her lips at both his words and his nervousness. *"Ja vell,* not *that* many, I suppose."

"Go on," she urged, her confidence and her happiness increasing by the second.

He took a deep breath and plunged forward. "We've been friends for a long time. It's high time that I marry, Emma Weaver, and there is no other woman that I could ever imagine caring for the rest of my life, no matter how long or short that may be."

"Long, I hope," she quipped.

Her comment caught him off guard and he gave a soft laugh. "Me too, I reckon."

"I should hope so."

He frowned. "There you go again, Always able to distract me with your words. As impossible as it seems, that is one of the very traits that I so very much love about you!"

And there it was. The one word she had longed to hear from him without really knowing it: love.

"I want to marry you, Emma." He looked down upon her, his eyes staring into hers. "There is no better matched couple anywhere in Lititz...no, Lancaster!...than us. *Mayhaps* we have flaws, grave imperfections, but together we are as perfect as we possibly can be. We complete each other." He reached out, and with a trembling hand, he touched her cheek, a simple gesture that said as much as his words. "I want you to be Gideon's Emma from this day forth."

This time, when the tears threatened to fall, she let them, for they were not tears of sorrow as she had expected, but tears of joy.

"Nothing would give me greater happiness," she whispered, clutching at his hand. "I will gladly be Gideon's Emma from this day forth!"

The look of elation that washed over his face made her laugh as the tears fell from her eyes. He pulled her into his arms and held her. With her cheek pressed against his shoulder and his hand warm against her back, he sighed. He kissed the side of her head, his lips brushing against her prayer *kapp*. "If you only knew how I have suffered these past months... *mayhaps* years!"

"It was unintentional, I promise," she replied lightly, feeling warm and safe in his arms. However, the word *suffer* triggered a new thought, one of practicality rather than emotion. "There is, however, one regret that I do have." She pulled away as she said this, a new look of worry upon her face.

"A regret?" He seemed surprised at the use of that word.

"*Ja*, a regret." She bit her lower lip and wondered how to phrase the fear that was on her mind. By agreeing to marry Gideon, the very thing she had not dared to consider a possibility, she had also agreed to move away from home. The news would undoubtedly cause a great shock to her *daed*. "Oh, help!" she muttered, taking a step away from Gideon as she contemplated the situation. "If we were to marry, my *daed* will be left to live alone after we wed. He'll feel abandoned!"

He seemed to ponder this, but only for a short moment, for Emma turned around and faced him.

"I could never do that to him!" She rubbed her forehead, distressed at the realization.

Taking a step toward her, he reached for her hand. "I cannot find comfort and happiness in our future if your *daed* is unhappy. There is, however, an easy fix to the problem. He will move in with us, then." The solution seemed amiable enough, a fair and honorable way to continue caring for the elderly while beginning their new lives together. It was not uncommon for parents to live with newlyweds, especially when the bride or groom was the last child to marry.

Emma, however, was not convinced. "*Daed* is a creature of habit, Gideon. You are well aware of that." She frowned at the difficulty that was presented by the situation. "He likes his walks at four o'clock, down the same road and by the same farms. He's familiar with this house for almost thirty years. He does not adapt well to change," she pointed out. "Remember the fuss he made when Irene married your *bruder?* To move him, at this stage of his life...I fear it would be rather traumatic for him."

There was validity to her argument, and Gideon knew better than to debate her on the issue. With a heavy sigh he nodded his head. "Then I shall have no choice but to move into your *haus.*"

His offer surprised her and she brightened at the thought. "You would do that?"

He laughed at her response and gave her another quick hug. "For you, Emma? I would do just about anything!"

"And I you," she whispered. For a brief moment Emma let him hold her, her cheek pressed against his shoulder. She shut her eyes and said a silent prayer, thanking God for the long, winding journey that led her to this moment. In all of her attempts to match others to their perfect mate, she had never contemplated her own. Clearly the hand of the Lord had guided her to this destination, a destination that she didn't know existed until the very moment she fell upon it.

❧ *Chapter Nineteen* ❧

OR AS MUCH as Paul's marriage to Alice had stunned
the *g'may* and Francis's betrothal to Jane had taken
everyone in the community by surprise, when word
began to spread around the church district about Gideon
King and Emma Weaver, it was met with broad smiles and
general happiness. Indeed, the reaction was just the opposite of what occurred with the two previous announcements.
Instead of the news being responded to with "Did you even
suspect?" or "How long have they known each other?" the
community greeted the unofficial announcement about
Gideon's engagement to Emma with "Why, what took them
so long?"

Only two people did not respond in such a positive
manner: her *daed* and Hannah.

During the week immediately following his proposal,
Gideon had made a point of stopping by the Weavers' *haus*
every day in the late afternoon. When Henry went for his
four o'clock walk, Gideon and Emma spent their time discussing the best way to tell her *daed*, for she had insisted on
delaying telling him the news of their engagement, fearful of
his reaction to the consequent changes that would undoubtedly befall all of them.

"He's going to be devastated," Emma fretted, pacing the floor with Gideon standing patiently as he tried to comfort her as best as he could.

"Time and repetition of the *gut* news will ease his worries, Emma. If we present it to him in a positive light, he should have little argument, don't you agree? He's stronger than you think."

So it was decided that the sooner they told him the better.

On Friday when Gideon arrived for his now-daily visit, they finally told Henry the news. Ten minutes had passed since Gideon's arrival. Henry had asked all of his regular questions and shared his own news, for he had visited with Daniel Zook earlier in the day. He had just excused himself for a moment to go upstairs and retrieve a sweater, realizing it was growing cold in the room.

With a quick glance in Emma's direction, Gideon nodded his head, indicating that now was the time. "Today, Emma," Gideon whispered when her *daed* was out of hearing. "We cannot delay this anymore."

She pouted. "He's dreaded this day since I was a little girl!"

Gideon laughed at her expression and reached out to touch her chin. "But you are no longer a little girl, need I remind you of that fact?"

She waited until he had returned and settled back into his recliner before she cleared her throat and, with one last apprehensive look at Gideon, took a deep breath and faced her *daed*. "I...I must tell you something that is quite *wunderbaar gut* news," she started, wringing her hands nervously in her lap.

Henry frowned at her. "News? What news? Did someone stop by earlier when I was away?" He looked genuinely confused, knowing that Emma had not left the house that day so any news that she had received should have been shared well before now.

She laughed an uneasy laugh and looked at Gideon, who was seated beside her *daed* in the rocking chair. Once again he nodded his head in encouragement. Bravely Emma swallowed her fear and forced herself to say the very words that she had practiced with Gideon. "The news is about the very two people seated before you," she said, gesturing toward Gideon. "We wanted you to be the first to know that the bishop will be announcing our banns at the next worship service."

He simply stared at her, no expression on his face. Had he heard her? She waited for a response but there was none. Just as she was about to repeat herself, Henry finally blinked twice and, with a shake of his head, spoke. "How can this be?" He looked first at her, then at Gideon. "I don't think I understand what you just said. Banns? The two of you?"

Emma nodded her head. "*Ju*, it's true."

Henry looked back at her, his eyes wide in disbelief. "Emma, are you sure?"

"*Daed*!" She gasped at his question. "Gideon is your friend! He's a right *gut* man! How can you ask such a thing?"

"*Nee, nee*," Henry started apologetically, quickly backtracking so that he was not misunderstood. "It's not Gideon I worry for! It's you!"

That was even more unsettling. "Me?"

"Why, you always said you'd never marry," he explained, his voice still exposing the shock that he was feeling from Emma's announcement.

Taking a deep breath, she admitted that much was true. "But I have changed my mind. When God leads one to unfailing love, one should not turn away." She smiled at Gideon. "And that is what God has done."

Henry's face paled. "Then you will leave..." As Emma had suspected, the thought of her marrying would be soured mostly by his fear of living alone.

Gideon cleared his throat and leaned forward. "If it is all the same to you, Henry," he said. "Emma and I have discussed this matter, and we, with your blessing, would prefer to stay on here."

"Here?" He looked from one to the other in complete disbelief. "Live here?"

"Ja, here!" Emma said quickly, her hand fluttering in the air nervously. "And, really," she said with a timid laugh. "What difference would it make? I mean, after all, you do enjoy Gideon's company so much anyway. You're always so excited when he visits. Now, he'll just 'visit' every day."

Henry seemed to digest this news while Emma chewed on her lip, her familiar gesture of anticipation when nervous and waiting for someone's reaction. She glanced at Gideon and he raised his eyebrows at her, an approving nod indicating that she had done well. Henry, however, clearly thought otherwise. As the realization that this marriage was truly going to happen sank in and that change was afoot, he turned his attention to Gideon.

"Are you sure?" He spoke slowly, questioning Gideon directly. "About living here? Your business is on your property."

"And so it shall stay there," Gideon quipped lightly. "Unless you wish me to move it here, of course."

"Nee, nee!"

Emma and Gideon laughed at the serious expression that

her *daed* wore upon his face. Only then did he realize that Gideon had spoken in jest.

Sobering, Gideon quickly explained. "It's not so far away. A simple ten-minute drive by horse and buggy," he said casually. "As for the *haus*, it's not as warm and lively as yours. Besides, I can always rent it out, perhaps to another young couple that is soon to be wed?" He didn't have to state that he was referencing Francis and Jane. It was a clever solution that Emma had thought up just the previous day.

Without any further arguments, Henry lifted his hands in defeat. "I see you have it all worked out," he said. "This news certainly has taken me by surprise."

"We know," Emma replied softly.

"It will take me some time to get used to this idea," he mumbled as he shook his head. "Gideon and my Emma. I never would have thought it."

The next day Emma harnessed the horse to the buggy and drove the short distance to Gladys's home in order to speak with Hannah. She dreaded the exchange, worrying that her friend's self-confidence as well as her faith would suffer when she learned that, yet again, she had been mistaken about the courtship of a man and that again, Emma was at the core of it. In order to delay the inevitable, Emma let the horse walk most of the way to the Getz *haus*, using the extra few minutes to take deep breaths and practice, once again, the words she was going to say to her friend in order to ease their sting.

Fortunately Emma found Hannah alone at home, sitting at the kitchen table and peeling potatoes for supper. Gladys had gone visiting. One look at Emma's face and Hannah already knew that bad news arrived with her friend.

"What is it?" she asked quickly, setting down the peeler.

"I must share something with you," Emma admitted slowly.

"I hesitate to do so because this situation is so similar to the last time I shared upsetting news with you, my dear friend." Hannah stiffened her back as the meaning of Emma's statement became clear to her. "The only difference this time," Emma added, "is the fact that the misunderstanding was not due to my encouragement," she said. "And it involves Gideon, not Paul."

Hannah did not respond. She merely stared at Emma.

"And I fear that, this time, it involves me as well," she said, hesitating as a dry feeling invaded her throat.

She found it hard to complete what she needed to say, for she knew her words would cause her friend certain pain. How many nights had Emma laid in bed awake, thinking that he was going to propose to Hannah? How many days had she paced the kitchen floor, fretting over the day that she would have to sit on a hard bench and watch as the bishop wed Gideon and Hannah? The pain that she had felt was how Hannah would undoubtedly feel when she realized that Gideon cared for another.

Swallowing her fear, she finally confessed what she needed to say. "I must confide in you that I have accepted Gideon's proposal."

A dark cloud passed over Hannah's face. Clearly this was news that she did not expect. Emma didn't blame her for looking confused. After all, the entire situation still seemed surreal to Emma too.

"I'm not quite sure how to respond to this," Hannah admitted.

"I'm sure it comes as a surprise."

"A surprise! *Ja*, to say the least!" There was a definite edge to Hannah's voice. She stood up and paced the floor, her arms crossed over her chest. "First Paul and then Gideon? I just don't know what to make of this!"

"Nor I," Emma confessed.

Hannah turned around, a frown upon her face. "You? You don't know what to make of this?" She exhaled loudly and lifted her eyes toward the ceiling. "You taught me to think highly of myself and I believed you."

"That's not fair," Emma exclaimed. "While I admit that I was in error about Paul's affection, I recognized my involvement and I apologized. I told you that I wouldn't do it again, and if you recall, I never encouraged you to have feelings for Gideon. In fact, when you told me about your suspicions, I thought his attention might be focused..." She paused, searching for the right word. "Elsewhere."

"Elsewhere?"

Emma remained silent.

Hannah quickly understood what Emma's silence meant. "Elsewhere. I see. You suspected his attention lay *elsewhere*, but certainly not with me. It's never with me, is it?" she sighed, leaving unspoken the part that, for as frequently as it was not "her," it was, however, "Emma." Her shoulders slumped forward and she stared down at the floor, her eyes misting over. She sat back down on the sofa and shook her head, a look of sorrow on her face. "My aspirations were too high, I reckon, to expect his to be so low."

Emma caught her breath at this late statement. Was *that* what this was about? Aspirations? Was she accusing Gideon of marrying Emma for her good standing in the *g'may*, instead of the real reason: that he loved her? While it was true that Hannah was still considered a newcomer to their church district and community and had not yet approached the bishop to become an official member of the *g'may*, that had nothing to do with Gideon's proposal. Did she honestly think that Gideon, of all people, would think less of her for that?

"Nonsense!" Emma stood up and faced her friend, trying patiently to not be motivated by emotion when she spoke. "This has nothing to do with 'aspirations' being too high or too low! I find that mildly offensive, Hannah. After all, our aspirations should be to honor God and not set ourselves above others by showing prejudice. Have we not learned anything in the past few months?" She tried to calm down and took a deep breath, shutting her eyes for a long moment as she formulated her next words. "I've already apologized for any part that I had in your disappointment with Paul, and my heart aches for your pain at the perceived loss of Gideon. Just as we were mistaken with Paul, you were mistaken about Gideon. But I can assure you that this has nothing to do with 'aspirations,' Hannah." She uttered the word as if it were poison.

She meant what she had said and felt a degree of disgust, both at Hannah for having voiced such a statement and at herself for her own past behavior living it. Hadn't it been Emma's hopes to help Hannah turn away Ralph Martin, a pig farmer, in the hopes of attracting the attention of Paul Esh, a young Amish man from a well-respected family in the *g'may*? Hadn't Paul expressed his own prejudice at the thought of marrying Hannah, considering her unknown background less suitable for the son of a bishop, and preferring to propose to a more notable young woman: Emma? And then there had been the issue with Hetty at the picnic, the moment when Emma had shown such an ugly face to so many, disappointing them as well as herself. Finally, Emma knew that Gideon had been correct when he had accused her of having prejudice against Jane, not just because she was the talk of the *g'may*, but also because she suspected Gideon of taking a fancy to her.

Oh, Emma had learned some valuable lessons indeed. The experiences of the past two months had humbled her, teaching her to accept people for who they really were and not what they stood for. It was a lesson well learned and not a moment too soon. She reflected frequently on how far she had come, often wondering if Gideon would have proposed to her if she had not traveled such a journey.

The tears were now falling freely from Hannah's eyes and she was covering her face with her hands, sobbing.

"Dear Hannah," Emma said, her voice softening as she moved to sit beside the distraught woman on the sofa and tried to console her. "I'm so terribly sorry for any pain that you might feel."

Quickly Hannah stood up and turned her back so that Emma could not see her tears. She tried to straighten her shoulders, attempting to put on a facade of strength that she clearly did not feel. "If you'll excuse me," she said softly, her voice wavering under her distress. "I'm suddenly not feeling very well and...and I think I might go lie down for a spell."

Emma hung her head, knowing that it was time for her to leave. With a deep breath she stood up and started to walk toward the door. She turned her head and took a final look at Hannah, who was standing in the same spot, not moving and clearly waiting for Emma to leave. "I hope you feel better soon," she whispered. She slipped out the door and headed for the buggy, thankful that with its help she could leave quickly.

When she arrived home, she found Gideon waiting for her on the porch. While she hadn't told him everything, not wanting to embarrass Hannah, she had indicated that she was headed to share news that would greatly distress her friend. Had he suspected anything, he was too much of a gentleman to put his thoughts to words. Instead, he had offered to take her to see her friend, a kind offer that Emma had politely turned down. This was something she needed to do alone.

Now as she stopped the horse and buggy in front of the small barn, she found herself relieved. His consideration, as he was waiting for her return, knowing that Emma might need extra support, was thoughtful. Yet, upon seeing him there, she realized that, in hindsight, she should not be surprised. Gideon King was truly an unselfish man with great compassion for others. It was just like him to be overly concerned and show up to comfort her when she needed it.

With an apprehensive look on his face, he regarded her countenance as he crossed the driveway to help her unharness the horse from the buggy. When she gave no indication of what she was feeling, beyond an unusual silent air about her, he merely started to unbuckle the traces connecting the horse's harness to the buggy.

They worked in silence, side by side, Gideon occasionally glancing at her and Emma still deep in thought. When they had finished tending to the horse, he walked with her to the *haus*.

"If you wish to talk about it…" he finally said as she sank onto the sofa, leaning her head against the back of it.

Shutting her eyes, she sighed and tried to think about how to share her emotions with him without harming Hannah. There was no easy way around it, so she chose to merely shake her head. "*Nee*," she responded but smiled gently at him. "What is the saying? 'Less said, soonest mended.' I think that applies nicely here."

"*Gut* advice, Emma," he said, taking a seat next to her. He reached out to brush aside a piece of stray hair that had fallen from her bun. "Now, let me tell you my news for the day!"

Not wanting to take away from his obviously good mood and interesting news, she sat up and tried to forget about Hannah. Time would heal that wound. "Please do tell me your news. I'm ready for a distraction, I think!"

"I spoke with the bishop today." There was a sparkle in his eye. He reached out and took her hand in his.

She questioned him with her eyes. "And that is such big news?"

He laughed at her. "*Nee*, it is not. You knew that I was going to speak to him." He lifted her hand and kissed the inside of her palm. "But it is the next part that I don't think you would have anticipated!"

"You delight in teasing me!" she protested.

"Indeed, I do!"

She threatened to withdraw her hand.

Again he chuckled and held it tighter. "*Ja, vell*," he began. "I was speaking with the bishop and informing him of our intentions. And wouldn't you know it that Alice was sitting in the next room, working on some mending. I do believe I caught her peeking around the corner while I made the arrangement for the banns."

Emma gasped. "She didn't!" He gently prodded her leg in jest. "She did indeed!"

Her mood began to lift and she joined him in laughing. "I can only imagine the reaction on her face!"

"And I wouldn't be surprised if half of the *g'may* doesn't know already!" He didn't seem disappointed by this proposition. "I do believe that there will be no secrets safe in our *g'may* as long as Alice Esh is part of it!"

Within two days word spread of their upcoming announcement. Upon hearing the news, Anna insisted that Samuel bring her to the Weavers' residence where, with one look at Emma's face beaming with mirth and happiness, whatever she had just heard was instantly confirmed. They embraced and the room soon filled with laughter. Anna insisted that Emma sit with her and share the details of this surprising news.

"I suppose I should not find it so shocking as some other recent announcements," Anna said, her way of indicating her own feelings toward Paul's rash marriage and Francis's unexpected engagement. "Gideon always did seem to be a fixture at the supper table, more so toward the end of my time living here, come to think of it."

In hindsight Emma saw it too. How she had missed Gideon's affection for her, she never could say. They had known each other for so long that, indeed, she thought of him as family already. "I can't say when it happened," Emma confessed, for in truth she didn't dare reveal Hannah's secret admiration of Gideon, which had triggered the discovery of her own feelings for the very same man. "But once I recognized how I felt, it was oh so clear!"

Anna laughed, delighted with Emma's admission. "It's such *wunderbaar gut* news, Emma. And to think that he offered to move here so that your *daed* would not become unsettled. Gideon King is the very best of men, I believe!"

"As do I!" Emma happily agreed. "Even when he does scold me so!"

At this, they both laughed, knowing full well that, despite their upcoming marriage and Emma's vow to improve herself, Gideon's days of scolding Emma were not over.

❦ *Chapter Twenty* ❦

To Emma, it felt strange to be standing in the sitting room of her *haus*, the room so familiar but the setting so surreal. The last time when so many people had gathered in their home had been years ago when Irene married John King. Today, however, the sea of people gathered there celebrated a different Weaver *dochder* getting married to another King: the older King *bruder*.

After the bishop had announced their engagement, only two Sundays ago after the worship service, Emma noticed that everything moved at an accelerated pace. Irene had been most helpful, visiting more frequently and outlining all of the things that needed to be done and organized: the house cleaned, a new dress made, invitations delivered, and food preparations assigned. These were not deeds that Emma would have either wanted or, for that matter, been able to undertake in such a short time. Emma's appreciation for her older *schwester*'s guidance and participation was almost as great as her relief that both Irene and John expressed enormous joy over the upcoming nuptials. If Emma had ever been fearful that the couple might react with anything less than an abundance of joy, she was quickly reassured that their reaction was quite the opposite.

"I always hoped that things would turn out this way," Irene had even confided in her as they were putting the finishing touches to the blue wedding dress that Emma would wear for the wedding ceremony and at the party that would follow. "Perhaps John might have taken a bit of convincing, but he was quick to see that the two of you are intended for each other! And knowing my John, I knew that his *bruder* would be a right *gut* husband to you. We've been hoping and waiting for this day for well over a year now!"

Something Emma hadn't expected, however, was her *daed*'s interest and involvement in the planning of the wedding. At this rather unpredictable time of year, he had been terrified at the thought that Emma might not be able to marry at home, so with Gideon's help, they had arranged for a temporary room to be built off of the sitting area that wrapped around to the porch. By enlarging that area and converting the wall of windows into an open doorway, the extra space permitted the wedding to be held at the Weavers' *haus*.

Now as Emma looked out at the guests, almost four hundred of them and still counting, she was glad that her *daed* had been so wise and Gideon so accommodating.

Earlier in the day the worship service had seemed extra lengthy to Emma. She did catch Gideon's eyes upon her a few times from across the room while the congregation sang from the *Ausbund*. She thought she saw him smile, which caused her cheeks to color. But then, just as quickly, he looked away, not wanting her to feel embarrassed.

When the time came for the ceremony, Emma rose from her bench and walked slowly to stand beside Gideon and in front of the bishop. Her *schwester* stood to her left while Gideon's *bruder* stood to his right. The resemblance between the two *schwesters* and their *bruder*-husbands was quite noticeable even for someone who would not have been aware of their kinships. To Emma it felt as if everything were falling into place, orchestrated by God Himself. Indeed, an aura of peace and rightfulness surrounded the congregation.

The bishop took a deep breath, pausing just long enough to look first at Emma and then at Gideon. For twenty minutes he spoke about the commitment they were about to make to each other, talking about marriage as a union before God that only death could separate. Emma listened to his words, words that she had heard many times over the years at other weddings in the *g'may*. This time, however, she not only heard them; she also understood them as well.

When the sermon was over, the bishop turned to Gideon as he slowly began to enunciate the beautiful wedding vows that everyone was waiting for. "Can you confess, brother, that you wish to take this, our fellow sister, as your wedded wife, and not to part from her until death separates you, and that you believe this is from the Lord and that through your faith and prayers you have been able to come this far?"

With a very serious nod of his head and affirmative tone of voice, Gideon clearly spoke the one-word answer: "Yes."

The bishop then shifted his body so that he was looking directly at Emma, his dark eyes peering at her from behind his round glasses. "Can you confess, sister, that you wish to take this, our fellow brother, as your wedded husband, and not to part from him until death separates you, and that you believe this is from the Lord and that through your faith and prayers you have been able to come this far?"

She bit her lip and nodded her head. But with all that emotion and the entire congregation's eyes fixed on her, the word seemed stuck in her throat. It looked as if no one breathed until she found the strength to softly whisper "yes" in response to the bishop's question.

"Since you, Gideon King, have confessed that you wish to take our fellow sister to be your wedded wife, do you promise to be faithful to her and to care for her, even though she may suffer affliction, trouble, sickness, weakness, despair, as is so common among us poor humans, in a manner that befits a Christian and God-fearing husband?"

Once again, Gideon nodded, "Yes."

"And you, Emma Weaver," the bishop continued. "You have also confessed that you wish to take our fellow brother to be your wedded husband." He paused and cleared his throat, reaching behind him for the glass of water that was on the windowsill. "Do you promise to be faithful to him and to care for him, even though he may suffer affliction, trouble, sickness, weakness, despair, as is so common among us poor humans, in a manner that befits a Christian and God-fearing wife?"

"Yes," she managed to say. She felt the weight of the eyes upon her back and her stomach seemed in turmoil. It was only because of Gideon standing next to her that she managed to find the strength to stand there before every person in the *g'may* as well as friends and family who had traveled from afar. His confidence and strength had helped her through the ceremony, for now she knew that life without Gideon was simply not living at all.

Finally the bishop gestured Gideon and Emma to take hold of each other's right hand. When they did so, he covered their hands with his and said, "The God of Abraham, the God of Isaac, and the God of Jacob be with you both and help your family come together and shed His blessing richly upon all of you. Now, go forth as a married couple. Fear God and keep His commandments."

And with that, they were married.

If the worship service seemed to go by far too slowly, the hour while she sat beside Gideon, on his left side, at the *Eck table*, reserved just for the bride and groom, seemed far too short.

She had enjoyed sitting there, her friends and relatives bringing both of them plates of food and desserts. Several times Gideon and Emma had managed to secretly hold hands under the table, the feel of his palm pressed against hers seeming as natural to her as breathing. If she had never felt the warmth of another man's hand touching hers, she now could never imagine anything as wonderful as Gideon's touch upon her fingers.

For the rest of her life she would be known as Gideon's Emma, a distinction that also felt natural, as if it always should have been that way. Over the past few weeks she had often found herself lost in her thoughts, tripping over memories that now, with the realization of Gideon's true feelings, took on an entirely different meaning. She could see the signs and hints of his affection. She could feel his pain when he thought that her interests lay elsewhere. And she continually heard his words on that day when he had proposed to her. To say her relief as well as her joy had been overwhelming was, indeed, an understatement.

During the second hour of sitting at the *Eck table*, people began to stop by, usually in pairs, to spend a few moments with the newly married couple and wish them well. It began with family, immediate and then extended, before friends and neighbors made their way to the table. For a few minutes the guests would talk with Gideon and Emma, congratulating them on their marriage and sharing advice, news, or compliments about their union. For Emma it was only the second time that she met many of Gideon's extended family, the first time having been at Irene's wedding just eight years ago.

As the clock struck three o'clock, a group of youths began singing a song, some of the older guests joining in. Emma felt Gideon reach for her hand again, his thumb gently caressing her wrist. She smiled but kept her attention on the song, singing along with the other guests.

It was much later when Emma finally saw her friend Hannah in the back of the room. To Emma's surprise, Ralph Martin was by her side.

All day Emma had not been able to speak to her friend. Before the worship service and the ceremony, there had simply been no time. Afterward there were so many people in the *haus* that she had lost sight of Hannah. Over the past few weeks she hadn't seen much of her, and Emma worried that their friendship was, indeed, strained. However, she had later learned that Hannah was working almost six days a week, stepping in for other young women who were busy traveling to attend their own family weddings. Still, Emma felt for her friend, knowing that it must be a strange and sad feeling to have been in attendance at the wedding.

As for Ralph Martin, Emma hadn't noticed him among the crowd earlier and experienced a moment of surprise to see him in attendance. Then she remembered that Ralph and his family rented that farm owned by Gideon in Strasburg. It was only natural that Gideon would have invited the Martin family to the festivities.

"If you'll excuse me a moment," she whispered to Gideon.

She made her way through the room, pausing to say kind words to people who smiled at her, reached out and touched her arm, sharing their congratulations and wishing her a long life of happiness with Gideon. By the time Emma stood before Hannah, Ralph had already moved over to join a group of men near the dessert table.

If Hannah felt discomfort, she did not show it. She smiled and gave Emma a warm embrace. "How happy I am for you!" she said, and from the glow on her face and sparkle in her eyes, it was clear that she meant it. "I'm ever so sorry that I wasn't around these past few weeks. With so many weddings, I volunteered to fill in for several people at the store."

"So I heard," Emma replied, smiling. "I'm so glad you are well! I was worried, you know!"

Unspoken between them lingered the issue of their last conversation. Hannah flushed at the reminder and shook her head, averting her eyes. "*Nee, nee,*" she assured Emma. "I am quite well. In fact, you might say that all of these experiences have taught me something." She glanced over Emma's shoulder and lowered her voice, making certain no one could overhear. "I did listen to your words, Emma, and I have come to understand so much better. You were quite right about a lot of things."

"And quite wrong at times too," Emma quickly added, humbly.

"Only God is perfect, anyway."

Emma smiled in response.

Several people who wanted to congratulate Emma interrupted their conversation. With a slight wave of her hand, Hannah disappeared back into the crowd and Emma, being distracted by all of the guests at her wedding, did not have time to spend with her again.

It was later in the evening when the last of the guests finally filed out. Emma was glad to see quiet fall upon the *haus* at last, for it had been a long day. She was exhausted, and rightfully so. After all, the festivities had started at eight o'clock in the morning, and already it was close to seven o'clock in the evening. She had been on her feet for most of the time.

The women in the *g'may* had already taken care of cleaning the kitchen so that Emma would not have to be bothered with that chore in the morning, but the rest of the first floor was in disarray. Furniture had been moved out, temporarily stored in the barn and upstairs in the spare bedroom. Gideon had recruited his *bruder* and some friends to help move a few items back before they too had departed for home. Still, she knew that they would have a long day tomorrow, putting the *haus* back in order; the sooner the better so that *Daed* didn't fret too much over the disruption to his daily routine.

"There we go!" Gideon announced as he came into the house, carrying the last kitchen chair. He placed it on the floor and slid it under the table, the feet of the chair scraping against the floor. "Samuel has offered to come in the morning to help with the larger pieces. We'll have everything back in order by noon!"

She smiled.

A silence fell over the room.

"So," he said quietly, leaning against the chair and watching her thoughtfully. "Emma King."

The two words sounded strange together, and Emma felt the color rise to her cheeks. For almost twenty-two years, she had been Emma Weaver. Having a new last name sounded foreign and surreal. The reality of the day hit her, and she fought the urge to feel overwhelmed, causing her blush to deepen.

He chuckled at her reaction and took a few steps toward her, reaching out to hold her hand. Gently he lifted her hand and pressed his lips to her skin before pulling her into his arms and staring down into her face, a look of adoration on his own. "It is done," he said softly. "You have done the one thing that you always declared you had no interest in doing!"

"And what would that be?" she asked, genuinely perplexed by his words.

"You've become a *fraa!*"

Another blush was met with soft laughter.

"You always were so adamant," he said. "So quick to insist that you, Emma Weaver, were independent and would never be agreeable to marry!"

"Mayhaps you wanted to marry me just to prove me wrong," she teased. "It wouldn't be the first time that you took delight in doing so!"

"Nor the last, I'm sure."

Despite wishing to disagree, she knew that he spoke the truth. *"Ja vell,"* she sighed. "Let's hope that it gets less frequent as time passes."

"Let's do, indeed!"

They both laughed, a sweet sound in the otherwise silent house.

Lifting his hand, he pressed it against her cheek and leaned down to place his lips against her forehead. She shut her eyes, enjoying the tenderness of the moment. It had been a long day and she knew that he was just as exhausted as she was. There was a lot of work to do the following day, but she appreciated the peaceful moment, alone with her Gideon in the kitchen, shrouded in the darkness which was broken only by the flickering from the small kerosene lantern on the counter.

He cleared his throat when he pulled away, a new gruffness in his voice as he spoke. "I need to go check on the horse. Make certain she's settled in. I promised your *daed* that I'd check on his too. Check that they were watered properly this evening."

"I'll just finish up here, then," she said with a soft nod of her head, even though there really wasn't much more she needed to do at this point.

"I'll meet you upstairs, then," he mumbled, giving her hand a soft squeeze before releasing it.

She stood there, her hip pressed against the counter as she watched Gideon walk away, his broad shoulders disappearing through the door and into the darkness. For a few moments, she stood at the kitchen sink, staring at the black window, her mind trying to commit to memory every wonderful moment of that day. When she felt she was ready, it was with a satisfied smile that she lifted the lantern, her finger carefully grasping the handle, and walked toward the staircase, quietly ascending so as not to wake her *daed*.

❧ *Epilogue* ❧

WHILE IN THE midst of fixing the noon meal, Emma looked up at the noise, to see Gideon walk into the kitchen. He had taken to coming home in the middle of the day, eager to spend more time with his bride, before returning to his business for the afternoon. Henry had found the extra company at dinner to be a delight. He liked to discuss business matters with his son-in-law and offer the occasional word of fatherly advice. Emma had taken pleasure in being able to cook a bigger meal; it was more satisfying to cook for three than it was for just two, as it allowed her to experiment with some more elaborate recipes.

The hint of a beard cast a shadow on her husband's cheeks and tickled her lips when she greeted him by returning his kiss. Her *daed* was upstairs, taking a short nap, so she welcomed his affection and smiled when he pulled back, his arms still wrapped around her.

"You are home early, then, husband," she observed, her eyes flickering to the clock on the wall. "I didn't expect you for another thirty minutes!"

"I couldn't bear to stay away from you!" he teased as he

gently touched the tip of her nose. "And I have news! News that, I'm afraid, you might find rather shocking!"

Emma gasped. "Yet you smile! How shocking can it be?"

"Ja vell, I find it delightful, but I do fear you will be rather irritated when you hear it," he admitted dramatically, in his teasing way.

Her curiosity was piqued. "What a riddle you give me!" She couldn't imagine what news would cause pleasure for her husband while causing her pain. The gleam in his eyes told her that, despite his words, she might not be vexed by it at all. "Do tell and don't keep me in suspense, I beg of you!"

"Prepare yourself for the very worst news imaginable," he said, trying to hide his delight.

"You tease! What could possibly bring you such joy while causing me so much misery?"

"There is but one subject, I believe," he said cryptically.

"I can't think of any subject!"

"Hannah," he said, the name causing Emma to pause.

She had seen her friend only once since her marriage to Gideon and that was at worship. To Emma's dismay, neither she nor Gladys accepted her invitation for joining the small gathering to play Scrabble and share coffee at the Weavers' *haus* afterward. This refusal caused Emma some distress, for she feared that, despite their talk at the wedding, Hannah was avoiding her. It didn't matter that Gladys claimed she was not feeling well and Hannah insisted she had other plans. Her downcast eyes when she politely refused gave Emma pause to question the truth behind the statement.

Could she honestly have perceived herself so enamored with Gideon that their friendship was over? The thought pained Emma, but she also knew that there was nothing she could do about it. It was up to Hannah to recover and move on, accepting the situation and being thankful no one else had been made privy to the intimate details that might otherwise cause them both great embarrassment.

"Do you know already, then?" he asked, made curious by Emma's unusual silence.

"I have not seen her since worship," she admitted carefully, worried that something dreadful might have happened to her friend.

"Ah, then I will be the one to tell you the horrible news," he said, looking forlorn and gloomy, despite the fact that Emma suspected that his expression was entirely feigned. "I have had a visit this morning from Ralph Martin, you see. It does appear that he will be taking a *fraa* at last!"

Emma felt her heart flip-flop. "Oh, dear! How will Hannah react to this news! It is horrible." She tried to pull away from Gideon, feeling the urge to pace the floor. She could only imagine what Hannah would feel when she heard. After all, this would be the third man who she had expressed interest in that married another. "That poor, poor Hannah. That would be the third time her heart is broken!"

Gideon laughed. "*Nee*. He is to wed your 'poor, poor' Hannah. It's to be announced this Sunday at worship!"

Emma stared at him, amazed at his announcement. "Is this true?"

"It is, indeed!"

"Oh, my!" A hand fluttered to her chest and Emma relaxed. "Why, this is not horrible news! This is the best news ever, Gideon!" She looked up at him. "Tell me everything! Do you know how this has come about?"

"I didn't question him, Emma," he said reproachfully. "Although Ralph did mention seeing her at our wedding. I do believe that was the rekindling of the flame. I suspect that is why she has not been around to visit, for he has apparently been visiting with her every evening."

Emma was delighted with this news, if not discouraged by her husband's lack of details. "Well, I shall have to get the longer story directly from Hannah, then!" she said, her mind already trying to figure out how to coordinate a visit with her friend as soon as possible.

For all of Emma's happiness about the upcoming betrothal of her friend, Gideon seemed equally pleased with her response. "I see you have markedly changed your opinion about this matter since we first discussed it so long ago," he remarked. "Or perhaps you merely lost your sense of smell?" he added, a smirk on his face.

"*Ja*, I have. I mean...*nee*. Oh, Gideon, stop teasing!" she exclaimed, momentarily covering her face with her hands to hide the blush that covered her cheeks. "I was foolish, I reckon."

He lifted an eyebrow. "Oh, *ja*?"

"But, *mayhaps*, a little less so now," she allowed herself to admit, which caused him to laugh as he embraced her.

"A little less, for sure and certain," he chuckled.

With a new cheerfulness to her step, she moved about the kitchen while Gideon settled down at the table, the *Budget* newspaper now in his hands. The noise of the paper crinkling whenever he turned the pages comforted her. Occasionally, as she finished preparing the dinner meal, she glanced over her shoulder to watch him, a smile upon her lips and joy in her heart. Seeing Gideon seated at the far end of the table felt natural and caused her great happiness.

Returning to her work, she said a prayer of thanks to God for all of His blessings. It was not the first time that she had paused to reflect upon the power of God's will. Despite her previous naiveté in thinking she could help shape the future of others, she had learned so much. Now she was humbled in the knowledge that God had far greater plans for His people than a mere human could ever imagine. Even with her interferences, regardless of how good her intentions might have been, God's plan would always prevail. All she had to do was have faith.

Outside the kitchen window, a gray-topped buggy pulled by a high-stepping brown horse could be heard, the noise of its heavy horseshoes clattering against the road. The gentle whirling of the buggy wheels grew louder as it passed the Weaver house. The sound reminded her of the voice of God, gentle at first, but, if ignored, becoming stronger and louder to draw the attention back toward Him.

It was a reminder that lingered in her soul, long after the sound finally disappeared from her ears.

Coming in 2015 From Sarah Price
Second Chances

❧ *Chapter One* ❧

ANNA EICHER SAT in the old rocking chair by the
wood-burning stove, quietly quilting as she listened
to her father and her two sisters talk with Lydia
Rothberger, an elderly woman from the *g'may* who had
taken on the role of dispensing maternal wisdom ever since
their mother passed away ten years ago. Lydia's presence in
the kitchen was always welcomed, even if she charged the
air with a tight energy of propriety.

With each stitch that Anna pulled through the fabric, her
dark eyes glanced up, just for a moment. No one noticed.
They were too engrossed in their discussion, the three other
women's attention focusing on her father.

With a silent resolve Anna tried to concentrate on her
work, knowing that the tiny stitches in the baby blanket she
was making for her younger sister Mary was the only input
she would make today. No one cared what *she* thought about
the possibility of her father losing their small family farm
anyway. The affront did not bother her. Indeed, she was just
as happy to stay out of the heated discussion.

"What will people think? They will talk for weeks! *Mayhaps*
months!" William said, his hands raised just slightly in the
air. The deep wrinkles under his eyes spoke of sleepless

265

nights and hard decisions. He looked first at Elizabeth and then to Lydia. "You know that Amish grapevine. Gossiping and speculating, all of them."

Anna bit her lower lip, too aware that the biggest contributor to that grapevine was her own father.

Elizabeth shook her head, equally as distraught. "There must be another way. Perhaps to hire young men to farm the fields."

That suggestion invigorated William. A new look of optimism lifted the cloud of despair that had rested upon his face. With great hope in his eyes, he pointed at his oldest daughter while he glanced over at Lydia for her response. "*Ja*! That's a right *gut* idea! Hire men to work the farm!"

"William," Lydia said, leaning forward and gently touching his knee. The gesture was one of familiarity without intimacy.

Almost thirty years had passed since Lydia stood beside her best friend, Anne Hershberger, at an early November wedding. The two women had grown up together in Sugarcreek, Ohio, and it was only natural that Lydia be her attendant when Anne married William Eicher. Best friends from childhood, the two young women remained just as close when Anne moved to the small town of Charm, just ten miles away.

Since that time, Lydia Rothberger's presence in the Eicher family had been constant: through births, deaths, baptisms, and one marriage. Her sensibility guided the daughters and, on occasion, their father. "It's time to consider alternatives. You simply cannot maintain it, William, and you have spent your savings. There is no money left to hire young men." She hesitated, glancing at Anna with a sympathetic look in her eyes. "Nor to even make it through the winter, I fear. You might consider selling it to live off the proceeds."

He stood up and began pacing the room, twisting his hands in front of him. "This *haus* has been in the family for generations!" His feet shuffled across the perfectly waxed and shiny linoleum floor. Anna worked hard to ensure that it was never dull or filmy. "Who would buy it?" He shook his head and continued pacing. "People will say I cannot provide for my family! Humiliating!" With stooped shoulders and glazed eyes, he paused to consider this thought. "*Nee!* Disastrous!"

"Scandalous, indeed!" Elizabeth added.

Anna looked up and studied her older sister. Ever since their mother died, Elizabeth had assumed the position of the female head of the house, helping their father make decisions. But it was Lydia who provided a maternal presence, at least to Anna. On most occasions Elizabeth deferred to Lydia. However, if Lydia was not around, there was simply no reasoning with father and eldest daughter. They seemed to agree on anything and everything as long as it maintained their image within the community. And that left out Anna.

As for Mary…

Anna looked at her other *schwester*. She was the prettiest of the three and, being married, the only one who wore a white prayer *kapp* at worship service. Her waist, while not quite as thick as Elizabeth's, still showed the extra weight that went with bearing children, although Anna wondered if she might be expecting another baby already.

Unlike Elizabeth who worried more about the conjecture of others in regard to the family reputation, Mary's concerns were about having to support her destitute father and sisters. "If you sold your house, where would you live?" She lifted her head and stared first at her father and then at Elizabeth. Anna offered a meek, "We could stay with you, Mary."

267

This idea flustered Mary and she responded with a quick excuse. "You know that our *haus* is already too small! Salome Musser refuses to give up the larger part!" She pursed her lips and sighed. "Imagine that! Putting us into the *grossdawdihaus* with two small *kinner!*" She clicked her tongue three times as she shook her head, clearly disapproving of her mother-in-law's decision. "Her own son, me, and two grandchildren! Living in such cramped quarters!"

No one responded to her complaints. Nor did anyone point out that she still had a spare bedroom, given that the two young boys shared one. However, Mary's family all knew what was required when Mary went on a self-indulging rampage: a proper moment's hesitation, as if permitting a respectful silence to acknowledge Mary's complaint, before continuing to address a situation at hand.

At last Elizabeth broke the compulsory silence. With her porcelainlike white hands folded together and resting so primly on her lap, she appeared almost like an austere school teacher as if she were reprimanding rambunctious young children. Only she wasn't: she was scolding her father. "I dare say that selling the house would raise eyebrows, *Daed.*" She paused, hesitating as if mulling over her own words. "But there must be something we can do. Why, the Hostetlers kept their family place even after all of those medical bills required not one but two rounds of aid from the *g'may!*" She turned her head and looked at Lydia. "Certainly we are better off than that!"

Once again a glimmer of hope shone from his eyes. For the second time that evening William pointed at Elizabeth as if her suggestion was the solution to his problems. "*Ja,* that's the truth!" A glow of eagerness returned to his face.

"No one can doubt that we have done much better than that Henry Hostetler!"

Lydia shook her head. "I've gone over your numbers, William. You have simply spent far more than you have earned...or saved. The maintenance on this property plus the taxes on the land are only part of the problem. You also spent almost ten thousand dollars on that new buggy last spring."

"And the horse," Anna whispered.

Lydia nodded at the reminder. "And the horse. That was a very expensive horse, William, especially considering the fancy harness you purchased from Benny Zook."

"Fancy harness?" He looked incredulous at the words spoken by Lydia. "I see nothing wrong with purchasing a good quality harness for a horse that is sound and capable."

"It was green as they come, William," Lydia reminded him, with just enough gentleness in her voice so that he did not become more irritated. "You had to pay John and Martin Wagler to break it."

"I'm sure that Cris would be happy to buy your new buggy," Mary cheerfully offered, as a way of moving the conversation along, ignoring the glare that Elizabeth sent in her direction. She smiled as if this alone would solve her father's money problem. "Although it is used now so it wouldn't fetch the same price, I reckon."

This suggestion did not sit well with William. "I just purchased that buggy! It has the new battery that recharges! I shall not part with it! Perhaps I should just sell a few acres."

"I'm afraid it's not as simple as that," Lydia said, a gentleness to her voice that did little to lighten the news. "Even selling those unused acres that you never farm wouldn't help,

William. And frankly it would make the property less valuable in the long run."

It wasn't a big property, just ten acres. Many years ago it had been much larger, but as customary among Amish families, parcels were divided and given to sons throughout the generations. Anna loved to walk through the tall grasses in the back acres, sometimes finding a broken piece of metal from an older plow or harvester in her path, especially after a sweet spring rain. She knew that her grandfather, *Grossdawdi* Eicher, had lived on the property, helping his own *daed* farm those acres a couple of generations ago. But when he married and acquired the small farmette, he chose not to farm but worked in minerals, instead. With only two children who survived into adulthood, he didn't have to worry about decisions regarding inheritance. His son, David, eight years older than William, had married and moved to the southern part of Holmes County. With his wife, he raised their five daughters and one son. Now that David was older and bound to a wheelchair, he lived on the same farm with that son and two grandsons, the oldest of whom ran the large farm.

As for William, he followed in his father's footsteps, and when *Grossdawdi* Eicher passed away, he had inherited the farmette, the perfect size for raising his own small family.

Minerals had been a valuable career path for William, given that there was limited competition. The rewards for his efforts were great from a financial perspective. The only problem was that he had sold the business three years ago, retiring when he hit sixty-one and his vision worsened. Too many years of refusing to wear glasses when the sun went down had quickened his visual impairment. Without a steady income, his unwillingness to decrease spending had begun to seriously deplete his nest egg. And though not spoken aloud, everyone knew that they could not accept assistance from the *g'may* without revealing that pattern of profligate spending.

Now he sat in his chair, trying to digest Lydia's words, while rubbing his hands as if attempting to ward off a deep pain. A flare-up. Again. Without being asked, Anna set down her quilting and quietly stole across the room to retrieve a small plastic container from the propane-powered refrigerator. She unscrewed the lid of the jar as she approached her father. Kneeling by his side, she dipped her finger in the jar and began to rub the waxlike ointment onto his hands, the scent of lavender slowly filling the room.

Only Lydia appeared to notice.

The older woman smiled as she observed Anna's attentiveness to her aging father's arthritis. It always seemed to flare whenever he became upset. Over the years, however, he stopped seeing doctors, claiming their *Englische* medicine was too suspicious and full of ingredients he couldn't pronounce.

He withdrew his hand from Anna's, motioning for her to leave his side. It was not an overtly rude motion, or at least Anna didn't take it that way. No, she merely picked up the lid to the jar and got to her feet, quietly returning the ointment to the refrigerator while he talked.

"I just don't understand how this happened." He frowned, the deep wrinkles by his eyes mirrored by the ones engraved in his forehead. *Lines of age meant years of wisdom*, Anna thought as she sat back on the sofa and watched him. Or in his case years of foolish spending. "So many years! So much work! Where has all of the money gone?" This last question, directed at Lydia, was spoken in a tone that bespoke genuine worry and fear.

"*Daed,*" Anna chimed in, her soft voice barely audible. "No one will think any less of you for selling the *haus*. There are worse things, I suppose."

"What could possibly be worse?" His voice cracked as he addressed Anna. Her sensible nature often conflicted with his vanity, a character trait so contrary to the Amish life that Anna often wondered how he had not once been reprimanded by the bishop. Now, and not for the first time, he stared at her, an expression of incredulity on his face, as if the words she had spoken were that of a child and not an intelligent woman. "It isn't *your* reputation at stake, need I remind you?"

"William!" Lydia gestured toward the reclining chair. "Please sit. You're working yourself into a tizzy."

Silently Anna watched as her father did as Lydia instructed. *Bless her heart*, she thought. Dear Lydia with her calming influence over stressful situations in the Eicher house. Without Lydia, Anna knew that there were times that even Elizabeth would not be able to handle her father's anxieties. Clearly this was one of those.

William took a short breath and lifted his chin. "*Ja vell,* I won't be letting that Willis get his hands on it, that's for sure and certain!"

"*Daed!*" The anger in her father's expression caught Anna off guard. As soon as the word slipped from her lips, she covered her mouth. She hadn't meant to reprimand him; however, his display of anger, especially so pointedly at one particular individual—and family at that!—upset her. She was thankful that no one else had paid attention to his outburst.

William turned toward Anna. Lifting his hand in the air, he pointed toward the heavens. "God is my witness, I don't care whether or not he's my nephew's son! The injustice he did to this family!" His anger dissipated just enough so that, when he looked at Elizabeth, there was less fire in his eyes. "Ach, the humiliation! It's unthinkable that his banns were read after he came calling on you!" He reached out to pat her hand, a gesture of comfort to his oldest daughter. "Why, the entire church district whispered for months, and not even John David would invite me to play checkers that winter!"

Anna looked away, the color flooding to her cheeks, but not before she saw Elizabeth's jaw muscles tighten.

Despite her own discomfort with her father's rebuke, Anna felt even more shame as she remembered her sister's stoic response when it was announced after worship service that Willis Eicher and Barbie King were to marry. At that time, seven years ago, there were plenty of unmarried young women in the *g'may*, five of whom sat between Anna and Elizabeth on the hard pine bench since they always entered single file in chronological order. Even though she hadn't been able to comfort her sister, Anna felt the sting of the announcement. Elizabeth, on the other hand, never once mentioned his name nor the four times that he had come calling at their house.

The intention had been clear and, frankly, presumed by all.

Instead, Willis Eicher chose to marry a woman from a far-away church district. That decision always brought out the fire in William's eyes, for the woman was the only daughter of that *g'may's* bishop. Besides the whispers about Willis snubbing Elizabeth, there had also been scuttlebutt over the motives behind his surprisingly sudden decision: the King family owned a rather large farm in another church district in a neighboring county.

Anna had never truly decided which one of them had felt more disgraced: *Daed* or Elizabeth. Even today she couldn't decide. The one thing she did know was that the wounds remained fresh for them both and reminded her far too much of the pain that she too had once caused.

Her thoughts were interrupted when Lydia reached out and, with a calm hand, touched William's sleeve. "William, that's pride speaking."

He ruffled at her words and shifted his weight in his chair.

"Besides, maybe we won't have to sell the *haus*. Not yet, anyway." Her eyes brightened from behind her glasses. "I have another possible, perfectly reasonable solution!"

"The only perfectly reasonable solution," he grumbled, "is staying in my own *haus*."

Elizabeth leaned back in her chair and rested her head against the cushion. "I just hate the thought of all those people talking about us."

"Speculating..." he added.

"I knew we shouldn't have donated so much money last year!" Elizabeth clicked her tongue disapprovingly. "You know that the amount we donated was shared by Preacher Troyer's *fraa*! Everyone knows and now speculates about our situation!"

"Scandalous!" William cried.

Anna felt as if the two of them were playing volleyball.

The kitchen clock chimed six times. Lydia glanced at it for she needed to leave in less than thirty minutes. *Certainly she had her own work to do*, Anna thought. Already Lydia had spent almost an hour with William and his daughters, reviewing the situation, a situation about which he merely grumbled and complained with no inclination to act upon a viable solution.

"If you should like to hear my solution?" Lydia interrupted. She spoke louder than usual but still with a degree of patience. Once William and Elizabeth settled down, she took a deep breath and began speaking. "It's simple, really. You have that small *haus* in Florida. Move there for a while. Winter and spring are lovely down there. It's less expensive to live there, and if you rent this *haus* for a year or so, the income will replenish your savings. If you find Florida to your liking, you can sell the *haus* without raising an eyebrow. If you don't, you can always return."

Anna looked up again from her quilt. "Why, that's the perfect solution!"

Lydia nodded and added, "Especially after last winter being so difficult and causing the flare-up with your arthritis. Certainly no one will question why you have left." Pausing, she let that suggestion register with William.

"If we move that far away, I'd still have to sell my horse and buggy," William grumbled.

Anna glanced up at him sharply. This was the first indication that her father might—just might—be willing to listen to reason.

Lydia nodded gravely to acknowledge William's loss before pressing her point home. "If you don't rent out the property, I fear you'll have to approach the bishop for assistance or, even worse, sell it. This way no one will be any the wiser and you can return for the summer to stay with Mary and escape the Florida heat."

A silence fell over the room. Anna waited, her breath caught in her chest. Elizabeth almost broke into a rare smile while Mary developed a typical scowl, the two very different reactions almost amusing to Anna except she knew the serious reasons behind them.

Finally Elizabeth nodded her head in approval, her agitation from moments prior quickly vanishing. "That's an agreeable solution!" She met her father's worried gaze. He often sought her validation on important decisions, and even those that did not qualify as very significant. She was, after all, the maternal head of the house, at least since their mother departed from her earthly life to begin her heavenly one. "Especially with the cold season soon upon us. I'm rather partial to that idea."

But the idea of William and his two unmarried daughters leaving Sugarcreek was not received as well by everyone.

"Florida?" Mary scoffed at the idea as if someone had just given her a glass of spoiled milk. "Oh bother! Who will help me with the *kinner*?" With a helpless expression on her face, she looked first to her father and then to Lydia. "You know I haven't been feeling quite well! The headaches and fatigue! And those two *kinner* are so active. Cris's family provides no help at all. Why! They return the boys to me in worse shape than when they left, what with all the cookies and sweets!" Disgusted, she returned her attention to her father. "If you move to Florida, you simply must leave Anna behind. It's not as if anyone would miss her..."

The comment, while seemingly harsh, didn't faze anyone in the room. With the exception of Lydia, Anna knew that it was an accurate statement and not necessarily spoken with malice. Her quiet nature often caused people, especially her family, to overlook her at larger gatherings. And to be needed by someone, *anyone*, was better than to be needed by none.

"And when we return, then what?"

Mary sighed. "If Salome Musser would let us move into the big *haus*, we might have room." She picked at a white thread on the blue sleeve of her dress. "*Mayhaps* this might be the catalyst for her to finally do the right thing, *nee*? Who ever heard of such selfishness? And with only Leah and Hannah living there." She looked up, suddenly aware that everyone watched her, stunned by her sharp words. "*Ja vell*, it's true! Her son did buy the farm, after all."

Another glance at the clock and Lydia suddenly stood up. "Think about it, William."

For a moment Anna's heart broke. Her father looked around the room, his eyes taking in the freshly painted walls (for he always hired three young men to repaint them in the springtime), wood-stained trim work (something that Anna worked tirelessly to clean each week), and perfectly waxed linoleum floor (another task that fell upon Anna). Cleanliness was, after all, next to godliness.

"To have another person sit in my kitchen?" Emotion welled up in his throat. "Tend my Lizzie's gardens? Who could I possibly entrust with such a valuable piece of my life?"

Gathering her black sweater, Lydia ignored his reservations. She spared a genuine smile in Anna's direction before picking up her basket. "I heard that George Coblentz is returning to Sugarcreek. His older sister is ailing and they may need a place to stay."

"They?" William's mouth fell open. "You mean he has young *kinner*?" He shook his hand in front of his chest as if warding off something bad. "*Nee*! I won't have undisciplined young ones tearing through this *haus*! They'll trample the rose bushes, for sure and certain!"

Laughing, Lydia placed her hand on his shoulder, the closest gesture of intimacy she ever shared with him. It was a simple touch that spoke of a deep friendship and even deeper tolerance on her part. "Oh, William! You fret over the most mundane things! Besides, it's just George and his *fraa*, Sara. Their children are all grown up now."

Anna picked up her quilting, readying herself to continue working on the blanket since Lydia was leaving.

"Coblentz?" William tugged at his neatly trimmed white beard. "I don't know anyone named Coblentz."

Lydia slipped her arms into her sweater and quickly extracted the strings to her prayer *kapp*. Her hand on the doorknob, she turned to wave one last time to the three young women before responding to his statement. "Of course you do," she said, opening the door. "George's *fraa* grew up here. Sara? Sara Whittmore?"

Anna's fingers froze over the material, the needle only partially pushed through the fabric. She dared not raise her eyes. To do so, she feared, would allow Lydia, of all people, to read her thoughts.

"They are the most delightful people, and you know what they say about a woman without *kinner*," she said, her voice light and breezy. "They take the best care of the *haus* and gardens!" One last wave and Lydia disappeared out the door. Behind her, she left four people in deep thought: three who wondered about this George Coblentz and how the *g'may* would react to the news of the Eicher departure while the fourth stared at her lap, her eyes glazed over and her fingers unable to extract the needle.

Whittmore. The name was far too familiar to Anna. While the voices of her family faded into the background, long repressed memories awakened. She lifted her eyes and looked around the room, her eyes seeing the very objects that so alarmed her father just moments before. Rather than fearing the hands that might touch them in just a few short weeks, her heart pounded at the very thought of them staying in their house.

She sighed, lifting her eyes to the ceiling as she fought the intense pounding of her heart. *Oh*, she wondered, a deep and hollow feeling forming inside of her chest. *Was it possible that, once again, he might actually walk these floors?* The very thought led her to distraction and made her so uncomfortable that she had no choice but to claim a headache and, soon after Lydia's departure, retire to the safety and isolation of her room. The only problem was that she was not alone, for the memory of Sara's brother, Freman Whittmore, accompanied her.

❧ *Glossary* ❧

ach vell—an expression similar to *Oh well*
aendi—aunt
Ausbund—Amish hymnal
boppli—baby
bruder—brother
buwe—unmarried man
daed—father
danke—thank you
Eck table—a corner table for the bride and groom to sit at
    their wedding feast
Englische—non-Amish people
Englischer—a non-Amish person
foresinger—the man who starts the hymn singing at worship
fraa—wife
g'may—church district
grossdawdi—grandfather
grossdawdihaus—small house attached to the main dwelling
grossmammi—grandmother
gut mariye—good morning
haus—house
ja—yes
kinner—children
maedel—older, unmarried woman
maem—mother
mayhaps—maybe
nee—no

onkel—uncle
schwester—sister
wie gehts—what's going on?
wilkum—welcome
wunderbaar—wonderful

❦ Books by Sarah Price ❦

THE AMISH CLASSIC SERIES
First Impressions
The Matchmaker

THE AMISH OF LANCASTER SERIES
Fields of Corn
Hills of Wheat
Pastures of Faith
Valley of Hope

THE AMISH OF EPHRATA SERIES
The Tomato Patch
The Quilting Bee
The Hope Chest
The Clothes Line

THE PLAIN FAME TRILOGY
Plain Fame
Plain Change
Plain Again

OTHER AMISH FICTION BOOKS
Amish Circle Letters
Amish Circle Letters II
The Divine Secrets of the Whoopie Pie Sisters (with Pam Jarrell)
Life Regained (with Pam Jarrell)
A Gift of Faith: An Amish Christmas Story

An Amish Christmas Carol: Amish Christian Classic Series
A Christmas Gift for Rebecca: An Amish Christian Romance

THE ADVENTURES OF A FAMILY DOG SERIES
A Small Dog Named Peek-a-boo
Peek-a-boo Runs Away
Peek-a-boo's New Friends
Peek-a-boo and Daisy Doodle

OTHER BOOKS
Gypsy in Black
The Prayer Chain Series (with Ella Stewart)
Postcards From Abby (with Ella Stewart)
Meet Me in Heaven (with Ella Stewart)

❧ About Sarah Price ❧

THE PREISS FAMILY emigrated from Europe in 1705, settling in Pennsylvania as the area's first wave of Mennonite families. Sarah Price has always respected and honored her ancestors through exploration and research about her family's history and their religion. At the age of nineteen she befriended an Amish family and lived on their farm throughout the years.

Twenty-five years later Sarah Price splits her time between her home outside of New York City and an Amish farm in Lancaster County, Pennsylvania, where she retreats to reflect, write, and reconnect with her Amish friends and Mennonite family.

Contact the author at sarahprice.author@gmail.com. Visit her weblog at http://sarahpriceauthor.com or on Facebook at www.facebook.com/fansofsarahprice.

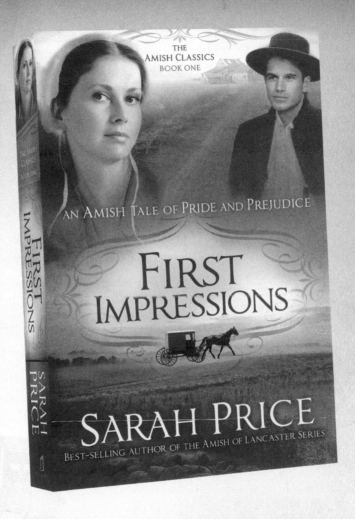

Be Empowered

Be Encouraged

Be Inspired

Be Spirit Led

FREE NEWSLETTERS

Empowering Women for Life in the Spirit

SPIRITLED WOMAN
Amazing stories, testimonies, and articles on marriage, family, prayer, and more.

POWER UP! FOR WOMEN
Receive encouraging teachings that will empower you for a Spirit-filled life.

CHARISMA MAGAZINE
Get top-trending articles, Christian teachings, entertainment reviews, videos, and more.

CHARISMA NEWS DAILY
Get the latest breaking news from an evangelical perspective. Sent Monday–Friday.

SIGN UP AT: nl.charismamag.com

CHARISMA MEDIA

P9780